THE KING SNAKE

BRIAN SHEA

TY HUTCHINSON

Severn River
PUBLISHING

Severn River Publishing
www.SevernRiverPublishing.com

ISBN: 978-1-64875-220-9 (Paperback)
ISBN: 978-1-64875-221-6 (Hardback)

ALSO BY THE AUTHORS

Never miss a new release!

SevernRiverBooks.com

Sign up and receive a free copy of

Unkillable: A Nick Lawrence Short Story

1

Charong Bunsong stepped up onto a small boulder and raised the night-vision binoculars to his eyes. His gaze moved up and down the lazy flow of the Mekong River, where it intersected with the borders of Thailand, Myanmar, and Laos: the Golden Triangle.

He stood on the Thai side, and directly across the river was Laos. In the middle of the river was a small island where the borders of Thailand and Laos met. It provided a marker for the boat they were expecting to pick up the cargo on hand.

"They're late," Bunsong said as he lowered the binoculars. "They should have been here at two a.m."

Standing next to Bunsong was another man dressed in the same military fatigues: a mixture of black, dark blue, and gray. He had an AK-47 slung over his shoulder. Behind them were five other men wearing fatigues and carrying the same type of rifles. They were keeping watch on the cargo: thirty women, ages nineteen to twenty-two.

Bunsong glanced back at his men, and a tiny glow of a red caught his eye. He walked over to one of his men and slapped a cigarette out of his mouth.

"Are you stupid? You want to get caught by Border Patrol?"

The man avoided eye contact while keeping his mouth shut. None of Bunsong's men ever questioned him. To do so meant a painful punishment at the very least, more depending on his mood, which lately seemed sour at best.

The women sat on the ground, huddled into a tight group. None of them dared look any of the men in their eyes, especially Bunsong. The rumors about his beatings were widespread. But this specific group of women knew exactly what they had signed up for.

Yes, they were being trafficked. No, they were not being held against their will, nor had they been tricked into coming along. They had been promised money for their families in exchange for marriage to single Chinese men. Decades of a one-child policy paired with Chinese couples only wanting boys had lowered the number of single and available women in China. Young Chinese men were left to find brides from other countries. Bunsong was happy to supply the demand.

Trafficking women into China was relatively easy, especially when the women were coming along willingly. Bunsong didn't have to worry about them running off or fighting back. Both of those scenarios always ended in death, which reduced Bunsong's profits. Not the news he wanted to deliver to his boss.

But that wasn't a current worry for Bunsong. His boss was out of the country and had entrusted Bunsong to manage the operations while he was gone. Who was his boss? Somsak Ritthirong, the most notorious human trafficker in all of Asia. As feared as Bunsong was by others, his boss was far worse.

Bunsong returned to the boulder and continued to monitor the river for the slow boat: a long, narrow boat capable of floating on the water's surface, even in the shallowest of waters. It was necessary for navigating specific parts of the river.

"There it is," Bunsong pointed. "Get the cargo ready. I want to load them quickly."

While Bunsong kept a watchful eye on the boat, his men moved the women down to the river's bank. In recent years, the Laos border patrol had increased its presence along the border to stem the flow of drugs from Myanmar; mostly opium. Drug traffickers preferred running drugs through Laos to get to Vietnam, where demand was high, rather than cross through Thailand and into Cambodia and then on to Vietnam. This caused more problems for Bunsong. He had to worry about both Thai and Laos border patrols.

That night, the quarter moon above shed just enough light to make the women noticeable on the banks of the river. From atop his perch, Bunsong kept watch of the surrounding area. This was always a critical moment. Once his men and the women were out in the open, it was difficult to hide what they were doing.

His men needed to quickly load the women onto the boat and collect the correct payment. Bunsong would only breathe a breath of relief once he knew both had been done. His payment from the Laos traffickers was four thousand US dollars for each woman, which amounted to a total of one hundred twenty thousand dollars. Bunsong did this once a week.

The Laos trafficker would sell each woman for six thousand, perhaps more depending on the woman or the scarcity of women being trafficked into China. No payment was made to the woman's family when Bunsong took them. Their daughter would have to negotiate how much money would be sent back to take care of her family with her new husband.

Only then would the woman see any sort of value from the arrangement.

The slow boat cut its engine and drifted toward the shore where the women waited. The women could only bring clothes on their backs and a small plastic bag filled with a few personal belongings. Most chose to take photos of their family.

Bunsong brought the binoculars up to his eyes again and studied the banks on the other side of the river. That's where he spotted movement—the faint outlines of what appeared to be a group of men moving slowly. He counted at least ten individuals, but there could easily be more. Bunsong spoke into his throat mic and warned his men a Laos order patrol was moving in.

No sooner had Bunsong given that order than he spotted individuals on the bank south of his position. It had to be Thai Border Patrol. What were the odds of both countries convening on that specific location at that time of the night? Low. It had to be a coordinated operation, which meant someone had tipped them off.

"It's a trap!" Bunsong shouted into the mic.

But it was too late. Gunfire erupted from the Laos side, and soon both patrols were shooting at Bunsong's men. The captain of the slow boat gunned the engine and pulled away, leaving Bunsong's men and his cargo out in the open with no cover.

Bunsong pulled the Beretta M9A1 from his hip holster and took aim, firing on the Thai patrol and killing one of their men with a clean shot to the head. Seconds later, a hail of bullets chipped at the boulder Bunsong had been standing on, forcing him to jump back off from it.

He peered above the top of the boulder, shooting when he could, but there were too many of them. At least twenty heavily armed men made up the Thai Border Patrol—and probably an equal number for the Laos patrol. Outnumbered and outgunned. Bunsong ordered his men to retreat.

"What about the women?" one of his men answered.

"They're replaceable. Get out now!"

But Bunsong's order came too late.

He watched hopelessly as bullets from both sides of the banks mowed down his men and his cargo. The Thai Border Patrol began to focus on him. Men were starting to climb the small hill to his location. He had no choice but to run or face the same fate as his men. To the Thai and Laos governments, Bunsong and his men were wanted traffickers. Their orders weren't to take them into custody but to eradicate them. And as for the women caught in the middle, both governments viewed them as collateral damage.

2

Its nickname is Monster Mansion, but its official name is Her Majesty's Prison Wakefield, where England's most dangerous and heinous criminals are housed. Approximately six hundred high-profile and high-risk inmates are imprisoned there. They can't be trusted *not* to escape—many have attempted it. Nor can they be trusted to *not* kill a fellow inmate —many have already done so.

Because of that, inmates are kept in single-occupancy cells. They are also required to prepare their own meals in a small kitchen where they are heavily guarded. It's irresponsible to think nothing could go wrong in a cafeteria. But the most stringent of rules are reserved for those for whom death really is the safest precaution.

Buried underneath Wakefield are two unique cells. Very few individuals have access to this area. In fact, to reach the unit, a person must pass through seventeen steel doors.

Each cell is approximately five and a half meters by four and a half meters. The side and rear walls are made of concrete. The entire front is made of transparent bulletproof acrylic, allowing the prison officers to easily see inside. It resembles the glass-cage prison that Hannibal Lecter is kept inside of in *The Silence of the Lambs*.

Inside the cell is a concrete slab that serves as a bed. One chair and one table are also included, but they are made out of cardboard. The toilet-sink combo is bolted down. A team of officers keeps around-the-clock watch on the cells. They never enter the cell while an inmate is occupying it. Food is always passed through a narrow slot. Conversation with the inmate by an officer is forbidden.

An inmate named Phillip Hunnicutt occupied one of the cells; he's the reason why the underground level was built in the first place. When Hunnicutt could no longer continue to kill outside of prison, he began murdering other inmates: casually, deliberately, and without remorse. Isolation was the answer.

Hunnicutt remained underground, segregated from others except for the officer detail. It was often asked why the prison built two cells. Aside from Hunnicutt, no one else came remotely close to fitting the requirements of being locked up inside of one...until two months ago, when Hunnicutt got a neighbor.

Special Agent Sterling Gray knew the drill. He'd made the trip to Wakefield in Yorkshire multiple times during the last two months. The two-hour-and-forty-five-minute train ride from London didn't bother him one bit. He enjoyed the scenic ride alongside lush green pastures dotted with quaint villages. That day marked his sixth visit to the small cathedral city.

Gray always booked a ticket in the first-class carriage and enjoyed the reclining seats and extra legroom required for his height. He always took advantage of the decent buffet since he liked to arrive in Wakefield by ten a.m. It meant an early start for him, and it was easier to fill his belly on the train.

The train stopped at the Wakefield Westgate station, which conveniently happened to be across from HMP Wakefield. It was a ten-minute walk from the station to the entrance gate of the prison, where the arduous process of multiple security checks began. Even though by his third visit everyone knew Gray, the protocol was still followed to a tee. Gray didn't mind. It was for his protection as well.

After his initial check-in, Gray was always escorted to Berry Summerfield's office, the prison governor who had been in that position for the past twenty-five years and was less than a year away from retirement. Gray had come to like the man and respected his tenacity. It took a particular type of person to run a correctional facility—no easy task. But Summerfield had always remained positive with a smile on his face. Gray remembered a few wise words from Summerfield the first day they'd met. He said, "Everyone deserves a second chance, even the people who screwed up their third."

"Special Agent Gray, welcome to Wakefield," Summerfield said with a smile as he motioned for Gray to take a seat.

"Governor Summerfield. Pleasure as always."

"How was the train ride?"

"Peaceful."

"I do love the trains, always did ever since I was a young laddie. But with my current schedule, it's not often I find the time to take long trips."

"You'll have plenty of time come retirement."

"And I plan on making the best of it." Summerfield shifted in his seat. "As you know, today will be your last visit. The paperwork is being filed as we speak, and the inmate will be extradited soon."

"Yes, I am aware. The past two months felt like two weeks."

"Did you find your visits enlightening?"

As an agent who worked in the FBI's Behavioral Analysis Unit, having a chance to spend two months interviewing this particular inmate had been a coup for Gray.

"I did. Talking to a man like him, and having him actually cooperate, is truly rare. It was fascinating to understand the mindset of someone like him."

Gray didn't fly all the way to England just to interview the inmate. His supervisor had transferred him to work alongside Interpol for an indefinite amount of time. Since Gray's arrival, Interpol had become accustomed to using his profiling skills and more to help facilitate investigations.

Summerfield drew a deep breath. "My job is to rehabilitate. Your job is to understand. We both need to enter the mind of the individual. I've watched every interview you've conducted with the inmate, and I do find them enlightening myself."

"I'm glad to hear that."

"Well, let's not hold up your final meeting." Summerfield stood. "Shall we?"

Visitors to the underground unit were required to be escorted by Summerfield himself. There were no exceptions. Their footsteps echoed throughout the hallway as they passed through numerous steel doors.

"What's his mood like today?" Gray asked.

"From what I've been told earlier this morning, upbeat. Be careful, though."

"I always am. Is he still bullying Hunnicutt?"

"He is, but instead of broadcasting his words during the day for everyone to hear, he does it late at night, between one and three in the morning. That's when he starts whispering into Hunnicutt's ear. We never thought to make the cells soundproof when we first built them, but we're considering modifying them."

"Is he telling Hunnicutt the same thing, that he's forgotten and no one cares?"

"It's harder for us to pick up on what's being said now that it takes place quietly, but I imagine it is for the most part. Hunnicutt's already been escorted out of his cell for his exercise. You'll have your privacy."

"I appreciate it."

Two prison officers met Gray and Summerfield once they passed through the last security door. A chair was in front of a cell with a video camera set up to record the interview.

Summerfield led the way to the cell. Gray could already see inside clearly because of the transparent acrylic. The inmate was sitting at his desk and appeared to be writing on a piece of paper.

They stopped in front of the cell. The man inside continued to write as if they weren't there. Gray looked at Summerfield, who simply shrugged.

"You're late, Special Agent Gray," the inmate said without lifting his head up.

"Just a few minutes," Gray answered. "I apologize."

"You know how I feel about tardiness."

"You've made it clear to me in an early conversation. Shall we get started, then?"

The man stopped writing and looked up at Gray. "I already have."

3

Summerfield left, and the two officers took their usual positions near the security door. Gray turned on the video camera and sat. The man inside the cell was named Somsak Ritthirong, a.k.a....King Rong. A play on King Kong.

"This will be our last meeting," Gray said.

Ritthirong raised an eyebrow. "And why do you say that?"

"Are you not aware of your extradition? The courts denied your final appeal. You are to be handed over to the Thai authorities as soon as possible."

Ritthirong was a Thai national wanted by the Thai government on charges of human trafficking. Not only had he already proven to be the worst trafficker in Thailand, but he also held the crown in Southeast Asia. Hence the nickname.

"Nothing is as it seems," Ritthirong said.

Gray watched him adjust the gold-framed glasses on his face. When he first learned of Ritthirong's nickname, he found it puzzling, for the man looked nothing like a giant beast. In fact, he was the complete opposite. An accountant was Gray's first thought when he laid eyes on him.

Ritthirong was five foot seven and probably no more than

135 pounds at most. He wasn't muscular, nor did he have intimidating looks. So how did a man of his stature become the biggest human trafficker in Southeast Asia? That was one of the questions Gray had set out to answer during his interviews.

One reason stood out right away. There wasn't a person that Ritthirong wouldn't traffic—nothing was off-limits. He'd trafficked men and women and children of all ages, covering sexual exploitation, organ removal, forced labor, and other criminal activities. What made Ritthirong worse than other traffickers was that he was known to squeeze every monetary worth out of a person before discarding them, dead or alive.

He had been on the run from the Thai government for the past five years. During that time, they'd caught him twice. Both times he escaped, and he managed to run his organization from outside of the country.

After Interpol issued a red notice for Ritthirong, Slovakian authorities had managed to apprehend him. Not only had Ritthirong escaped, but he also left a trail of bodies in the process. Three months ago, British authorities arrested Ritthirong. Wanting to take no chances, they brought him immediately to HMP Wakefield. They locked him in the unoccupied cell next to Hunnicutt while he fought extradition. Both Thailand and Slovakia wanted him.

"I think it's a done deal...your extradition," Gray said. "But you can keep clinging to that lifeboat of denial if you wish."

Ritthirong chuckled. "Tell me, Agent Gray, did you really learn anything substantial from our conversations?"

"I might ask you the same question. What we discussed should have benefited us both."

"You never answer my questions," Ritthirong answered with surprise. "What does that say?"

Gray smiled at Ritthirong. "Let's talk about remorse."

"We've discussed that. You've already determined that I have none."

"Have you always felt this way about others? Indifferent?"

"I treat things accordingly. You don't have the same feelings for your phone that you do your family, do you?"

"Of course not. These people you traffic, in your eyes, they really are a commodity, aren't they?"

"You say that like it's breaking news. It's not just me. Other traffickers are the same. Sometimes you let me down, Gray. I expect more from you."

"A lot of your victims were children. Didn't that bother you?"

Ritthirong stood up from behind his desk and walked right up to the acrylic. "You sit there dressed in your pressed suit and your clean buzz cut, passing judgment on me like you're better, but you're not. I know all about the man you killed in London with your bare hands. It takes a certain type of person to squeeze the life out of someone. Did you look into his eyes while you did it? Tell me, what was that like, to watch a man die slowly in your arms?"

"You really are something, aren't you, bringing that up. Did you google that yourself or convince one of the prison officers to feed you that information?"

"You didn't answer my question."

"I was cleared of any wrongdoing. That man was a serial killer. He had taken the lives of three young women and was working on the fourth. I still don't see how this has any similarity to the atrocities you committed."

"I've never strangled a person. What's it like when they're gasping for air and struggling to free themselves? What's it like when you have to struggle harder to continue killing them? I'm curious to know your answer."

"You really are a piece of work, aren't you?"

"Tell me, Agent Gray, what wakes you in the middle of the night in a cold sweat, gasping for air? Does killing that man in cold blood do it? Or is there something much more heinous that you're hiding from me?"

Gray had always believed his role was to protect, save, and do the right thing. Joining the Air Force and Pararescue only grounded this belief inside of him even more. It's why he felt uneasy when Hunnicutt mentioned the man he killed in London. Taking a life wasn't something Gray took lightly. His role was to save lives, not end them, even that of a killer. A flashback to his time serving in the Air Force came to Gray. A mission in Ethiopia had gone sideways. He lost a lot of men because of bad intelligence. These were men who trusted him to not only lead them into danger but safely out of it. Even in that instance, where he was not in the wrong, Gray blamed himself.

"There is something, isn't there?" A smile formed on Ritthirong's face. "Something worse than the man you strangled."

During Gray's second meeting with Ritthirong, he had Ritthirong's IQ tested. As Gray had suspected, it was high: 150. Further tests revealed Ritthirong had an ENFP personality. No surprise there. Most geniuses are. Gray picked up reasonably quick on how intuitive Ritthirong was. Nothing he did or said was without an alternative motive.

"I'm not playing this game with you," Gray said.

"I'm simply asking a question. You did tell me during our first meeting that I had a right to ask questions."

"The rule was you had to answer all of my questions if you wanted me to answer one of yours. You failed to do that."

His family was the one subject that Ritthirong refused to talk about. He would shut down anytime Gray brought up his family or even anything related to his upbringing. Even childhood friends or time spent at the university was a no-go. As far as Gray knew, Ritthirong had never married, nor did he have any known offspring.

The only information Gray knew about Ritthirong's family was what had been in his file. He came from an upper-middle-class family and graduated from the top university in Bangkok. His father was an influential businessman, and his family ran in the same circle of Bangkok's elite.

Instead of following in his father's footsteps, Ritthirong grew his power in another way. By the time he was thirty, he had trafficked more than half a million people throughout Southeast Asia and the world while amassing sizable wealth in the process.

However, that all came at a cost. His family disowned him. In fact, the tip that Ritthirong was in London came from his family. It was well known that they very much wanted to see him dead. He was the blemish on the family's legacy that could not be washed off.

It's no secret that Ritthirong got to where he was because of his smarts and not because of his brutality. Though there was plenty of that from the reports, Gray had read. But when he questioned Ritthirong about how involved he was with that part of the business, thinking he only ordered his men to carry out the task, Ritthirong answered with a resounding yes. Ritthirong was capable of being both a strategist and a monster.

What made him even more successful in that arena was that he looked and acted nothing like a ruthless human trafficker. He was well spoken, polite, and charming when needed. A true chameleon.

"When I am gone, what will you do with your time, Agent Gray? Seems to me you have a dull future upon you."

"I think not. Plenty of interesting cases to keep my mind

occupied. Sadly, I can't say the same for you. The charges the Thai government will bring against you carry the death penalty. You will be found guilty; the evidence against you is overwhelming. Your last days alive will be spent incarcerated at the Bang Kwang Central Prison. You might know of it as the Bangkok Hilton. It'll make this place seem like a resort."

"Will you miss me?"

"Why would I miss you?"

"Because you don't have all the pieces to the puzzle. You haven't figured out everything you want about me."

"It would be naive of you to presume what I know or what I don't know."

"I know more than you think. I might entertain the thought of..."

"The thought of what?"

Ritthirong drew a deep breath. "Our time is up. Run along, Agent Gray."

4

After Gray wrapped up his meeting with Ritthirong, he stopped by Summerfield's office on the way out and invited him to lunch. Gray wasn't sure if he'd ever make a trip back to Wakefield, but he wanted to show his appreciation for Summerfield's willingness in accommodating his petition to interview Ritthirong.

The two enjoyed a bite at a nearby pub. Conversation hovered mostly around Summerfield's retirement.

"I've worked my entire life. It'll be odd not waking up and heading into an office somewhere," Summerfield said.

"If you don't have an office at home, you can always put one in. You know, to tide you over when the urge arises."

"The missus wants to turn the spare room into a proper exercise room. I like the idea myself."

"There you go. That can be your new office."

After lunch, Gray caught the next train back to London and arrived a little after five. He had plans to meet a friend for a few pints at six thirty. He didn't really feel like heading all the way back to his flat, only to turn around and head back out. He also didn't want to wait in a pub for an hour. *You know what? I'll just swing by his office and hang out there.*

The office Gray was heading to was the Metropolitan Police headquarters, or the Met, as most Londoners referred to it. The building was located between Whitehall and the Victoria Embankment along the river Thames. The person he was meeting for pints was DI Chi Gaston.

Gray had first met Gaston when he was recruited by Interpol to consult on an investigation involving a serial killer in London. Not only did the two work well together, but they both also enjoyed pints and laughs.

Gray exited the elevator on the second floor, where Chi's unit was located. He spotted his friend at the rear of the room, hunched over his laptop, tapping away. As always, Chi's hair was a mess, and a five-o'clock shadow clung to his face.

"Chi," Gray called out as he approached his desk.

Gaston looked up in surprise. "Sterling, did I get the time wrong?"

"No, pal, you're good." Gray took a seat next to Gaston's desk. "I'm early. Thought I'd come here and bug you instead of wait in the pub, unless you're knee-deep into something serious."

"Nah, I'm just finishing a report. I'll be done in fifteen minutes. Feel free to get yourself dolled up if you want."

A short while later, Gray and Gaston sat in a nearby pub with freshly pulled pints.

"Today was your last meeting in Wakefield, ain't that right, mate?" Gaston said. "How did it go?"

"Bittersweet. I'd love to keep talking to Ritthirong, but at the same time, I feel like the more attention I give him, the more I feed his ego."

"What's it to you? That psycho's got a short lease on life.

The Thai government will convict him, and that'll be the end of King Rong." Gaston took a large gulp.

"You're right. I can't prevent the next low-life from filling the void Ritthirong will leave, but I'd like to think I've learned enough that I can help others apprehend people like him quicker."

"What do you think made him so hard to catch him in the first place?"

"Besides being incredibly smart and having money to get things done? I'd say it's the way he carries himself. He can be charming and polite when he wants. Physically, he's not threatening. He's everything you *wouldn't* suspect. I think that's what kept him free for so long. If you think you're hunting for a beast, you start looking for one. Ritthirong looks nothing like that."

"A wolf in sheep's clothing."

"Exactly. When law enforcement in Slovenia was looking for Ritthirong, they actually stopped and questioned him. He even walked with the officer for a bit, trying to help them with the search. That's how good he is. He'll hide right in front of you."

Gaston scratched his chin. "I'm glad our boys were able to catch up with him, and you got to learn something from your interviews."

"Here, here." Gray lifted his pint and clinked glasses with Gaston. "You know Lillie's flying to Thailand."

"You don't say?"

"She's overseeing the extradition."

Gray had met Lillie Pratt on the same investigation that he worked on with Gaston. She was a Criminal Intelligence Analyst with Interpol. She was the one who actually pulled Gray in on Gaston's investigation, which then led to his indefinite consultancy.

"Yeah, she's tagging along until the very end. She's making sure everything goes smoothly during the handoff between the UK and Thailand."

"I wasn't aware of that," Gaston said. "I invited her to meet up with us. Maybe she'll stop by. I'd like to hear more about that."

"Look who just walked in," Gray said as his eyes lit up. "Lillie. Over here." Gray waved to the petite blonde in a pantsuit.

"Sterling, Chi. How is everything?"

"We've got pints. What could be better?" Gaston said as he stood. "What are you having, Lillie? This round's on me."

"Pint of London Pride," she said as she sat on the stool next to Gray.

"How did your meeting go today?"

Gray filled her in quickly, mentioning that he'd wished he had more time with Ritthirong.

"I think I can grant you that wish."

"What are you talking about?"

"If you want, you can tag along with me on the trip."

"Really?"

"Sure. You're essentially working at Interpol. What do you say? Are you game to come along?"

"Yeah, of course. Will I be able to continue interviewing him?"

"I hope so. That'll be a primary reason for you to be there. Plus, we'll need all the backup we can handle. Ritthirong is considered a flight risk."

Gaston returned with Pratt's pint just then.

"Chi, Lillie just told me I'll be helping escort Ritthirong back to Thailand."

"Brilliant. You just mentioned wanting more time with the bloody bastard. Now you got your wish."

"What kind of security detail is being planned?" Gray asked Pratt.

"On our end, there'll be you and I from Interpol. A six-man detail from the Aviation Security Operational Command Unit will be assisting us. They'll transfer and guard the prisoner from Wakefield to Heathrow and ensure he's on the plane. Our government is only responsible for Ritthirong up until that point. The Thai government is sending two individuals to the UK to escort Ritthirong back on the flight back."

"Two? That's it?"

"My understanding is that they're members of Thailand's elite Special Branch Bureau force. They provide protection for the king and other VIPs. I don't know what the Thai government has planned once the plane lands."

"They must have already forgotten about his successful escape from the Slovenian police force," Gaston said as his forehead crinkled.

"Just so I understand: It's just you, me, and the two men from the SBB force on the flight to Thailand?" Gray said.

"That's correct. Once the door to the plane is shut, he's Thailand's responsibility."

"Is this normal? I've actually never been a part of extradition."

"It depends on the country, but for the most part, it's par for the course. If a prisoner was being extradited back to the UK, we'd send a team from the Met to escort that individual on the flight back. I imagine we would send a larger team if it was someone like Ritthirong, with his past and all."

"Is a date set yet?"

Pratt nodded as she took a sip. "End of the week. Are you sure you're good to go? We'll stick around for a few days, as I'd like to rendezvous with Interpol's NCB in Thailand. Then we'll catch a flight back."

"It all sounds good to me. Have you been to Thailand?"

Pratt shook her head. "This is a first. I take it you've visited before?"

"I have, but it was a long time ago when I was younger. I'm sure it's changed a lot since then."

"Well, if we're able to peel some free time away, you can show me a sight or two."

"The food in itself is a sight." Gray delivered a chef's kiss. "Delicious, from what I recall."

Gaston raised his glass. "Well, while you two are gallivanting halfway around the world, I'll be holding down the fort. Not to worry."

5

After escaping the shootout with Thai Border Patrol, Bunsong drove nonstop until he reached the sleepy town of Saraburi, about two hours north of Bangkok. The sun had just started to rise at that time. The city didn't have much to offer except a stopover point to Khao Yai National Park, the largest and most popular park in the country. Visitors came to see the wild elephants.

He wasn't happy about losing the cargo, but losing his men angered him more. He could always find women, but trained and loyal men weren't easy to come by. He had spent a great deal of time preparing those men to do a specific job: procurement. Specifically, women he could traffic to China for the purpose of marriage. That's the only responsibility those men had. Nothing more. Nothing less.

It was that way with everyone that worked for Bunsong. Everyone had a specialty, and they were expected to be very good at it. Working this way made his men more efficient and productive. But Bunsong couldn't take credit for this. His boss, Somsak Ritthirong, had developed this specific system and made sure it was applied to all aspects of his business. He wanted every man who worked for him to have a specific job, and he wanted him to excel at it.

The black pickup turned off the highway and continued along a dirt road for about half a mile. That's where the first checkpoint was established. Bunsong stopped the truck near a one-room stilt house. Underneath were two old sofas and a small table. Empty beer bottles littered the ground.

He honked his horn, and a man stuck his head out the window. Three men with compact assault rifles slung across their chest climbed down a ladder while rubbing their eyes. Clearly, they'd all been sleeping.

"You idiots. You're supposed to be watching the road," Bunsong said.

The three men nodded.

"And clean this place up."

The men immediately did as they were told as Bunsong drove away.

When Ritthirong went on the run, he placed Bunsong in charge of the entire operation. For years he had done an excellent job. Everything ran smoothly, as if Ritthirong were right there. But in the last six months or so, things had begun to deteriorate. Turnkey operations, like the one the night before, went sideways. Men like the ones at the first guard shack were slipping, becoming complacent. Bunsong had several tactics to counteract those issues, but nothing really seemed to work as of late. And that worried him. If he dropped the ball, he might as well just put a gun to his head, because that would be better than facing Ritthirong.

Deeper into the jungle, he drove until a thick, concrete wall came into view. It stood twelve feet tall and had a solid steel gate guarding the entrance. On top of the wall, spaced out, were battlements with guards inside. Bunsong honked the horn once more, and the gate slid open, revealing a stunning two-story mansion inside.

The palatial residence was the last thing anyone would expect to find in the jungle. But that was the point. Not many people would think to come looking there. And for those that knew of the place, they kept their mouths shut. Bunsong drove past two armed men and then around a water fountain that anchored a roundabout. He climbed out of the truck and headed into the home.

A man greeted Bunsong as soon as he entered. "How did it go?"

This man was Bunsong's right-hand man. Everyone called him Rooster because he had a long neck and kept his hair in a mohawk.

"We got screwed. I lost everything," Bunsong said.

"What happened?"

"Someone tipped off Border Patrol. I want you to find out who did it."

"No problem. I'll ask around. We'll find the rat, and then we'll skin him."

Bunsong continued walking into the kitchen. "Is that coffee fresh?" He pointed at the coffee maker, and Rooster nodded.

"Any news?" Bunsong asked as he poured himself a cup.

"The best kind. The boss is coming back to Thailand."

Bunsong choked on his coffee. "What? When?"

"Soon."

"Why am I the last to know about this?"

"You were busy up north. Our contact at the prison sent me a message. The Thai government is extraditing him back to Thailand."

Bunsong placed his cup on top of a granite island. "We

don't have much time. Every bit of our operation needs to be working flawlessly, just as he had left it. Call a meeting with the men this afternoon and make sure they understand what is expected of them. Reach out to our contacts; you know which one. Tell him we need to talk tonight. I'll drive into Bangkok."

"A meeting has already been arranged for ten thirty tonight. Same place."

Bunsong drew a deep breath. "I can't believe it. After all these years, he's finally coming home."

6

At eight p.m., Bunsong had climbed into his truck and begun the drive into Bangkok. The meeting he had scheduled was located in the Bang Rak district just off Si Lom Road. Bunsong left his vehicle in a parking structure not far from the meeting location. At that time of night, that stretch of Si Lom Road didn't have a lot of foot traffic, as it was the heart of the financial district. Once the offices cleared out at six, so did the area.

The place Bunsong was heading to was a tiny bar called Madrid. It was hidden in a narrow alleyway off the beaten path and saw very few customers off the street. That's precisely why Bunsong liked it. Plus, he thought their pizza was delicious.

Bunsong pushed open the wooden door that had a port window built into it. The low-lit bar was skinny and long. Five circular booths with black vinyl seating and laminated tables occupied the left side. On the right side, a bar ran the length of the space. Unrecognizable liquor brands filled the glass shelves behind the bar. Three cobweb-covered paintings were hanging on the wall; all featured a matador in a bullfight.

Standing behind the bar were three elderly Thai women.

They ran the joint. They nodded at Bunsong as soon as he entered. He took his usual seat in the booth at the rear of the bar. One of the ladies brought him a bottle of Singha. Another got to work on his favorite, Laab Moo pizza, which is pizza topped with minced pork that's been pan-fried with chilies, lime juice, fish sauce, and shallots. The women never spoke a word to Bunsong. It was better to serve him and keep the peace.

Bunsong glanced at his watch. It was five after ten. The men he was due to meet were late. Bunsong couldn't stand tardiness, a habit he picked up from his boss. It was a strange quirk because, in Thai culture, tardiness was about as common as breathing air. To question one's tardiness was akin to complaining about the hot weather. Pointless. He took the last sip of his beer, and another bottle was placed in front of him on cue.

Another ten minutes passed, and Bunsong's pizza was delivered, but still no show of the men he was there to meet. Bunsong swore under his breath while he munched on a slice. If it weren't for the pizza, he would have left.

But that's not really true. The men he was there to meet were important. Bunsong didn't like them, but he had no choice but to work with them.

Halfway through his pizza, the front door opened, and in walked two men wearing leather jackets and jeans. Bunsong noticed both were wearing thick gold chains with a large Buddha amulet as a pendant. He had worked with them on two other occasions, and they were professional, serious, and not cheap.

Bunsong put on a smile, placed his palms together, and bowed slightly: a wai. He motioned for one of the ladies to bring beers for his guest.

"Are you hungry? The pizza here is good," he said as he picked up a slice and took a bite.

Neither answered as they stared back with stone-cold faces. They both had athletic builds and closely cropped hair. One of them had a noticeable scar near his right eye. His name was Sawat Chantha, but everyone called him by his nickname: Gun. In addition to the thick chain he had around his neck, Gun was fond of large rings made from twenty-four-karat gold. Rumor had it that he often had to replace them because he would beat men, disfiguring their faces and his rings in the process.

The other man, Narong Wongsawat, never spoke. But he was equally as dangerous as Gun. Everyone called him Ped.

The two bottles of beer that had been placed in front of them sat ignored. Bunsong returned the slice of pizza to the platter and brushed his hands before drawing a breath.

"Somsak Ritthirong is being extradited back to Thailand. I would—"

Gun held up his hand. "Three million baht," he said.

Bunsong's eyebrows popped up. He didn't expect to hear that number right out of the gate.

Neither man flinched at it, nor did they crack a smile as if it were a joke to lighten the mood. If anything, it tensed the situation. In his head, Bunsong would have easily paid a million-baht price tag. Even two million wouldn't have been a problem. Three million would have been a first, but not necessarily out of line. Bunsong just didn't expect that to be the first number thrown out.

"Three million is a lot of money," Bunsong said with a smile. "I was expecting something—"

Again Gun stopped Bunsong with a raised hand. "Three million baht each."

Six million baht? That's almost one hundred and ninety thou-

sand dollars. Are these assholes crazy? But Bunsong already knew the answer to his question.

"By noon tomorrow," Gun added.

Bunsong drew a sharp breath. That wasn't much time. As he gathered his thoughts for a response, the two men stood without uttering another word.

Bunsong sat speechless as he watched them walk out of the bar. The meeting was over. There would be no negotiation on the amount. No alternative forms of payment to consider. No half now, half later. No nothing. The price for their help was made very clear. If Bunsong wanted to see Ritthirong again, he had to deliver the cash. There was only one problem: Bunsong didn't have it.

7

On the drive back to Saraburi, Bunsong racked his brains on how to raise that much cash. He had quick access to at least three million baht, but he still had to make up the three-million shortfall. Bunsong's first thought was to squeeze his partners to pay in advance for cargo to be delivered later. It was a long shot but an option worth keeping on the table.

The second option was to steal the money. Bunsong knew someone who would easily have that amount on hand. More importantly, he knew this individual personally and where the money would be. There was a hurdle, however: he would essentially be starting a war with someone who had a long-standing working agreement with his boss. Neither was to interfere with each other's business. Ritthirong stuck to trafficking humans, and this person stuck to trafficking drugs. But Bunsong felt he had no choice.

By the time Bunsong arrived back at the mansion in the jungle, he had already decided to hit the drug dealer. Rooster waited out front with a group of men dressed all in black tactical gear from head to toe with balaclavas over their heads. Slung across their shoulders were compact assault rifles.

"The men are ready," Rooster said as Bunsong approached him.

"No assault rifles. We take handguns with suppressors only. I want to move in fast and make as little noise as possible."

"When do you want to do this?"

"As soon as I change into my gear, we go."

Thirty minutes later, the men had climbed into two black SUVs and were on the highway back to Bangkok, except this time they were heading to an area south of the capital.

Samut Prakan was a province sandwiched between Bangkok and the Gulf of Thailand. It was mostly known for factories that employed the locals. It was also home to a woman named Pornthip Chaichana, but everyone that knew her called her by her Thai nickname, Cake.

Cake was five foot seven and slim. Her silky black hair was long and straight, and her golden-brown skin made her tempting to most men that passed her by. By all accounts, Cake looked just like any other Thai beauty walking down the street. She was anything but.

From the age of four, her father had trained her in Muay Thai. By the time she made her professional debut at age fifteen, she had acquired a reputation as a fierce fighter who was lightning fast with her deadly elbow strikes. She went undefeated for the next four years, holding the champion's belt in her weight division at every age. She stopped fighting professionally at age twenty, when her father and coach suddenly died from a heart attack. Her father had been the heart and drive for her tremendous rise in a sport dominated by men. But with her father gone, Cake no longer had the fight in her needed to continue. She disappeared for three years, until one day...

Cake's new game was yaba. She controlled the distribution

in all of southern Thailand and into Malaysia. Almost all yaba production was done in Myanmar and then brought into Thailand for distribution throughout Southeast Asia. No one quite knew how Cake acquired her territory, but she had an iron grip on it. Over the years, other drug dealers—all men— had challenged her for that lucrative territory. Every single one of them had disappeared without a trace.

A Muay Thai champ turned ruthless drug dealer—two mountains that couldn't be farther apart. Not many people could claim that. There was one other thing about Cake that made her stand out from the ordinary. If you didn't know her, you'd never suspect she was a ladyboy.

"Are you sure about this?" Rooster asked as he adjusted his hands on the steering wheel.

"The boss is coming back," Bunsong said. "We need Gun's help, and that money needs to be in his bank account before lunch tomorrow."

"I'm just saying...Cake isn't someone we want on our bad side."

"We'll be fine so long as she doesn't know it was us that hit her. Think positive. There are a lot of people who are jealous of her territory. There are also a lot of people who don't like her because she is a ladyboy. She embarrassed a lot of men during her Muay Thai reign, and now she's doing it again as the Queen of the South."

"You think the boss will get angry? He's the one who made a deal with Cake. We traffic a lot of people through her territory."

"We don't have a choice. This needs to be done. Cake can't know it was us."

8

Cake lived in a secluded villa on the banks of the Chao Phraya River, right where it emptied into the gulf. She owned all of the lands around the estate, creating a gated community just for her. There was only one reason for someone to venture down the single-lane road leading to the front gates. And it wasn't to go fishing.

Rooster turned off the highway onto the road that led to Cake's villa and stopped. The other SUV with the rest of the men pulled up alongside.

"She has guards at the gates," Rooster said.

"Is there another way in?" Bunsong asked.

"There is, but we need to go in on foot."

Bunsong and his men climbed out of the vehicles and did a weapons check. Every man was outfitted with handguns with suppressors. They also had knives.

"If you think someone recognized you, kill them," Bunsong said. "Cake can't suspect it was us. Understand?"

The men nodded.

"What if we run into Cake?" one of them asked. "Kill her?"

"We can't kill her," Rooster said quickly.

"He's right," Bunsong said. "It would create an unstable vacuum in this area and affect our business. She needs to think this was just a robbery by one of her enemies. Wound her if it comes to it."

The road leading to the entrance gates to her estate was land populated with mangrove trees. It was dense, but cutting through them would keep them hidden. Rooster led the way. It was slow going, but eventually, they reached an iron fence at the edge of Cake's property.

One of the men looked through night-vision binoculars. "I see the home. The lights are on inside," he said.

"Can you see anybody?" Bunsong asked.

"Three men are sitting outside around the table. They're eating and drinking."

"What about the other women?"

Cake's inner circle was made up of five individuals—all ladyboys. Each one had been personally trained in Muay Thai by Cake. They were just as dangerous and very loyal to her. Everywhere Cake went, they went, whether it was to a business meeting or to a nightclub. Cake called them her Fierce Five.

"I don't see them," the man said.

"I wonder if Cake is even here," Rooster said.

"It's better if she isn't. Let's go. In and out. Fast!"

All seven men climbed over the fence and crouched as they made their way toward the villa. The area ahead of them was manicured grass, followed by a pool. Cake's men were gathered by a cabana. Bunsong and his men were able to approach unseen in the dark. As they neared, it was clear that the men were drunk, a good indication Cake was not in the villa.

Bunsong drew his weapon and motioned to his men to do the same. Rooster had long ago come across information that

Cake always kept large amounts of cash in her office on the second floor. The plan was for Bunsong and Rooster to head to the office while the rest of the men secured the villa.

As the group of men closed in on the unsuspecting guards, Bunsong fired first, hitting one of the men in the center of his chest. Seconds later, all three men were dead, still propped up in their chairs. Into the villa, Bunsong and his men went.

"There," Rooster pointed to the stairs.

He and Bunsong headed up to the second floor while the others had been ordered to secure the home.

"Where's her office?" Bunsong asked. The hallway continued to the left and right. Both ways had numerous doors—all shut.

"I'm not sure."

Just then, they heard a toilet flush, and the door next to them opened up. Rooster shot the guard exiting in the forehead.

"We need to check each room," Bunsong said. "You go that way. I'll go this way."

One by one, they cleared the rooms. It was already apparent to Bunsong that Cake and her Fierce Five were not in the home. They couldn't have picked a better time.

"Over here!" Rooster called out to Bunsong. "Her office."

Bunsong hurried to Rooster, who had already headed inside the room. He was searching through the drawers of a large desk. Bunsong began looking through a bookshelf, pulling the books off as he searched for a safe or a hidden compartment. So far, neither man found anything. Rooster tore through the cabinets of a wet bar while Bunsong ripped down paintings that hung on the walls. They came up empty.

"Shit! Maybe she doesn't keep money here." Rooster breathed hard as perspiration rained down the sides of his face.

"Her bedroom," Bunsong said.

He ran out of her office and down the hall to a door at the very end. He leaped up into the air into a flying kick. The impact splintered the wood around the doorknob. Another forceful kick, and the door flew open. Bunsong and Rooster tore the bedroom apart as they searched for cash. Bunsong headed into the walk-in closet and ripped the clothes off the rack. He found three stuffed duffel bags and quickly unzipped one of them. Inside he found stacks of baht.

9

The day had come for Ritthirong to travel back to Thailand. Gray and Pratt set out for HMP Wakefield early that morning, as they needed to be there before noon. It also took longer by car than it did by train. Pratt wanted to be on the road by seven a.m. She didn't want anything, even unexpected traffic on the M1, to screw up her schedule that day. Even though Ritthirong wasn't scheduled to fly out until nine thirty at night, many procedures needed to take place when transporting a high-risk prisoner. Pratt was required to be a part of that every step of the way.

"It's going to be a long day," Gray said before taking a sip of his coffee.

"Sorry about the early start," Pratt said as she switched lanes, "but I always get a little anal when it comes to making sure extradition goes according to plan."

"No worries. It'll be interesting to see you in action. What time is the flight tonight?"

"Nine thirty on Thai Airways."

"Heathrow, right?"

"That's correct."

"How does that part work?"

"Aviation police will take custody of Ritthirong at Wakefield and retain custody until they arrive at Heathrow. At that point, the officers that Thailand sent will then assume joint custody of the prisoner until he is on the plane. Technically, they won't have full custody until we exit our airspace."

"And this will be a normal flight with civilian passengers?"

"Yes. Flight arrangements are the responsibility of the Thai government. Some governments send a chartered plane, while others are fine with a commercial flight. The plane we're flying on is an Airbus A380-800. First class is located on the upper deck. There are twelve seats, and they purchased all of them. We'll have that entire part of the cabin to ourselves."

"That works. Did you get clearance on whether I'll be able to speak to Ritthirong during the flight?"

"It's been signed off by the Thai government, but they have a provision that the men they sent will have the final say. If at any time they feel that it needs to stop, they can stop us from having any contact with Ritthirong."

"They seem to be entrusting a lot to this team."

"That's my thinking, but, hey, it's their call, right? I did a little research online on the men they're sending."

"Yeah? Anything interesting?" Gray asked.

"The Royal Thai Police has eight or nine special forces divisions. SBB is responsible for providing protection to the monarchy and VIPs. But within that unit is a small elite force known as the Black Tigers. They're very secretive and are deployed on a case-by-case basis. There was zero information on them."

"Hmm, seems like the government sent the best they had."

"When we arrive in Bangkok, I assume they'll have a larger contingent of law enforcement meeting us at the airport. It's their prisoner, so their rules. We're just there to make sure everything runs smoothly."

"Basically a cover-our-ass-in-case-something-goes-wrong deal?"

"That's it."

"You mentioned Interpol had an office in Bangkok. Will your colleagues also be at the airport?"

"No. There isn't a need, since I'm there."

"Sounds pretty straightforward. Shouldn't have any problems."

Gray and Pratt kept quiet for the rest of the drive, content to listen to the radio. When they arrived at the prison, they checked in at security and were escorted to Summerfield's office.

"Have you met the governor?" Gray asked.

"No, I haven't. What's he like?"

"He's down to earth. Calm. Patient. He's also a year away from retirement. He spent his entire career in corrections."

"A true rehabilitator."

"He believes he's done well. I like the guy. He comes across as genuine."

Summerfield's assistant had Gray and Pratt wait a short moment as the governor was on a call. A few minutes later, Summerfield peeked his head out from behind the door to his office.

"Special Agent Gray. I thought I'd seen the last of you."

"You can't keep me away."

Summerfield eyed Pratt. "I don't believe we've met yet."

"I'm Lillie Pratt. I'm an analyst with Interpol, and I'm here to help coordinate efforts between the agencies involved."

"Wonderful. There are many, and things aren't off to a great start."

"Is there a problem?" Pratt asked.

Summerfield motioned for them to come into his office.

"Shortly after three a.m., Hunnicutt began banging his head against the wall in his cell. He did a great deal of damage to himself. We had to rush him to the hospital for an emergency operation. They call it decompressive craniotomy. It reduces the swelling in the brain."

"Why would he do that to himself?" she asked.

"We have a pretty good idea. When we watch the footage from the security cameras, it looks like Ritthirong had been whispering to Hunnicutt again. I can't prove it, but I'm convinced his words provoked Hunnicutt to injure himself."

"Do you mind if I take a look at the footage?" Gray asked.

"Not at all."

Summerfield pulled the video clip up on his laptop and then turned it around so that both Gray and Pratt could watch it. Ritthirong had his face pressed against the acrylic near Hunnicutt's cell. They could clearly see his mouth moving. He had been whispering to him for almost forty-five minutes. During that time, Hunnicutt had become increasingly agitated until he snapped and began slamming his head against his cell wall. Three powerful strikes until he collapsed.

"I'm surprised he didn't kill himself," Pratt said.

"Almost did. He's still at risk of dying," Summerfield said. "Agent Gray, any thoughts as to what happened here?"

"As graphic as it is to watch Hunnicutt do this to himself, I think what is even more disturbing is Ritthirong's actions during those seconds. He appears to be taking joy in what happened."

"What could possibly be the reason?" Pratt asked. "Was there a problem between them?"

"As far as I know, there wasn't," Summerfield said before looking at Gray. "Did you sense anything during your conversations?"

"I didn't, but I actually don't think this had anything to do with Hunnicutt. You see here, right before Hunnicutt collapses? Look at Ritthirong. He looks at the camera."

"Is he smiling?" Pratt leaned in for a closer look.

"This was intentional. It was Ritthirong's way of saying goodbye."

10

Immediately after the incident with Hunnicutt, Summerfield had Ritthirong sedated and secured to his bed.

"He woke an hour before you two arrived," Summerfield said as he led Gray and Pratt to the underground unit. "Don't be alarmed when you see him. I felt it necessary to gag him so he wouldn't speak to anyone. I'll leave it up to your team on how you want to detain him while in transit. My advice is not to take any chances until you deliver him to the Thai authorities."

Through the seventeen steel doors they passed until they reached Ritthirong's cell. The guards that were usually there to keep watch were ordered to remain in the room next door and monitor Ritthirong through the security cameras. Summerfield had additional microphones installed near Ritthirong's cell so they could hear every movement and every grunt, no matter how soft.

They stopped in front of Ritthirong. He was secured to his concrete bed with a ball gag in his mouth, and his eyes were shut.

"Looks like he's sleeping," Gray said.

"He's not."

Summerfield had brought a collapsible baton with him. With the flick of his wrist, the baton extended and locked into place. He tapped the acrylic, and Ritthirong's eyes opened.

"Are you sure you want to speak to him?" Summerfield asked.

"I'm sure," Gray said.

"I'll remove the gag, but I'll keep him secured to the bed. You'll still have to remain outside the cell."

"That's fine."

Summerfield radioed for a prison officer to come and remove the gag from Ritthirong. Once that was done, he ordered the officer to remain with Gray and Pratt while he headed back to his office.

Ritthirong turned his head. "Special Agent Gray, I didn't expect to see you again. Who's your friend?"

"My name is Lillie Pratt. I'm a crime analyst with Interpol," she answered.

"Do you know who I am?"

"Of course. Your name is Somsak Ritthirong."

"Are you here to babysit me on the flight to Thailand?"

"My job is to oversee the extradition."

"Forgive me if I can't look you directly in the eye. You're much shorter than Agent Gray."

Pratt moved farther to the side of the cell.

"Much better... Have you and Agent Gray been dating long?"

"We're colleagues."

"Yes, I'm aware, but my question was whether you've been dating long."

"We're not dating."

"Somsak," Gray cut in. "Why did you want to hurt Hunnicutt?"

"I didn't. He hurt himself."

"Yes, that's what it looks like, but we both know that's not what happened."

"Agent Gray, are you trying to entrap me? Don't you think I have enough problems?" Ritthirong shifted his attention back to Pratt. "Lillie—do you mind if I call you Lillie?"

"You may refer to me as Ms. Pratt."

"Very well, Lillie. How long have you worked for Interpol?"

Before Pratt could answer, Gray placed a hand on her shoulder and then spoke into her ear. "It's important we don't let him control the conversation. That's what he wants."

"What did you tell her?" Ritthirong shouted. "No secrets!"

"We're here to talk about what happened to Hunnicutt," Gray said.

"Why should I care about what happened to him? He's not my responsibility."

"He hurt himself pretty bad. Does that bother you at all?"

"If you care so much about Hunnicutt, why are you here with me?"

"Answers."

"Agent Gray, you're so focused on finding the truth, it blinds you. Aren't you bored with this chase?"

"I'm bored with your attempts to make yourself seem like a bigger man than you really are."

Ritthirong was about to say something, but he held his tongue. He turned his head away from Gray and Pratt.

"Looks like that last one got under his skin," Gray said quietly to Pratt.

Pratt proceeded to tell Ritthirong how the day would play out. Not once did he look toward her or acknowledge anything she said, but Gray knew he was listening. In his situation, it was impossible to ignore her voice.

"On the flight to Thailand, you will officially be in the custody of the Thai government."

Ritthirong looked at her. "Will it just be me and those men on the flight?"

"No. Special Agent Gray and I will also be there."

Ritthirong shifted to his side as best as he could to get a better look at them.

"Looks like we got his attention again," Gray said, speaking out the side of his mouth.

"Agent Gray, I didn't realize you were coming," Ritthirong said. "A romantic getaway disguised as extradition business. Very clever. How long will you be visiting my country? If you want, I can show you around and recommend a romantic restaurant for dinner. Are you interested?"

Neither Gray nor Pratt answered.

"Oh, I get it. You need to keep your relationship quiet. Don't worry. Your secret is safe with me. See you on the plane."

Ritthirong closed his eyes and looked away. Gray and Pratt slowly made their way back through the security doors.

"I've never met someone quite like Ritthirong before," Pratt said. "Have you?"

"I've met a lot of interesting people. In some ways, they're the same, and in some ways, they're different. Ritthirong would be defined as a narcissistic psychopath, but what really makes him interesting to me now isn't trying to understand why he's committed all those crimes. I'm more interested in his family and upbringing. He comes from a wealthy family in Thailand that runs in the high society crowd. He had all the opportunities to be a productive member of society. Instead, he did a one-eighty."

"But psychopaths are born that way, right?"

"There is evidence it's a genetic disposition. But that's why

I'm interested in learning more about his upbringing. Not all people born with this condition turn into raging lunatics. The family environment plays a large role."

"Are there reports of other criminals or wrongdoing in the family?"

"Not that I could find, but I wasn't able to dig very deep into the family. Really, just surface stuff."

"Maybe my colleagues in the Interpol office might have some knowledge on that."

"That would be great if they did. While my conversations with Ritthirong were intriguing, and I learned a lot, I still have many unanswered questions. I only wish I had more time to continue our talks."

Pratt pointed her finger at Gray and smiled. "Be careful what you wish for."

11

After Gray and Pratt left Ritthirong, Pratt had a bunch of meetings lined up. There was no need for Gray to attend them, so Gray opted to tour the prison, thanks to an offer by one of the prison officers who had just finished his shift. His name was Newton Parish, and he'd been working at Wakefield for eleven years.

Gray wanted fresh air after being underground, so Parish started the tour outside in the recreation yard, a large paved area the size of a football field.

"I was twenty-five and wasting my life away in the pub," Parish said as he and Gray walked. "My girl at the time left me, and I guess you can say that was my rock bottom. My father wanted me to come work for him. He was a master plumber and made a decent living. I had no complaints growing up under his roof. My childhood was happy."

"Plumbing wasn't lighting any big fires under your butt?" Gray asked.

Parish shook his head. "I felt like I needed to be my own man. Working for my father would prevent me from doing that. A mate mentioned to me that the prison was hiring. I thought it might be interesting. I came in, applied for a job, and I've been here ever since."

"I take it you like it here," Gray said.

"I do. It gives me purpose. I feel like what I do daily makes a difference, whether educating an inmate or disciplining them. I know I did something."

"Fair enough."

"What about you? Working for the FBI must be exciting."

"Never a dull day. But it's also not a nine-to-five. You really do end up living the job, and the lines between personal and professional life blur quite a bit. But we do have one thing in common: we meet a lot of dangerous people."

"I won't argue that. I've had my fair share of run-in's with the inmates." Parish cuffed the sleeve of the white dress shirt he wore. "I got bit by an inmate a few years ago. He cannibalized one of his victims, and he tried to eat a piece of my arm. I clocked him right there on the spot. Thankfully, the tests were negative for any diseases. But I did end up with this scar. But this kind of stuff doesn't get to me. It's the psychopaths, the people like Ritthirong, that get under my skin. You deal specifically with people like that, right?"

"Mostly. Often they don't come across as human. They have zero remorse for anything that they've done. They don't deny doing any of the terrible things. Ritthirong fits that bill."

"I'm glad he's leaving. Let the Thai government deal with him. Two months was enough attention for Wakefield. You know when he first arrived, the media camped outside the prison twenty-four seven, three days straight?" Parish glanced at his watch. "Let's head inside. I'll show you the area where a few inmates are allowed to work or study. You know we have two inmates who convert books to braille?"

"I didn't know that. That seems like a good program."

"It is. In fact, we have a lot of programs set up that can

benefit the prisoners, but they can't be trusted. Personally, I don't trust any of them. You know I spent a year working in the underground unit watching Hunnicutt. I didn't like it. He appeared so normal. It creeped me out. I would never turn my back on one of those psychos. Are you traveling to Thailand with Ritthirong?"

"I am."

"You want my advice, mate? Don't turn your back on that guy. I know he'll be cuffed and you'll have armed guards with you, but I would always keep one eye on him."

"I'll do that."

Gray spent the next hour touring the prison's main buildings that were in the shape of a half star, with four wings. Parish and Gray had lunch in the officer's area. After Parish bade goodbye and good luck to Gray.

At five p.m. sharp, the prison officers started getting Ritthirong ready for his trip. A spit guard was placed over his head to prevent him from spitting or biting anyone. A belly chain was then used to secure his hands and feet. The Aviation Security Operational Command Unit, along with the prison officers, escorted Ritthirong through the seventeen security doors. Once secured in the transport van, the convoy of vehicles left Wakefield for Heathrow International Airport. Gray and Pratt brought up the rear of the convoy.

About forty minutes outside of Heathrow, Pratt received word that a few aviation police had already rendezvoused with the security team sent by the Thai government.

"When did they arrive?" Gray asked.

"This morning."

"Flying in and out on the same day. Talk about efficiency."

"They were invited to come to the prison but refused, preferring to wait in the Thai Airways lounge. They weren't even interested in heading over to the Met. They did bring a change of clothes for Ritthirong with a request he put it on."

"Hmm, all business, I guess. Still just the two?"

"Yep. We're on a direct flight. It'll take approximately eleven hours and thirty minutes to get to Bangkok. I believe we're arriving tomorrow afternoon around four. It should be an easy flight. You may or may not get a chance to talk to Ritthirong, even if you get the okay."

"Yeah, he might conk out for the entire flight. Does the Thai security team know I'm on the flight and what my intent is?"

"They were informed through the proper channels."

"So fifty-fifty?"

Pratt laughed.

Gray shifted in his seat. "You know, observing Ritthirong around other Thai people will be interesting as well. Especially Thai law enforcement."

"Oh? Why is that?"

"The easiest way I can explain it is like when you're a kid, and you have a teacher as an authoritative figure versus your mother or father. It hits differently, if that makes any sense."

"It does. His games might not fly with them."

"He might not even try. Like I said, it'll be interesting to see if his demeanor changes at all."

12

When Gray and Pratt reached Heathrow, the aviation police needed to bring Ritthirong inside through an alternative route. The two men sent by the Thai government were still waiting in the Thai Airways lounge. Pratt's responsibility was to meet them. When the aviation police were ready, she would escort them to a designated waiting area, away from any civilians.

After entering the lounge, Gray spotted the two men first.

"Straight ahead, the two serious-looking dudes in leather jackets," he whispered to Pratt.

They walked toward the two Asian men with brown skin dressed casually in civilian clothes, not that Gray expected them to be outfitted in tactical gear.

"Mr. Chantha. Mr. Wongsawat, I presume." Pratt said.

Both men stood, pressed their hands together, and bowed slightly.

"I'm Lillie Pratt with Interpol. This is my colleague Special Agent Gray. It's a pleasure to meet you two."

When they stood, Gray noticed the shoulder holsters under their jackets. They also wore utility belts. Most likely equipped with handcuffs, pepper spray, an extra ammo maga-zine, and a mini flashlight.

"It's very nice to meet you," Chantha said. "You may call me Gun, if you wish. It's easier for you than my Thai name. My colleague also has an easy nickname, Ped."

"Very well. Somsak Ritthirong is here. Members of the Aviation Security Operational Command Unit are currently escorting him into the building to a private holding area. Before we head there, do you have any questions for me?"

"Not at the moment," Gun said.

"Shall we?" Pratt led the way out of the lounge.

"Special Agent Gray," Gun said. "I'm surprised to see the FBI involved."

"I work in the Behavioral Analysis Unit. I've been inter-viewing Ritthirong for the last two months to understand his thinking."

"I see. And what have you learned?"

"If I had to boil it down to one point: strategic. It's probably why he's been able to stay at large for so long."

"The Thai government is thankful for the help of Interpol and the Metropolitan Police. Will you be on the flight to Thailand?"

"I will be. I was hoping for one last conversation with Ritthirong, if that's okay with you and your colleague."

"Let's wait and see."

"Fair enough."

The special waiting area was nothing more than a sectioned-off part of the gate where civilians could not go. It was common to see armed personnel at airports, so there wasn't much attention being drawn to the group. Ritthirong was sitting in a chair with a man on either side of him. He was no longer dressed in prison clothing but had on a pair of jeans, a white polo shirt, and trainers. The spit guard had been removed from his head, but he was still secured in the belly chain. Unless he stood up, one wouldn't suspect he was a prisoner.

When the time came to board the plane, Gun and Ped took custody of Ritthirong and escorted him onto the plane, followed by Gray and Pratt. Ritthirong had said nothing to the two men who'd been sent for him, nor did Gray notice them trying to communicate with Ritthirong.

When they reached the private business class cabin, Gun had Ritthirong sit in a middle seat in the front of the cabin. He then fastened Ritthirong's seat belt. Gun had also asked that Gray and Pratt sit in the last row of the cabin, away from Ritthirong. Gray and Pratt took their seats and settled in for take off.

After the first meal service, Gray stood to stretch his legs. He saw that Gun and Ped were busy on their phones, not paying any attention to Ritthirong. Gray made his way to the restroom at the front of the cabin. He didn't have to use it. He just wanted to see if Ritthirong was awake.

Gray squeezed into the bathroom and splashed a little water on his face before re-tucking his button-down into his pants. He flushed the toilet, and when he exited the bathroom, Ritthirong caught Gray's eye with a smile.

Well, if that's not an invitation to talk. Gray walked up to Gun, as he appeared to be the leader of the two.

"Have you given any thought to letting me talk with Ritthirong?" he asked in a lowered voice as he leaned in a bit.

Gun looked up from his phone and said, "No."

"No, as in you haven't given it any thought?"

"No, you can't talk to him." Gun went back to his phone.

Gray wasn't about to push the issue. Of all the people there, he was the least important person. He headed back to his seat and peeked over the divider that separated him and Pratt. She was watching a movie. He waved his hand to get her attention.

"Yeah, what's up?" she asked as she lifted the headset off her ear.

"I just had a weird moment with Gun."

Gray explained what had happened, and as the words left his mouth, it sounded like he was complaining over a little thing.

"Never mind. It's not a big deal. I don't know why I even brought it up."

"Do you want me to ask? I'll probably get the same answer, but I have no problem speaking with him."

"Nah, forget about it."

Gray sat down in his chair and reclined. The image of Ritthirong staring at him with a smile as he exited the bathroom stuck in his head. *Was he trying to say something, or was he just screwing with me?*

13

Gray ended up sleeping until the cabin lights came on. Breakfast service had started, and whatever he was about to be served smelled delicious. While he waited for his meal, he checked the flight path on the inflight entertainment system. They were about two hours away from Bangkok.

"Good morning, Mr. Gray," the flight attendant said with a cheery smile. "Will you be having the Western or Thai breakfast?"

"I'll go with the Thai breakfast."

A bowl of noodles along with a plain omelet, fresh-cut fruit, and a basket of bread was placed on his tray. Gray demolished the breakfast so quick, the flight attendant asked if he'd like another bowl of noodles. Gray took her up on her offer. After he finished, he stood and peeked over the divider and found Pratt working on her Western-style breakfast: scrambled eggs, sausages, potatoes, and a couple croissants.

"Good morning, Lillie."

"Good morning to you too. Did you take the Western or the Thai breakfast?" she asked.

"I did two Thai breakfasts. Any news from our friends upfront?"

"I haven't spoken with them the entire flight. What are they doing?"

"Same thing the last time I checked. They're on their phones. I can't see Ritthirong's face from here, so I have no idea if he's up or not. I'm guessing he is."

"You think they fed him?" Pratt asked before taking a bite of her croissant.

"Not sure."

Gray stopped a passing flight attendant. "Excuse me, do you know if the passenger in the front middle seat had breakfast?"

"We were given instructions not to serve him any food. He's only had water to drink on the flight," she said before continuing up the aisle.

Gray turned back to Pratt. "Is that normal?"

"Every country has their way of treating their prisoners. This is a walk in a park compared to what he's facing. His future isn't bright."

"No, it's not. Do we part from them the minute we exit the plane?"

"If there are no requests, then yes. Technically, we're already out of the picture. We have no jurisdiction whatsoever."

The remainder of the flight was smooth sailing until they touched down at Suvarnabhumi Airport. While they waited to disembark the plane, Gun put Ritthirong's spit guard back over his head. Both men seem pretty casual with their handling of Ritthirong. They weren't shy about turning their backs to him or standing too close. It was as if they viewed him as an average prisoner. But Gray figured it was probably a cultural thing because not once did he see any of the behavior that Ritthirong had exhibited in prison.

When they were finally given the okay to exit the plane, Gray and Pratt stayed back, giving Gun and Ped plenty of room to maneuver without interference. Not once during those final moments did they acknowledge Pratt. Again, Gray thought it strange, being she was the liaison between all agencies involved. But whatever. With their carry-ons in tow, Gray and Pratt exited the plane.

When they emerged from the jetway, they walked right into a tight area packed with a large contingent of men in brown uniforms: members of the Royal Thai Police. There were also a group of men dressed in black tactical gear. Gray recognized them as members of the elite Black Tiger unit with the SBB. After hearing what Pratt said earlier about the SBB, he did his own online search. Ritthirong was in the middle of the crowd. Gun and Ped were standing right next to him while they spoke to the other unit members. It was a murmur of the Thai language.

Outside of the small area, there wasn't any place else to go. Anyone exiting the plane had to funnel through that bottleneck of men. It was probably the reason why the other passengers on the aircraft were allowed to get off beforehand. The cabin crew and pilots emerged from the jetway and squeezed through the crowd, right past Ritthirong, as if he wasn't even there.

"Doesn't seem like they have a plan out of the airport," Gray whispered.

"Not our problem," Pratt answered.

"Couldn't hurt to stick around, just in case."

Gray and Pratt stepped off to the side and watched. No one paid them any attention, nor did anyone come up and inquire why they were there. The two groups of men continued to have multiple discussions as they pointed at Ritthirong. To Gray, it appeared as if they were figuring out who would escort Ritthirong from that point on.

After much discussion between the Black Tigers and officers with the Royal Thai Police, Gun and Ped each grabbed one of Ritthirong's arms and started walking forward.

"Looks like Ritthirong is sticking with the Black Tigers," Gray said. "If you don't mind, I'd like to follow and see how they handle Ritthirong from this point on."

"I don't mind. All we have is time."

Gray and Pratt remained a good twenty feet behind the pack as they moved forward. It looked like they weren't taking an alternative route out of the airport and were heading straight toward baggage claim. As Gray and Pratt made their way through immigration, Ritthirong and his handlers had moved off to the side, and another lengthy discussion began, this time with immigration officers.

"I'm sort of getting the impression that the left hand doesn't know what the right hand is doing here. You'd think a memo would have been sent that a high-profile prisoner was arriving on this flight, and the path would have been cleared."

Gray and Pratt cleared immigration right around the same time immigration allowed Gun and his men to continue. The group of men passed through the multiple baggage carousels to the one exit. Gray and Pratt followed behind them.

Once outside, the men gathered in a tight group near the curb for more discussions.

"I'm guessing no one thought to prearrange transportation," Gray said. "This can't be normal, can it?"

"I've seen prisoner transports happen in a variety of different ways, but I wasn't expecting anything like this."

The heat and humidity weren't lost on Gray as he immediately started to perspire. He wiped his forehead as he looked around for the taxi stand.

"I'm going to ring the Interpol office and let them know we've landed. If they don't need us to go there now, we can head to our hotel."

As Pratt stepped off to the side to make her call, Gray kept an eye on Ritthirong. He didn't seem to be at all disturbed by the unorganized efforts. He seemed to be rolling with it as if it were standard practice. For all Gray knew, it might have been.

Suddenly, Ritthirong did something that gave Gray pause. He scratched the back of his left calf with the front of his right foot. There was nothing unusual about that—except Ritthirong shouldn't have been able to do that while in a belly chain.

Did they free his legs? Gray studied Ritthirong's ankles, but it was hard to tell if the chains were attached from where he stood. He was about to ask Pratt to take a look, but she was still on her call.

Gray moved closer for a better look but still couldn't determine if Ritthirong's legs had been freed. He'd been so focused on Ritthirong that he didn't notice one of the members of the Black Tigers had come up to him quickly, placing a hand on Gray's chest to stop him.

"I'm with Interpol. My colleague and I were on the same flight as your prisoner."

The man just stared back at Gray with an expressionless face. Gray was about to apologize when a booming noise caught their attention: a truck had rear-ended another car. RTP officers headed over to the accident as the passengers of both vehicles exited and began shouting at each other.

Without warning, one of the vehicles caught fire, making an already-chaotic scene worse. Travelers began to run from the area as the fire quickly engulfed the car. Other cars near the accident honked their horns for other cars ahead to clear the way.

Boom!

The vehicle exploded, and Gray felt the heat of the explosion before shielding his face with his forearm. People were shouting and screaming as they ran in every direction. Gray moved toward the accident to see if he could lend help. The second explosion happened right then, forcing Gray to stop.

Pop!

Pop!

Pop!

The sounds rang out. It took a beat for Gray to recognize the popping sounds. It wasn't coming from the fire. It sounded like gunfire. Gray, taller than everyone around, searched the crowd for the gunman.

A whizzing sound passed just over Gray's head, forcing him to drop low.

Holy crap! That was close.

Someone was definitely shooting. Gray's initial thought was that someone was having a severe case of road rage. Everyone around him had already hit the ground. Gray scrambled back away from the curb. While doing so, more gunfire erupted. And it didn't sound like a man firing a pistol. It was automatic gunfire.

People everywhere were running for cover. Some of the men from the Royal Thai Police had their guns drawn and were shooting, but Gray couldn't tell what they were firing at from his location.

More bullets whizzed by him, and Gray scurried back behind a standing desk for cover. He looked over to where Pratt had been standing, but she wasn't there. He assumed she had ducked for cover. Members of the Black Tigers had also taken cover, with their weapons drawn. There definitely was an attack happening, but by who and why Gray couldn't quite tell.

Then he spotted what had to be one of the attackers. A man wielding an automatic assault rifle was dressed in black tactical gear like the Black Tigers, except he had a balaclava over his head. Then it clicked.

Ritthirong! This is an escape.

Gray searched for Ritthirong but couldn't find him. He didn't see Gun or Ped, either. The entire group of Black Tigers and the RTP force had spread out because of the gunfire.

Just then, an officer with the RTP joined Gray behind the standing desk for cover. He had his weapon drawn, but one look at his eyes, and Gray could tell this guy was frightened to death and wasn't about to do anything to stem the attack. The officer peeked out from behind the desk, and a bullet struck him in the forehead. He slumped over, eyes open and vacant.

Legally, Gray wasn't allowed to carry a firearm in Thailand, but he wasn't about to risk taking a bullet to the head like the man lying next to him did. He grabbed the handgun, a SIG P320SP, from the dead officer's hand and ejected the magazine. It looked only a quarter full—at most four bullets. *Better than nothing.* He popped the magazine back in. Even though there was an active shooter, he had no jurisdiction in Thailand. All he wanted was to not get shot.

He peeked around both sides of the desk but didn't see the shooter. Most of the people in the area had cleared out. A few members of the Black Tigers and the RTP were still in hiding. They were shouting back and forth to each other in Thai. Gray also hadn't spotted Pratt yet. Maybe she'd retreated back into the arrivals hall.

More shouting prompted Gray to take another look. This time he saw members of the RTP force walking around. It appeared the attackers were either down or they had disappeared. Gray motioned for one of them to come over as he pointed at the officer next to him. Gray pulled out his FBI badge so they wouldn't mistake him as one of the shooters. He still didn't see Gun and Ped anywhere.

He did his best to convey to the officer that came over that the gun he was holding was his colleague's handgun. He seemed to understand as he called for help.

Gray headed inside the arrival hall to look for Pratt, but he didn't see her immediately. He dialed her cell phone and waited for her to answer.

"Hello?"

"Lillie, it's Sterling. Where are you? Are you hurt?"

She didn't answer right away, but Gray heard a muffled voice. A beat later, a man came on the line.

"Hello, Special Agent Gray. How are you enjoying my country so far?"

Ritthirong?

14

Cake must have watched the footage from her home security system more than fifty times. Frame by frame, she went through it, trying to figure out who had killed her men and robbed her of almost four million baht. What made her even more irate was the Fierce Five coming back with no actionable intel.

"How could nobody have seen or heard of anything?" Cake growled as she sat behind her desk.

The Fierce Five stood in a half circle facing her, their heads lowered to avoid eye contact. The group of Muay Thai–trained ladyboys ranged in age from nineteen to twenty-four. And Cake had given them each nicknames.

Chompoo, or Rose Apple in English, was the oldest of the group and also their leader. Cake relied heavily on her to ensure the other four fell into line and there were no problems. As a little girl, Chompoo had idolized Cake from the moment she first saw her fight in Muay Thai tournaments. Chompoo's father was also a professional fighter, so she began training at the gym as soon as she was old enough.

Mint was the second oldest in the group. Her father was

German and her mother Thai, and as a result, she was born with green eyes. She also happened to be the most beautiful of the Fierce Five. Cake named her Mint after the fragrant green herb.

Nok was the tallest in the group, with her long legs. So naming her after a bird, a stork, seemed fitting.

Joke's name didn't need much explanation. She was the funniest in the group. She was also the most well-rounded fighter of them all, having a background in mixed martial arts. Because of that, Cake designated her as the group's trainer. She wanted everyone to develop fighting skills beyond Muay Thai.

And last, there was Tukta, which translated to Doll. She was the smallest and the youngest. With her big brown eyes, she looked a lot like an anime character.

Chompoo stepped forward. "I can't explain it. Either people are afraid or someone paid them off."

"Who has that much control in my territory? I care for the people here. I built two clinics and fixed up the schools. I helped the farmers and donated food to the poor. These people should be loyal to me. Someone knows, and I want you to find out!"

"I agree, someone does know, but not anyone from around here," Chompoo said. "It isn't one of our known enemies. It could be someone we would never suspect but who knows enough about your operations to do the job."

"What are you saying?"

"I think we should look at our allies."

Cake took a moment to consider Chompoo's advice. She trusted her allies. She thought they had good working relationships that benefited both sides. To double-cross would only hurt both businesses. It really made no sense. Peace between them made money.

She let out a breath. "Start looking at our partners and see what you can find out."

The Fierce Five left Cake's office. She looked at the security footage, paying close attention to a man walking down the hallway toward her bedroom. She paused it right when he looked at the camera. The lights were off in the hall, and there wasn't enough ambient lighting to give much detail. He was dressed all in black and had a balaclava over his head.

Who are you?

Cake scratched her head as she replayed that section of footage, hoping to see some small detail about the man that would give away his identity. But nothing at the moment stood out to her. He was of average height and build. Nothing about the way he walked stood out. *If only I had a good look at your eyes. I would know who you were.* Cake had tried playing with the saturation, the exposure, the black point, the shadows, and the brightness of the footage, but none of it gave her a clearer look at his eyes.

But Cake was never one to give up so easily. She thought more about what Chompoo said, that it could be someone they'd least suspect, someone not from their province.

If they weren't from Samut Phrakan, they were either from the southeast side of the gulf or the southwest. Cake controlled everything south of her. She knew all her enemies operating in those areas. She thought she would be able to pick them out, even if they were dressed all in black. Chompoo's point was starting to make more sense.

Bangkok, the capital of Thailand, wasn't that far north. Were the police there involved? Was the local government involved? Cake paid a tax to the police so that she could operate with impunity. As far as she knew, they were happy with their monthly payments. So was the governor of Bangkok and other influential politicians that could make life hard for her.

She mentally ran through a list of people who might have become disgruntled, but again, she'd heard or seen nothing to indicate that unless a more lucrative opportunity had developed. Was someone trying to take over her business? Did someone want her out?

Cake no longer felt she could rely entirely on her Fierce Five. She'd have to do a bit of detective work herself. And she knew exactly how to go about it. She picked up her phone and tapped out a message. A few minutes later, there was a knock on her office door, and in walked Mint.

"Do you need something?" she asked after she closed the door behind her.

When Cake and Mint got all dolled up, they were a force to be reckoned with. Together they always drew the attention of every man and woman in the room. Part of Cake's success in the drug trade had a lot to do with knowing the right people, which wasn't always easy. But Cake had learned early on that her looks and her charm could get her anything she wanted. So much so, rarely did she use violence.

"Tonight, you and I are going out," Cake said with a smile.

15

Gray still couldn't believe what had just happened, as he stood there dumbfounded. One minute he and Pratt were getting ready to take a taxi to their hotel. The next thing he knew, Ritthirong had apparently kidnapped Pratt.

And what made it worse was that no one at the scene cared. No matter who Gray spoke with, whether with the RTP or the Black Tigers, no one seemed to believe him or even wanted to listen. He learned real fast that their smiles and nods weren't signs of willingness to help but of empty politeness.

Frustrated, Gray left the crime scene.

I'm not responsible for that mess. Let those guys figure it out. Gray had hopped into a taxi and was on the way to the Interpol offices. He had to inform them about Pratt.

They would know who to talk to in Thailand to get the ball rolling. Also, I'll contact the UK Embassy. They need to be notified that she was abducted. Gray also knew the Bureau had a legal attaché, essentially, an FBI liaison, stationed in the United States embassy. He was aware he could reach out to that person as well. The more people alerted at the higher levels, the better chance of forcing the RTP to act. And they needed to. Not only was their high-profile prisoner on the loose; Ritthirong, for all accounts, kidnapped a Criminal Intelligence Analyst with Interpol. Surely those aren't the headlines the Thai government wanted to be broadcast.

With all of the possibilities of real help floating around in his head, one major hurdle stood in the way: the day was just about over. Unless people worked past five in Thailand, Gray wasn't sure who he could get in touch with right away.

I'll make a call to the Bureau back in the US if worse comes to worst.

Each of Interpol's member countries hosted a National Central Bureau, or NCB, that connected that country's law enforcement with other countries. The NCB office was located inside RTP headquarters, about a forty-minute ride from the airport, in the heart of Bangkok.

On the way there, Gray put a call into the Interpol offices. Pratt had given Gray an itinerary of their trip, and her Interpol contact was on it: Khemkhaeng Suthisak. It wasn't the easiest call to make. There was a lot of explaining to the reception in regard to who he was. Once past that hurdle, he had to explain who he was trying to reach.

"I'm not sure how to pronounce his last name, but it's spelled S-U-T-H-I-S-A-K."

"Kehmkhaeng Suthisak?" the woman asked.

"I believe that's the person."

"Just a minute."

Gray held the line as he was transferred.

A few moments later, someone else answered. "How may I help you?"

"I'm trying to reach Suthisak?"

The woman corrected his pronunciation and then asked what it was regarding. Not wanting to explain what happened to someone he didn't know, Gray opted to explain who he was and why he was in Thailand.

"Yes, we are aware of the extradition," she said.

Gray waited for a beat to see if she'd heard the news. Surely, the word of the explosion and the attack by armed masked men had spread by now. But the woman said nothing.

"It's urgent that I speak with Mr. Suthisak in person regarding the extradition. I'm en route now by taxi."

"He's unavailable at the moment."

"Will he be available in, say...forty minutes?"

The woman didn't answer.

"I'll see you in forty minutes. Please don't let him leave the office. Something terrible has happened."

Gray debated if he should make a call to the Bureau's legal attaché at the embassy. He did a quick search online to find the location of the embassy. It was located in the same part of town as the RTP headquarters. They weren't even aware that he was in town. And they would just involve Interpol, anyway. Gray opted to wait until he met with Suthisak.

Sixty minutes later, the taxi dropped Gray and his carry on off at the RTP headquarters. Two buildings greeted him. The first looked like a 1920s seaside hotel—the original headquarters, he guessed. Right behind it was a tall concrete office building—the new addition.

The sun had set by then, and it was clearly after office hours. All Gray could do was hope that the woman he'd spoken to took him seriously. Gray was met at the door by a security guard.

"Closed," The security guard said.

"I need to see Mr. Suthisak with Interpol. He's expecting me."

The guard gave him a blank look.

"Mr. Suthisak? Do you know him?"

He smiled. "Suthisak. Me know."

"I need to see him."

The guard shrugged.

It was clear he didn't understand much of anything being asked. Gray pulled out his cell phone, called the Interpol offices, and got a recording stating that it was after hours and that he should call back after nine the following morning.

"Crap!" Gray muttered under his breath.

His mind raced for the next steps. He knew both the UK and US embassies would be closed, and he didn't have the personal cell number for the legal attaché.

A tap on Gray's shoulder grabbed his attention. The guard pointed at two men in the lobby walking toward the entrance. Both men looked Thai.

"Suthisak," the guard said.

"Mr. Suthisak," Gray called out.

One of the men looked in his direction.

"Mr. Suthisak. I'm Special Agent Gray." He held up his identification. "Please, I need to speak to you."

Suthisak said something in Thai to the other men, and they parted. He then looked at Gray curiously.

"How can I help you?"

"It's about Lillie Pratt."

"Yes, Ms. Pratt. Is she here with you?" Suthisak looked around.

"That's why I'm here. This will sound crazy, but hear me out. I believe she's been kidnapped."

"Kidnapped?"

Gray spent twenty minutes explaining what had happened at the airport and how he had tried to alert both the RTP and Black Tigers to no avail. Suthisak listened patiently, nodding every so often until Gray finished.

"Special Agent Gray, how sure are you Ms. Pratt is

missing?"

"As sure as I can be. I called her on her phone, and Somsak Ritthirong came on the line. I'm positive it was him. I know that voice."

Suthisak drew a deep breath. "Maybe she stepped away for another matter."

"She had actually stepped away to call your office."

"My office? I didn't receive a call from her. But regarding your other statement about Mr. Somsak Ritthirong, I'm not sure I understand what you're implying."

Gray shook his head in disbelief. "*I* don't understand. Everyone I try to notify about this has trouble believing anything I'm saying. There was an explosion. Shooting. An officer with the RTP was killed right in front of me. Ritthirong has escaped, and he's taken Lillie with him."

Suthisak gave Gray that same look he'd seen from RTP officers at the airport.

"Let me show you something." He tapped at the screen of his phone. "This just aired on television not too long ago."

Gray watched the video playing on Suthisak's phone. It was news footage of a man being escorted to a van by police at Suvarnabhumi Airport. Holding the man by his arm was Gun and Ped from the Black Tigers. A spit guard obstructed the man's face from view, but he was dressed exactly like Ritthirong.

Gray was at a loss for words as he watched the video unfold. "It...it can't be. What about the attack? Right here, this is where the car exploded," Gray said, pointing as he looked up at Suthisak.

"Agent Gray, maybe you're jetlagged from your flight." Suthisak patted Gray's arm. "Some rest might help, because, as you can see, Mr. Somsak Ritthirong is safely in custody and on his way to prison."

16

Suthisak had already left, and the security guard had returned to his post behind a small desk, leaving Gray alone on the steps outside of the RTP building and questioning his own memory. Was he really jetlagged? Could that have all been a dream?

Get a hold of yourself, Sterling. You know what you saw. If it were a dream, Lillie would be with you right now.

Gray shook off the cloud swirling around his head as he dragged his luggage behind on the way to the entrance gates of the RTP.

You may not be able to explain the footage you just witnessed, but the fact of the matter is Lillie is missing.

Gray tried ringing Pratt's cell phone once more, but it went directly into voicemail, signaling that it was switched off. Gray mentally started a checklist of things he could do immediately.

Identify and contact his legal attaché. Contact both UK and US embassies first thing in the morning.

Contract Gun and Ped from the Black Tigers.

Look into obtaining security camera footage from the airport.

Gray paused for a moment. *Should I inform Evie?*

Evie Jones was Lillie's wife, and Gray had gotten to know her well while working alongside Pratt.

Surely, I have a responsibility to tell her what happened. But what good would that do? She'll have a ton of questions, and at the moment, I have zero answers. I'm still trying to wrap my head around it. Wait a little, Sterling.

Gray flagged a taxi and climbed inside. He pulled his laptop out of his luggage and immediately logged into the FBI's website. It didn't take long for him to identify the legal attaché assigned to Bangkok: Agent Bennett Nickle. Gray immediately called the contact number listed for him. The voicemail system at the US Embassy picked up, and he was directed to Nickle's voicemail.

"Agent Nickle, this is Special Agent Sterling Gray. I've just arrived in Bangkok today, and I must speak with you as soon as possible. It's regarding the abduction of a colleague who also arrived with me. I'm available at this number night and day. Please call as soon as you get this message."

After disconnecting the call, Gray began to map out his plan of attack. He struck out with Suthisak at the NCS. The UK Embassy would be his next stop since Pratt was a UK citizen. After that, it was over to the US Embassy to track down Nickle and find out what help he could lend. Last, getting in touch with Gun or Ped. He had no idea what steps to take to make that happen in the quickest way possible. Hopefully, Nickle could help with that. In reality, Gray would need to lean on Nickle to get anything done. Gray didn't know the ins and outs of how things worked in Thailand.

Gray's cell phone rang. "Gray speaking."

"This is Agent Nickle."

"Agent Nickle. I appreciate you calling back so quickly. I—"

"Not now," Nickle said as he cut off Gray. "It's better we speak in person. Where are you?"

"I'm in a taxi heading to my hotel...the Hyatt Regency. I don't know the address offhand."

"I know it. I'll meet you there shortly."

About fifteen minutes later, the taxi arrived at Gray's hotel. He hadn't had a chance to exchange money, but the driver was willing to accept overpayment in pounds. While Gray checked in to the hotel at reception, he took a moment to look around. He thought Nickle might already be there, but no one fit the profile: an elderly Indian couple, a Singaporean family, a few businessmen, and a white guy dressed in a Tommy Bahama floral shirt, cargo shorts, and flip-flops.

"Here's your key card, Mr. Gray. You're in room 1910 on the nineteenth floor. The elevators are that way."

"Thank you."

Gray grabbed the handle of his roller carry-on and started toward the elevator when the Tommy Bahama fella intercepted him.

"Agent Gray. I'm Agent Nickle. Welcome to Bangkok."

Gray did a double take, noticeable enough to prompt Nickle.

"I know. You were expecting someone dressed in a suit like you. I took today off. I was heading to the Hooters around the corner for beer and wings when I received your message. Why don't you drop your stuff off and meet me back down here?"

Before Gray could manage a response, Nickle spun around and headed back to the chair he'd been sitting in earlier.

Gray continued up to his room and changed into something more suitable: jeans and a polo shirt. He splashed a little water on his face, pulled himself together, and went to meet Nickle.

"First time in Bangkok?" Nickle asked as they walked out of the hotel.

"I visited twelve years ago for about a week."

"Business or pleasure?"

"Ah, pleasure. I'm sorry, Agent Nickle. I'd like to steer the conversation to my colleague."

"I know you think I'm making small talk, but I'm not. I'm trying to assess what you know about Thailand and how it works here. Since you've only visited as a tourist, I will assume you know nothing."

"I'm not sure I understand what you're getting at."

Nickle slapped Gray on the back. "You will, all in due time. Hooters is down the next soi. 'Soi' is what we call the small streets that branch off the main roads."

Nickle took the lead, making his way around the other pedestrians on the narrow sidewalk. Gray couldn't help but think how Nickle looked nothing like an FBI agent. He had a mop of curly blond hair sitting on his head that appeared as if he'd used his fingers to comb it. He was shorter and bulkier than Gray, and his attire would be well suited for a captain of a deep-sea fishing boat in the Florida Keys. *So much for my profiling skills*, Gray thought.

Nickle took a seat at a tall round table in the corner of the restaurant. Gray sat opposite him, still wondering why their important conversation couldn't occur in the hotel lobby.

The server, a short Thai woman with energetic steps that bounced her enhanced chest, appeared at their table. Her nametag read *Joy*.

"Money! So long I did not see you," she said with a cheerful smile. "Where you been?"

"I'm here now. That's all that matters."

"The usual?"

Nickle looked over at Gray. "You a beer drinker?"

Gray nodded.

"Double that order."

"She called you Money," Gray said.

"The locals I know in Thailand call me Money because of my last name. Feel free to call me either one."

"I'll stick with Nickle," Gray said.

"And I'll stick with Gray, though don't be surprised if the locals give you a nickname. They're fond of them."

"How long have you been stationed here?"

"I'd say for the better part of fifteen years."

"That's unusual. Is that by your doing?"

"One hundred percent. I love it here in Thailand. It's become home for me. Don't get me wrong, the Bureau has on numerous occasions tried to replace me, but every agent they assign here doesn't last very long."

"Why is that?"

"They have trouble acclimating, and they never gain the trust of the locals. You need that to be effective at the job. Me? I'm fluent in the language, know the ins and outs of how Thai bureaucracy works, and am practically a local. Plus, I can stomach the spiciest food any Thai person can throw at me."

Joy quickly returned with two bottles of Leo. Nickle grabbed a bottle and held it up.

"Cheers. Now, how about you fill me in on this abduction?"

17

Cake had a plan that night, and it revolved around collecting information. As much as she could from people who had their ears to the ground. And it would start with dinner at the members-only Pacific City Club.

The club was located on the top three floors of a thirty-story office building located on the lower end of Sukhumvit Road. It was there that politicians, businessmen, dignitaries, and celebrities gathered to hobnob. They were the elite, the privileged, and the established. A lot of old money is connected to elite families that have been in power for generations. In Thailand, they have a nickname for these people: hi-so, which is short for "high society." On the other end of the spectrum, the low-society people, or lo-so, clung to the bottom rungs.

Cake gained membership at the club shortly after her father had passed. His good standing in the community and her success in the ring was enough to secure an invite to apply for membership.

Spending time at the club had shaped Cake's thinking and

the decisions she made. She'd learned early on that the people who frequented the establishment controlled all of Thailand. If she could fall in with them, she'd also have a role in influencing her country. The connections she made, coupled with her natural ability to charm, were what helped Cake make inroads into the drug trade and gain her territory.

Cake's occupation was no secret. Everyone there knew what she did. It's just that they also benefited. And in the end, that's what the club was genuinely about: maintaining the status quo for Thailand's elite by any means possible.

"Cake, we're so happy you could join us tonight," the man at reception said as he greeted Cake and Mint.

"You remember, Mint, right?"

"Of course. How could I forget those green eyes?"

The man turned his head so that Cake could see his profile. "Notice anything, darling?"

"You have a new nose."

"I do." He clapped his hands excitedly. "I absolutely love it. Now, is it just you two? Do you have other guests joining you tonight?"

"It's just us."

He leaned in with a coy smile. "Do you want privacy, or are you here to be seen?"

"I need to work the room."

"Of course. You're Cake. You do what you do," he said as he playfully pointed at her. "Follow me. I have the perfect table."

The man sashayed as if he were working a runway. Head up, back straight, legs crossing over each other with every step. When Cake entered the main dining room, heads turned and fingers pointed as conversations about her arrival arose.

"Cake!"

A spunky woman appeared in front of Cake. She wore a

sheer black top with no bra underneath and a matching schoolgirl skirt. The sides of her head were shaved, and the hair on top slicked back with gel. She had more bangles on her wrists than anybody should really have—all gold. Her neck was fully tatted, and her knee-high leather boots added a foot to her short stature.

"Oh my God, Cake! I haven't seen you in ages. Who are you meeting here?"

"No one. We're here to hang out."

"Join me at my table." The woman grabbed Cake by the hand and began pulling her over to a large table where eight other people gathered.

The upbeat, insistent girl was Phukdat, a Thai rapper based on the island of Phuket who had exploded on the scene a few years ago.

"What are you doing in Bangkok?" Cake asked as she sat next to Phukdat.

"I'm shooting a music video in Chinatown this week. I have a dope song dropping soon. And you? What brings you out of Samut Prakan?"

Word hadn't yet spread about Cake's misfortunes. And she wanted to keep it that way. It was also imperative that she deal with it as soon as possible while keeping up appearances. Nothing was more important to the superficial crowd dining there that night than appearances. It's what people see, not what they know. Cake intended to not only find the person who had stolen from her. She would paint a new narrative that suited her, and that's what everyone would remember.

But Phukdat wasn't like everyone else. Cake didn't have to pretend around her. They both came from meager backgrounds, not established hi-so families. Most everyone in that room had the privilege of backing them.

Cake leaned in and lowered her voice. "I got hit a few days ago."

"No way. By who?" She grabbed a bottle of champagne from the ice bucket stand near her chair and poured them both a glass.

"That's what I'm trying to figure out."

Cake proceeded to tell Phukdat about the robbery and the theories floating around in her mind.

"Have you heard anything about this?"

Phukdat shook her head before downing her champagne and urging Cake to do the same. She then quickly refilled both glasses.

"But if I do, believe me. I'm ringing your ass. I can't believe someone did that. I bet it was Sin and Satra. You know those guys were always jealous of your power."

"I don't think it was them. They're too stupid to pull off anything like this. The men who hit my place had training."

"I wouldn't cross them off the list. I heard they're barely making any money with their business. You should take it over."

"Not my style. Even I know if it smells like shit. It's shit."

Sin and Satra ran the local mafia in Samut Sakhon, the province directly to the west of Cake. Most of their business dealings involved the massive seafood industry. Almost all seafood that is processed in Thailand takes place in Samut Sakhon. They essentially squeezed the owners of the canneries and the fisherman for a cut. In addition, they also tax the migrant workers. They really were leeches that had no standing in Thailand. The only reason why they hadn't already been eradicated was that their uncle was a high-ranking officer with the RTP. Sin and Satra were the sons of his sister-in-law. They might be the screwups of the family, but they were still family.

"So, what will you do?" Phukdat asked.

"See what people know."

"You mean like if someone is shopping and spending a lot of money?"

"No, not like that. Whoever took my money was strapped for cash. They needed quick money. They were in trouble."

Phukdat crinkled her brow. "That rules out everyone here."

"It's definitely not a hi-so."

"Probably not, but there are some fake-ass people in this room." Phukdat refilled their glasses again.

"Did you hear?" she asked after taking a sip.

"Hear what?"

"King Rong is back in town."

"Ritthirong? What? How? I thought he was running from the police. Why would he come back?"

"He didn't. He got caught. It was on the news today. The police in the UK caught him and sent him back to Thailand. You honestly didn't know?"

Cake shook her head. "But it's interesting. Are you sure it was really him? You know how things work. Nothing is ever what it seems."

Phukdat shrugged. "It's what I saw. Hey, after dinner, we're heading to Sing Sing. I'm meeting up with my cousin. She's the one dating a hi-so police officer. I can never remember his name, but anyway, he'll be there. I'm sure he knows more details than the media. Plus, he might be able to help you out with your problem."

Phukdat began posing for a bunch of photos with other guests dining at the club that night.

"You have that look on your face," Mint asked. "You think Ritthirong had something to do with it?"

"No, we have a good relationship. I'm just surprised he was caught, that's all."

"But?" Mint arched an eyebrow.

"I still think we should tag along with Phukdat and see what this policeman knows."

"Sounds good to me. I love Sing Sing."

18

All Nickle did after Gray finished explaining was to smile and polish off the rest of his beer before motioning for Joy to bring two more beers.

"I don't get it," Gray said. "Why does everyone think I'm making this up? You, of all people, should be taking me seriously. Do you really think I thought it would be fun to meet up with you on your day off only to make up a story like this?"

"Gray. It's not that I don't believe you. It's just that I'm not sure what you want me to do about it."

"Do about it? She's been kidnapped by Ritthirong."

"Ritthirong was on TV being escorted to jail. I'm sure he's sitting in some disgusting cell right now."

"It was his voice on the other end of that phone. I know what Ritthirong sounds like. I spent a great deal of time interviewing him."

Joy put down two fresh bottles of beer and walked away.

"Look, let's assume what you're saying is true. How do you explain Ritthirong being escorted by the RTP, the Black Tigers no less?"

"I don't know. I can't."

"Okay, say your colleague... What's her name?"

"Lillie Pratt."

"Okay, say Lillie *is* missing. I want you to set aside the idea that Ritthirong is behind her abduction for now.

"But he is behind it."

"Humor me, okay? Let's focus on Lillie's disappearance for now. Did she mention friends or family that might be here?"

"No."

"Could she have set up other appointments or engagements without informing you?"

"It's possible, but I don't think that's what she did. She doesn't operate that way, and she would have, at a minimum, sent me a text if she couldn't answer her phone."

"Fair enough." Nickle took a swig of his beer. "You've already informed Interpol about her disappearance."

"Yeah, they don't care."

"It's not that they don't care. They have no jurisdiction. They don't investigate. They facilitate. They're liaisons to help coordinate efforts between various law enforcement agencies."

"I fully understand how Interpol works," Gray said, getting a little heated under the collar. "I don't need the lesson."

"Stay calm. I'm here to help. So whether our friends at Interpol believe you or not, there's not much they really can do. In other words, they won't take action based on your word. So it's a dead end with them."

"Exactly, but I thought it was a good way to start and that they would help, as you said, facilitate my investigation. You know, put me in touch with the right people who can take action."

"You see, that's where you've taken a wrong step."

"What do you mean?"

"This isn't your investigation. You have no jurisdiction here in Thailand. You are not an FBI agent. You're a guest here."

"But Lillie is missing. We have to do something."

"We work for the United States federal government and their interest. Heck, even I have no jurisdiction in Thailand. I'm the equivalent of Interpol. I help facilitate cooperation between the RTP and the FBI."

"Right, so that's why I contacted you."

"Lillie is a UK citizen."

"You got to be kidding me. I get the feeling that all you're doing is making excuses. You're arguing semantics. You know damn well that what I'm saying is true about Lillie."

"Gray, calm down. I'm your best shot you have at making any progress right now. What I'm trying to do is make sure you understand the game. You can't play it unless you know the rules."

"What game are you talking about?"

"This is Thailand. It doesn't operate the same way the US does, or even the UK. There is minimal emphasis on the procedure here. There are no laid-out steps to take. There is the only interest."

"I don't understand. What do you mean by that?"

"What I mean is to get anything done here, you need to grab people's attention. And telling people that Lillie, an Interpol analyst, has gone missing won't cut it. Sadly, that's the real truth. There needs to be other motivators put into action. This needs to be handled the right way. Not the way you've been trained to tackle investigations."

"But surely, at the very least, the UK Embassy would be able to help. She is a UK citizen."

"Embassies are, again, there to further the interest of that country. They have no authority to investigate. What they will do is file a report with the Metropolitan Police back in the UK. They will then contact Interpol so that they can get the ball rolling with the Royal Thai Police."

"Are you kidding? She could be dead by then. Ritthirong is a psychopath, and this is some sick game he's playing."

"So you need to play the same game to get back at him. It's the only way, Gray, or else you'll never see Lillie again. I promise you that. Any evidence of her being here in Thailand will be swept under the rug and forgotten."

Gray ran a hand over his buzz cut as the wheels in his head got to work. "So are you suggesting we do nothing until the UK Embassy opens tomorrow morning? Surely you're not suggesting I walk into the nearest police station and file a missing-person report?"

"Not at all. That would be a monumental waste of your time. But visiting the embassy tomorrow is an item I recommend crossing off your list of useless things to do but they have to be done. I have another idea on how we can get started right away, tonight, in fact, at a place not far from here."

"What is it?"

"Blade Runner Alley."

19

Cake spent a little more time at Phukdat's table before she and Mint got up to make the rounds. They decided to split up to cover more ground. While conversations were guaranteed, it was impossible to tell whether they would bear fruit.

"Cake." An elderly gentleman dressed in a dark suit called out.

"Khun Vidura." Cake placed her hands together and bowed slightly. And then turned to an elderly woman dripping in diamonds. "Khun Ying."

"Please sit and have a drink with us."

Vidura and his wife, Ying, were old-school elite. Both came from wealthy families, but Vidura had built up his father's already-successful exporting-and-importing business into a conglomerate. Not only did they export a lot of Thai spices and goods, but they had also secured a firm grip on the importation of all liquor into Thailand. They were also the owners of a high-end chain of hotels and shopping centers. Vidura had retired eight years ago, entrusting the running of the business to his three sons and two daughters. They were frequent visitors to the Pacific City Club.

Vidura loved drinking Macallan fifty-year-old single malt scotch. He kept numerous bottles at the club. The average price for a bottle was two hundred thousand US dollars. A server came over—they always had a server dedicated to their table—and poured a glass of whiskey for Cake.

"Chon kaew," Vidura said as he held up his glass.

"Chon kaew" was a popular way to say "cheers" in Thailand. Its literal translation was "to bump glasses."

Cake took a sip of the smooth whiskey, holding it for a moment on her tongue to allow the spicy vanilla flavor to spread. Only then did she swallow.

"How is everything with you?" Vidura asked.

Cake wasn't sure if he was asking to be polite or if he had heard about her misfortune. Vidura had always been a father figure for Cake.

"To be honest, I've had a run of bad luck."

Vidura leaned forward with a frown on his face. "What happened?"

Cake explained in a way that didn't force her to say the word "robbery" out loud, but Vidura would still understand. He nodded as he leaned back.

Why would Vidura care so much that a drug dealer got ripped off? It's because he owned the largest palm plantation in southern Thailand. In fact, the majority of his income was currently derived from the plantation. Vidura was responsible for close to 75 percent of all palm oil exported out of Thailand. That equated to 2.7 million tons of palm oil per year. His operation employed thousands of workers to farm the land. It was an operation that ran twenty-four hours a day and still had trouble meeting the market's demands for palm oil. It generated significant profits for Vidura. But to keep his plantation producing at its optimum, he needed his employees to be on their toes. Yaba was one way to make that happen. He also required stability in the area.

If Cake's distribution of yaba pills to the south was disrupted or if she became distracted and her business suffered, or worse, Cake went on a rampage and started a war, that would create a lot of instability in the areas, thus affecting Vidura's plantations. So long as she kept the peace and the distribution flowing, his plantation hummed along smoothly. In return, he used his status to grease the politicians and the police in the area so that Cake's operations were overlooked, aside from the occasional PR bust needed.

Vidura knew what Cake was asking without her having to verbalize it. He knew every single influential person in Thailand. If there was anything to be found, he would have a very good chance at hearing about it.

Vidura placed his hand on Cake's forearm and gently patted it. "Be strong. Stay focused. Don't let this be a distraction that leads to more distractions. All will work itself out."

"Yes, I hope so."

Vidura raised his glass once more, and the two clinked their drinks. Cake politely excused herself from their table to continue the rounds. But no sooner had she walked away from Vidura's table than Somchai Thapthong, whom everyone referred to as Hi-So Charlie, intercepted her.

Hi-So Charlie was the opposite of the moniker Cheap Charlie. He loved to show off his wealth by spending vast amounts of money. He always wanted to make a splash with whatever he was doing, and he could. Hi-So Charlie was an heir to a family fortune that very few in Thailand could come close to competing with. Of course, no one dared call him that name in front of his face.

"Cake, dear. You're looking fierce tonight," Somchai said.

Cake's face brightened up immediately. "Somchai, it's been so long since I've seen you."

Somchai greeted Cake with a kiss on the cheek. "Who are you here with?"

"Mint is with me."

"Oh, she's darling. Where are you sitting?"

"We were sitting with Phukdat."

"Yes, I saw her earlier. She's a wild one. She wants me to invest in a music company with her? It seems like everyone I meet wants me to partner in a business with them." He leaned in and lowered his voice. "Only they don't have any money to contribute."

"Sounds like a lot of people require cash."

"So true. I don't know what it is, but everyone needs it right now."

"Besides Phukdat, who else has hit you up, if you don't mind telling?" Cake flashed a coy smile.

"You're a sly one. What *are* you getting at?"

"I'm interested in knowing who has money problems."

"Uh, everyone, apparently." Somchai motioned to a man sitting at a table full of pretties.

"Pretties" was a slang term used to refer to young and beautiful Thai women hired to work for promotional or enter-tainment events. It could be as simple as standing there and looking beautiful, pouring drinks all night, or accompanying a guest to dinner. There were twelve pretties sitting with this one man, a high-ranking officer with the RTP.

"I don't know why he has all those women with him. He can barely afford to pay his expenses," Somchai said. "The little brown envelopes that he receives every week, well, they've been light. Someone needs to put him on a budget." Somchai chuckled.

"Who else have you heard of that's light on cash?"

"Why are you asking, Cake? You never bothered with this sort of gossip before."

"Let's just say someone borrowed a large sum of money from me without asking."

Somchai raised his eyebrows. "Ah, I see. I'll tell you now it's not him. He's too stupid to do anything like that."

"I heard Ritthirong is back in town," Cake said.

"I heard too. Do you think it's him? I thought you guys were cool."

"We are. It's just that I find it hard to believe he was arrested, that's all. I don't think he's involved."

"You and I both know what we see isn't always the truth. This is Thailand. There is no real truth." Somchai gave Cake a hug. "I'll keep my ears open."

Cake continued to mingle with the diners but hadn't heard anything that would point her in a concrete direction. However, the night was young, and there was always Sing Sing.

During the short time that Gray and Nickle were holed up inside the Hooters, the skies over Bangkok had grown cloudy and unleashed a torrid rainfall.

"I swear the skies were clearer earlier," Gray said as the two men stood by the entrance, peering out through the glass door.

"It's monsoon season. Rain will come in like rocket, piss all over the place, and split before you can crack an umbrella."

Joy approached them with two umbrellas. "We loan them out to special guests."

"Thanks, Joy," Nickle said. "I'll make sure these find their way back here."

Nickle led the way down the sidewalk filled with uneven concrete squares.

"Watch your step. It's easy to tweak your ankle and eat a mouthful of asphalt."

"How far is this place again?" Gray asked.

"It's about a fifteen-minute walk. We're heading to Sukhumvit Seven. We just came out of Sukhumvit Fifteen."

"Why do you call this place Blade Runner Alley?"

"You'll see."

By the time they reached Sukhumvit 7, Gray's jeans had soaked up enough water to drench his pants up to his knees, and his shoes were waterlogged.

"Now I understand why you wear shorts and flip-flops," he said to Nickle.

"Living in Thailand, you're forced to adapt or be miserable. The alley is just ahead."

Sukhumvit 7 was a small one-lane road. They headed in about thirty yards and then made a left into a small restaurant with an open kitchen up in the front-facing the street. They slipped inside through the narrow opening off to the side of the kitchen. The place was tiny but brightly lit. There were seven metal tables, each capable of sitting four people. Mostly foreign men with Thai women were seated at the tables and eating. A menu written in Thai and English hung on the wall. A short and pudgy Thai woman served the diners.

"This is Blade Runner Alley?" Gray asked as he closed his umbrella.

Nickle pointed to the rear of the restaurant. "No. Though there is the alley."

To Gray, it looked like the entrance to where the bathrooms would be, but Nickle made a beeline straight toward it.

The alley was more like a narrow pathway lit mostly with varying types of colorful Christmas tree lights, small hanging bulbs, and neon signs. The uneven asphalt ground was wet with puddles of water, a mishmash of paper debris, and old takeaway boxes.

The first thing to strike Gray, aside from the sour stench of a nearby pile of garbage, was the music blasting out of a bar just up ahead on the right side. Gray peeked inside and saw men and very tall women drinking and playing pool as they walked past it. Gray tilted his head, as he hadn't seen very many tall Thai women since his arrival.

"It's a ladyboy bar," Nickle said. "Music's great. They have a live band on the weekend."

Opposite the ladyboy bar was a beauty salon large enough to barely hold two chairs. Both were occupied by women having their hair done.

Right after that were two smaller bars on opposite sides. Each one housed a small bar, five barstools, and a shelf with your standard liquor and beer on hand. They looked identical, except the left bar had only an old man singing karaoke: a Thai song. The other bar blasted techno music and had a monkey sitting on top of the bar. He wore a glow-in-the-dark collar leash held by the owner, who stood behind the bar. She smiled at Gray. Her front teeth were clearly missing.

They passed by more small bars that could hold no more than four or five guests at a time—one or two of the seats were occupied by bargirls. Equally sized massage shops also dotted the alley. There were vendors grilling meat on a stick and selling small bowls of noodles. People stood as they held their bowls and ate. There was no room for a table, let alone chairs.

The makeshift aluminum roofing that covered the walkway pinged loudly from the rain. Water dripped through cracks catching Gray's head every few feet or so.

"Now I understand why you call it Blade Runner Alley," Gray said. "But I'm lost on why we're here."

"That's why we're here." Nickle pointed up ahead.

A standing wooden bar blocked half of the walkway ahead. A lone light bulb dangled above, the only normal light he'd seen thus far. An old man stood behind the bar, and sitting on the bar top were three large glass jars filled with a brown liquid. Leaning up against the bar was a Thai man downing a drink.

Nickle bellied up to the bar and ordered three drinks. The old man lifted the glass cover from one of the jars and ladled three small cups full. Nickle passed a glass to Gray.

"What is this?" he asked.

"It's ya dong: Thai firewater. Drink up. It'll put hair on your chest. Plus, we need to catch up." He pushed the other glass over to the obviously drunk Thai man.

"Nickle, what are we doing here? We're wasting time. I thought you would introduce me to someone who could actually help."

"I am. Special Agent Gray, meet Detective Senior Inspector Chaemchamrat. Everyone calls him Chet because his last name is too hard to pronounce, even for Thai people."

Just then, Chet grabbed the shot glass and downed the ya dong.

"This is the detective that's supposed to open the door for me and help me locate Lillie?"

"I know he's not making the best first impression, but trust me, he's the best street fighter I've ever seen this side of the Mekong and one of the few incorruptible members of the RTP."

"You're kidding me, right? He can barely hold himself up."

"Hey, asshole," Chet said with a Thai accent. "What did you say?"

Gray ignored Chet, focusing instead on Nickle. "Look, maybe you got the wrong idea about me, but I'm not here to party."

Gray turned and was about to leave when Nickle grabbed him by the arm and stopped him.

"Trust me. You'll want his help. Now finish that drink." Nickle picked up the glass and held it out to Gray. "You got nothing to lose right now," he said.

Gray let out a dismissive breath before downing the liquor. It burned from the tip of his tongue to the back of his throat.

"What the hell is in that?" he coughed out the words.

"It's a special blend of who-knows-what mixed in with a bunch of Thai herbs."

"A little warning," Gray uttered in a breathy voice as he was still trying to swallow the last bit.

"Why are you here?" Chet shouted out as he grabbed hold of the bar to regain his footing.

"Are you sure about this guy?" Gray whispered to Nickle.

"Trust me. This guy can kick your ass blindfolded right now."

"I seriously doubt that."

Chet slammed his shot glass down hard on the bar top before walking right up to Gray with his chest puffed out. He was smaller than Gray, about five foot eight, but he ran his mouth like Goliath.

He stabbed his finger into Gray's chest to emphasize his question. "I said, why are you here?"

Gray slapped Chet's hand away, and Chet swung back, catching Gray on the chin with a fast and tight right hook. The punch knocked Gray onto his butt.

"You little son of a bitch."

Gray got back up onto his feet and charged Chet, tackling the man into a wall made of corrugated plastic. With Chet's back flat on the floor and Gray in the dominant position on top, he got ready to deliver a ground-and-pound. Only Chet deflected the blows and slipped in a snapping punch to Gray's nose. Chet then clasped his hands together and slammed his double fist straight into Gray's chest.

Gray fell over to the side, gasping for air. Chet punched him again in the face. As he wound up for a second strike, Gray kicked Chet hard in his gut. Then reached over and slammed his fist into the side of Chet's face, causing his head to bounce off the asphalt.

From the bar, Nickle watched both men climb to their feet and proceed to beat the living crap out of each other. The old man behind the bar placed a five-hundred-baht note down before pointing at Chet.

"All right, I'll match you. I gotta root for Team FBI."

Nickle placed his money on the bar.

Both men seemed to be equal in striking. Neither was advantageous in defense, resulting in both of their faces swelling up into a bloody mess. Both men collapsed to the ground with heaving chests and heavy eyelids. It appeared the fight was over.

Nickle looked back at the old man. "It's a draw."

They each took their money back. Nickle walked over to Gray, sitting with his legs sprawled out and leaning back against a panel of wood, and knelt down.

"Hey, buddy." He slapped Gray's face to grab his attention. "Looks like you and Chet are off to a great partnership. I need to take care of some business. I'll be in touch tomorrow."

Before Gray could manage a response, Nickle disappeared.

21

The cool kids in Bangkok hung out at Sing Sing, a cabaret nightclub located in the Phrom Phong neighborhood. If old money settled in at the Pacific City Club, then the new, brash money definitely vibed at Sing Sing.

The decor inside the club resembled Shanghai early 1900s with a bunch of metal and woodwork featuring geometrical designs and dancing dragons. Red Chinese lanterns lit the venue, giving its speakeasy feel and its patrons the privacy they craved. It was the perfect place to be seen without being seen.

Cake and Mint took a taxi to the club rather than tagging along with Phukdat and her entourage. She had hired a large shuttle bus to ferry them around town that night. Plus, Cake was in the middle of a conversation when Phukdat wanted to leave.

Mint didn't have much luck working the dining room, but every man she spoke with did ask her to meet up later that night. She politely declined.

"You keep bringing up Ritthirong," Mint said. "Do you really think he's involved?"

"No, I just can't believe he's been caught. I've always pictured him returning to Thailand and not caring that he was a fugitive. If he wanted to, he could settle any differences with the police and continue to 'elude,'" she said, using her fingers to signify quotes around the last word.

"Well, he didn't because he was on TV with the police," Mint said. "What do you think will happen to his operation?"

"Nothing, it's been running fine ever since he went into hiding. Charong Bunsong has been managing things without problems."

"That's his number two?"

Cake nodded as she checked her phone for messages.

"I agree with you. It doesn't make sense. He's too smart to be caught."

The taxi came to a stop outside of Sing Sing, and the two women exited the car. Once inside the club, they headed up to the second floor. Private tables lined the balcony that over-looked the dancefloor below. Deep house music gave the place a laid-back groovy feel, saving the upbeat tempos for later in the night. But beyond the private tables, through a maze of narrow hallways were the hidden backrooms reserved for VIPs. That's where Phukdat and her entourage would be.

An attendant greeted Cake and Mint in the hall. Cake said her name, and after a brief check of his phone, he allowed them to pass. They didn't need to know what room Phukdat had reserved. They could hear her rapping from outside.

Inside, red lanterns hung from the ceiling, giving the sofas and lounge chairs that opium den–like feel. Phukdat wasn't actually rapping. Her song was playing on the speakers as she stood on a couch, grooving to it.

"I'll fix us a whiskey," Mint said before walking over to the liquor table.

"Cake!" Phukdat motioned for her to come over. "This is the new song I'm dropping. What do you think?"

"I love it. It'll be hit just like all your others," she said.

"Over there." Phukdat pointed to the corner of the room. "That's the policeman I was telling you about. His name is Ped."

Cake looked where Phukdat was pointing and saw a man who, at first glance, appeared out of place among the younger, more energetic crowd. He sat quietly, sipping whiskey from his glass while he observed. Cake had never seen him before, which she thought was strange. She either knew all or at least *knew of* the important people, at a minimum by face.

"What police station does he work out of?"

Phukdat shrugged. "I have no idea. Go talk to him."

Phukdat's cousin was sitting right beside Ped, but she was involved in an intense conversation with another woman.

"Will your cousin freak out if I talk to him?" Cake asked.

"Nah, she's not that into him."

Mint returned and handed a whiskey soda to Cake, and the three women clinked their glasses.

"That's the police officer Phukdat was mentioning earlier," Cake said to Mint.

"Doesn't look like he's having fun here."

"It doesn't. I think we should both sit with him and see if we can get him to smile."

Cake led the way and then wedged herself between Ped and Phukdat's cousin, who obviously didn't mind because she hadn't stopped chatting and simply moved over. Since Ped was sitting up against the edge of the sofa, Mint plopped herself down on his lap.

"I don't think we met. I'm Cake, and this is Mint."

Ped cracked a smile and nodded in acknowledgment.

"Do you like Phukdat's new song?" Cake asked.

"Yes, it's very good. How do you know her?"

"We come from the same village: Rawai, Phuket."

"I know it. Very beautiful there."

"Like me?" Cake smiled.

"Yes," Ped nodded.

"Do we know each other?" Cake asked.

"I have heard your name before, but this is the first time we've met."

"I know most of the senior officers at the Lumpini and Thonglor stations."

"I don't work out of those stations. I work for the SBB."

"Oh?" Cake leaned in. "You are important."

"No, really."

"And modest. What is your specialty? Intelligence? You look like a smart man. I'll say you work in Intelligence, but you have big muscles, too. Hmm, let's see... Smart and fit. Do you provide protection to the royal family?"

"Not really."

"Okay, don't tell me. I'm having fun guessing."

Cake looked directly into Ped's eyes as she continued to deduce what he did.

"It's a very important job, behind the scenes. I feel I'm right about that. You're not someone who craves attention. You're a mysterious man."

Ped now had a lasting grin on his face. "You're getting warmer."

"Only one division works in such secrecy."

"And what is that?"

"You're a Black Tiger. Am I right?" Cake playfully jabbed Ped in his rib cage, causing him to giggle.

"Okay, you win."

"You're the first Black Tiger I have personally met."

"We don't hang out in situations like this too often." Ped

motioned around the room with his hand. "We work a lot. I just came off an important detail and took a few days off to relax."

"Can you tell me what it was about? Please, please!" Cake begged as she batted her eyelashes.

"Can you keep a secret?"

"Of course. I promise I won't tell anyone."

Ped whispered into Cake's ear. "I brought Somsak Ritthirong back to Thailand."

Cake drew a sharp breath as she pulled her head away so she could look at Ped's eyes to see if he was joking.

"You're serious, aren't you?"

He nodded. "I picked him up in London."

"Oh my God. That's amazing. I can't believe you caught him."

"We worked with the Metropolitan Police and Interpol. It was a group effort."

"Still, it's amazing. I never, ever thought he would be captured. Wait..." Cake arched an eyebrow. "You're not locking me up, are you?" She made puppy eyes at him.

"No, no, no. You have nothing to worry about."

"Good, because I like talking to you. So what will happen to him now? Will he go to jail?"

"Ritthirong's in jail waiting for his trial. It's up to the courts to decide his fate."

"What jail is he at?"

"Bang Kwang."

"I heard that is a really bad place to be, the worst out of all of them."

Ped nodded. "All high-profile criminals are kept there."

"Enough about my work. I'm on holiday. Why are you in Bangkok" Ped asked. "Don't you live in Samut Phrakan?"

"You have heard of me," Cake smiled. "I do live there, but I came here for a night out to find out the latest gossip. I took time off from work just like you. We had dinner at the Pacific City Club earlier. A lot of people in Bangkok are having a rough time."

"What do you mean?"

"Money problems."

"I heard the same too. It's slow now. I'm glad I have a lot of work. I don't have to worry too much about money."

"I bet they paid you a lot to go to the UK."

"It's my job. I get a salary."

Cake knew Ped understood what she was really getting at. No high-ranking officer could afford their lavish lifestyles without receiving weekly brown envelopes, no matter what division they worked in. Ped was no different from the rest.

"I'll admit, it's been a little hard for me to make my weekly payments, if you know what I mean," Cake said softly. "That's one of the reasons I'm here. I'm hoping to make different arrangements."

"How is that working out for you? Everyone needs to be paid."

"I don't know yet. We'll see what happens."

"I'm surprised you have this problem. I always heard you did well in the south."

"I do okay, but I have enemies. They attack me every now and then."

"I see. You have to be careful about retaliating. It could bring more problems for you."

"I know. But I don't even know who attacked me the last time. So I can't really retaliate." Cake giggled.

"Yes, that would make it harder." Ped took a sip of his drink. "What happened?"

Cake thought carefully about revealing details. But

someone like Ped would have access to another level of information that most didn't.

"While I was away, a group of men hit my home. They took my stash, and I lost a few men from my security detail."

"How much did they take?"

"A little under four million baht?"

Ped pulled his head back in surprise. "That's a lot to take, even for a group. They had problems, and they knew you had money on hand. Who has that information?"

"Not many, but it doesn't appear to be any of them."

"You don't have video cameras?"

"They wore masks. Trust me when I said I looked through the footage a hundred times."

Ped nodded and took a sip of his drink.

"That's why I'm in Bangkok, to see if anyone has heard about large amounts of money moving around recently."

Ped smiled. "What do you want from me, Cake?"

"The engine of Bangkok only works when it's properly greased, and we all work together," she said.

Cake saw the wheels in Ped's head move into motion.

"You sure it isn't one of your enemies that took your money?" he asked.

"I have to keep an open mind."

"That is true."

The two stared at each other quietly for a few moments, neither changing the expression on their face.

Ped drew a breath. "If I hear anything, I will let you know."

"That's all I ask. And you should know, I always return favors generously."

22

The last thing Gray expected when he woke up in his hotel bed was to be wearing a pair of damp jeans. He had removed his shirt but not his shoes. He rubbed his eyes and pulled away quickly, as it was tender to the touch. Gray sat up and threw his legs over the side of the bed and winced in the process. He felt like he'd aged ten years overnight as every part of his body ached. He walked over to the bathroom mirror, and one look triggered his memory. He'd been in a fight.

Gray examined his face. *Slight bruising on my cheek... Jaw pain when I open my mouth... A fat lip and caked blood in my nostrils. I hope the other guy looks just as bad.* Gray splashed cold water on his face and then grabbed a cola can from the mini fridge and placed it gently against his lip. It instantly felt better.

He sat down on the edge of the bed and did his best to piece together what had happened the previous night. He'd definitely remembered meeting Nickle in the lobby and then heading over to Hooters. All was okay during that time, except Gray did recall Nickle having trouble believing Pratt's situation. He had remembered walking out in the rain with

Nickle, the reason for his wet jeans. No way Gray could forget the name of the place they went to, Blade Runner Alley. And last but not least, his memory, now fully regained, painted a fresh picture of the man he got into a fight with—an inspector with the RTP, a drunken one, no less. Of course, everything from that fight until he woke was a no-man's-land.

Welcome to Thailand, Sterling. You got a fat lip, and your partner's missing.

Gray balled his hand into a fist. He couldn't believe Nickle led him down a rabbit hole.

What the hell did he think when he took me there? A drunk detective with the RTP would somehow get the ball rolling? I doubt it.

Here was a celebrated agent with the FBI's prestigious BAU, and nothing he'd done since leaving the airport had come remotely close to launching a search for Pratt. Not only that, but Gray had served in the Air Force as a member of the Pararescue unit. Being dropped into the middle of a hot zone, which is what it felt like, was nothing he hadn't been put through before. So why was he fumbling around as if he were as green as Gumby?

Gray checked the time. It was already after nine. Both the US and UK embassies would be open. He took a quick shower and got dressed. Before heading down to the lobby, Gray slammed a quick cup of instant coffee just to get the blood flowing.

When the elevator doors opened, and Gray walked into the lobby, he had the mindset that he wouldn't squander another second. Pratt's life depended on him making decisions that were smart and on point. He'd want Pratt doing the same were the situations reversed.

Gray zeroed in on the entrance at the other end of the

lobby, determined to not let anything unnecessary distract him from the task at hand. Until...

"You FBI agents always start your day this late?"

Gray looked toward where the voice came from. Sitting in a chair was the drunk he'd gotten into a brawl with the night before: Chet. He had a smirk on his face as he slowly stabbed chunks of cut watermelon out of a plastic bag with a wooden skewer and popped them into his mouth.

"You got a lot of balls showing your face around here," Gray said as he moved closer to Chet.

"Oh yeah? For a guy who needs my help, you have a stupid way of showing it."

Gray frowned. "Look, pal, no offense, but I don't need your help."

Chet stood up. "Let me guess. Your plan is to visit the UK and US embassies and file a report. Your next step is to follow up with your supervisor back in America and see what he recommends doing. Then you'll visit Nickle and tell him what an asshole he is and that he's lucky you don't report him for whatever shit you think he did wrong. Am I right? Is that pretty much what you had running through your head as you walked out?"

Gray waved off the assessment and then started toward the door. Chet quickly caught up and remained in step with Gray. He was dressed casually in jeans and a tight black T-shirt.

"Where's your brown uniform?" Gray asked.

"I don't need to wear that unless I have a meeting. Look, we got off to a bad start. I'm not the guy you met last night. I mean, I am if I'm drinking."

"I can't remember anything after Nickle left."

"Ya dong can do that if you're not used to it. I grew up on it. Someone like you drinking as much of it as you did last night isn't good."

"I did one shot."

"With Nickle, but after he left, we did a bunch more. And we sang karaoke. You sound just like John Denver."

Gray swore under his breath. "Since we're being honest here, that guy who you say sang karaoke with last night, that's not me, normally."

"No shit. Last night you couldn't shut up about how you were this badass profiler with the FBI."

Gray gave Chet a look of disbelief. "No way."

"I'm not bullshitting you, but I believe you. I did a little research this morning into your background. You're not just some dumb suit sent over here that ends up getting in the way, even though that's all you've done since your flight landed. You need someone like me helping, whether you realize it or not. I'm sorry for kicking your ass last night. Let's forget about it."

"You kicked my ass? That's debatable. The way I remember it, I kicked your ass. The shiner on your left eye is proof."

"Yeah, and that fat lip isn't?" Chet ate another piece of watermelon.

Once outside, Gray turned to Chet. "Okay, I'll bite. How do you think you can help me?"

"First, my recommendation is to forget about the embassies. They can't help, and they'll make things worse."

"How is that?"

"Because they're all corrupt."

"I can't speak for the people at the UK Embassy, but no way my government would have corrupt officials running the embassy unless you are talking about Nickle. He's not getting away with that crap he pulled last night."

"Trust me when I say it. They are as corrupt as my colleagues are."

"Why should I believe you?"

"Because I'm Thai. I know how things work in this country. If you go there and make waves, you'll make a lot of people nervous. They'll suppress anything you try to do to find your friend. Right now, you still have a chance to find her alive. You'll only screw things up by trying to do it the way it works back in your country."

Gray continued to shake his head in disbelief. "It can't be like that. These are government officials. You're telling me the ambassador is corrupt?"

"I'll give you some advice, be careful who you trust in Thailand. Don't be quick to listen to people because of who they are or what their job is."

"Does that mean I shouldn't trust you?"

Chet smiled. "Of course not." Chet popped another piece of watermelon in his mouth. "What I'm saying is if you want to see your friend alive, you need to listen to me and do things my way. If you do things your way, your friend will end up dead... Maybe you, too."

23

The way Gray saw it, he had made zero progress. It wouldn't hurt to listen to how Chet thought they should proceed.

Chet stopped in front of a black motorcycle and handed Gray an extra helmet he kept under the seat.

"Maybe we should grab a taxi," Gray said.

"This is faster. Are you scared?"

Gray put on the helmet and had hopped on the back. About fifteen minutes later, they'd come to a stop in a small soi. It was loaded with street vendors, most of them selling food to hungry Thais.

Gray hopped off the back of the bike and removed his helmet. "What are we doing here?"

"Breakfast. I need something more than watermelon. Over here is one of the best stalls for jok."

Gray had no idea what jok was, but he went along and took a seat on a small metal stool at an equally small table. Hanging directly above was a tangle of black electrical wires that flowed from concrete post to another.

"Is it safe?" Gray asked as he looked at the dangerously low wires.

"Sure, just don't bump your head against it."

A few minutes later, a server returned with two bowls of thick white porridge.

"This is jok, a rice soup," Chet said. "Those tiny meatballs are made out of pork, and that's ginger shavings on top. Try it."

Gray was pleasantly surprised after his first bite. "This is good."

"I've been coming here for years. So, tell me about your friend. Tell me everything that happened, not just at the airport. Everything back in London too, okay?"

In between bites, Gray briefed Chet, starting with picking up Ritthirong at the prison, then the flight to Thailand, the attack at the airport, and everything else that led to him meeting with Nickle.

After hearing him out, Gray half expected Chet to give him the same condescending smile everyone else had given him, but he didn't.

"Did you talk much with the two Black Tigers assigned to the detail?" Chet asked.

"A little. It was mostly small talk. You think they had something to do with it?"

Chet shrugged. "Maybe not, but their monthly salary can't support their spending."

"How do I know you're not corrupt?"

Chet laughed. "Because we're sitting on the side of a road eating jok that cost thirty baht each, about a dollar a bowl. And I'm splitting the bill with you."

"Okay, fine, but I'm convinced Ritthirong escaped. I don't believe he's sitting in some jail cell. I don't know who was being paraded around on TV, but it wasn't Ritthirong. He was on the other end of that phone call."

"I believe you."

"So we should schedule a meeting with Gun and Ped?"

"It doesn't work that way. Even suggesting they helped Ritthirong escape is dangerous. We need more information. Understand that we're not trying to investigate and find out who is responsible. We're trying to find your friend Lillie."

"So you're saying the best-case scenario is we find and rescue Lillie, but no one involved is charged with a crime?"

"Can you understand why your way would never work?"

Gray nodded.

Chet shrugged before scooping a spoonful into his mouth. "Plus, you have no jurisdiction here, so no one will take you seriously."

"I have a question. What's in it for you? If this can't become a formal investigation, what are you getting out of it?"

"Believe it or not, Nickle is one of the good guys, but he understands the game that is played here. He vouched for you. I like solving crimes, especially something like this. An investigation like this would never be given to me. Normally, something like this would just end up being wasted breath: 'We'll put our best men on it. We'll work hard to bring the culprits to justice.' Blah, blah, blah. After a few weeks, it'll just disappear. The news media will move on to something else. But handling it the way I want to, we have a chance to do something."

"Don't worry, I can find a gun for you." Chet lifted his bowl up to his face, tilted it back, and spooned the remaining porridge into his mouth.

"I'm not allowed to carry a firearm here."

"There are a lot of things we're not allowed to do here, but we do it anyway." Chet wiped his mouth with a napkin. "I have a serious question for you. Think about your answer, because maybe I'm the wrong person to help with your problem."

Gray lowered his spoon. "What's your question?"

"Are you willing to step into the gray area, Agent Gray?"

24

"Are you willing to go rogue?" That's the question Chet should have really asked. In all of Gray's years of working for the FBI, he'd always worked hard to uphold his oath and do his job to the best of his abilities. Sure, Gray had crossed a few lines and dipped a toe into the so-called gray area. But he had always carefully thought through whether it was necessary.

What Chet had asked went beyond anything Gray had done. On top of that, Gray had absolutely no jurisdiction in Thailand, nor would he have the backing of his government for taking any questionable steps. If he were caught doing something unlawful, he'd be at the mercy of the Thai government.

Chet returned to the small table after paying for the food. "Do you have an answer to my question, Agent Gray?"

"I'm not on duty. Call me Sterling."

"Stirring is hard," Chet said as he mispronounced Gray's name. "I'll stick to Gray."

"Fine. I have a few concerns. One, I'm obligated to report Lillie's disappearance."

"You reported it to her contact at the NCB and to Nickle.

That's Interpol and the FBI, two organizations that deal with criminal activity. The embassies aren't responsible for that. You feel like you didn't report it because you didn't see any action take place."

"Exactly."

"But the action did take place after you talked with Nickle. You're here with me. But you were looking for something official to happen, like a form filled out and stamped."

"That's not what I meant."

"Yes, it is because what we're doing here is off the books. I understand you feel uncomfortable, but you know you have no choice. And I know this is true because you would have left me back at your hotel."

Chet had nailed it. If Gray were being honest with himself, he was with Chet because he knew the path he was initially on was a dead end. It was either see what Chet could do or fly back to the UK alone and hope for the best.

The truth of the matter, Lillie's disappearance wasn't a United States federal crime. There was no reason for him to be involved other than providing a statement, which he'd already done. In fact, if he were to notify his supervisor, he'd be ordered to let the Thai authorities handle it. End of story.

Chet shifted in his seat. "Try thinking about it this way. All you're doing is gathering information. There's nothing wrong with that."

"But I'm also withholding information about Lillie's disappearance."

"Not really. You let some people know. Look, Gray. You need to make a decision." Chet tapped his watch. "If you keep waiting, there will be no Lillie to find. We have days to make progress. After that, my advice would be to catch a plane home and inform her family."

"Sheesh, when you put it that way... What are you suggesting we do now?"

Chet smiled. "We start by confirming if the man in jail really is Ritthirong."

"Will we be granted access to him?"

"From now on, ignore any thoughts you have on needing permission."

Gray and Chet made the short walk back to his bike and drove out of the small soi.

"Where are we heading?" Gray asked when they were stopped at a traffic light.

"Nonthaburi. That's where the prison is."

"So we are going inside the prison?"

"No. We're going to a place where the prison guards eat after work. There might be some of them there that worked the night shift."

Bang Kwang Central Prison was located just off the Chao Phraya River in the Nonthaburi province, about eleven miles north of Bangkok. Before his trip to Thailand, Gray had done a little research on the prison and knew it was where the most dangerous criminals were held and most of the foreigners who end up being incarcerated. It's also the only prison in Thailand that houses death row inmates.

It took about forty minutes for them to get there. Even with the wind blowing, the heat from the sun made his back feel like it'd been sunburned.

"Is this restaurant next to the prison?" Gray asked when they came to a stop at a traffic light.

"No. If you want, we can drive by later."

Chet parked the bike near what looked like a small number of crudely built dwellings. Kids played outside. An elderly woman washed clothes in a bucket. A man grilled unidentifiable meat on wooden skewers next to another vendor selling cut fruit.

"Where's the restaurant?" Gray asked as he looked around, confused.

Gray followed Chet through a narrow opening between two small structures and down a winding pathway until they reached a small area with a couple of tables with buckets as chairs under a tarp roof. Four men were gathered around a table. They weren't eating, but Gray recognized the brown liquid in the shot glasses.

"Sit," Chet said, pointing to a table. "I'll be right back."

Gray watched Chet walk over to the group of men and speak to them in Thai. Chet motioned for a young woman standing nearby to bring another round of drinks for the men. They cheered and downed the liquor. After Chet had a private conversation with one of the men. A few moments later, Chet returned with that man.

"Sterling, this is Film, like a movie."

Film pressed his hands together and bowed slightly before taking a seat.

"Film is a guard at the prison and works the night shift. He said he hadn't seen Ritthirong with his own eyes. No one has, as far as he knows. He's being kept in his own cell, and very few people have access to him."

"So where does that leave us?"

"Film said he will do his best to take a picture with his mobile phone of the man."

"So he'll be able to do that tonight?"

"I hope so. But now we must help him."

"How?"

"How much baht do you have on you?"

"I actually don't have any baht. I haven't had a chance to

exchange money. I can't even remember spending anything last night."

Gray removed his wallet and counted what was inside. "I have two hundred and seventy pounds. How much are we giving this guy?"

"Give me two hundred."

"Two hundred each?"

"No. I paid for breakfast this morning. You pay for this."

Gray let out a breath as he handed the notes over to Chet, who placed them in Film's hands. Film immediately gave Chet and Gray a wai and then returned to his table.

"You're buying lunch and dinner today," Gray said,

"Fine, no problem."

"What about the other guys? They can't help?"

"They will all help. That money will be divided up between them."

Gray felt a bit more hopeful knowing he had four men working for them. Maybe that two hundred pounds would do some good.

"There's no way we can gain access to the prison?" Gray asked.

"Right now, we have the advantage. No one knows you're digging for information. Once you make a formal request, the cover-up will begin. If that wasn't him on TV, then they are already covering up Ritthirong's escape."

"It just doesn't feel like we're doing a lot."

"We are. You're just used to being in control of your investigations and taking the lead." Chet stood up. "Don't worry, there'll be plenty enough for both of us to do."

25

Cake walked away from her night out knowing two things. One: A lot of people were hurting for money. Two: She was no closer to finding out who took her money.

She sat behind her desk, sipping tea from a mug. Mint sat on the other side of Cake's desk.

"Our pool of suspects just got bigger," Cake said. "If money is a problem for so many people, how can we narrow it down?"

"The more I think about it, the more I think it's not one of our enemies."

Cake eyed Mint. "What do you mean?"

"The men that took the money may not operate in our world. Maybe they only hired people to come here and steal your money. Businessmen need money. Politicians always need money."

"I don't think it's anyone hi-so," Cake said.

"Why not?"

"Businessmen have access to banks and investors. That's how they solve their cash shortages."

"And politicians?"

"They have their supporters."

"But their supporters could be involved."

"My gut tells me that's too far of a reach."

"I know what you're saying. Wait... You're not thinking—"

"I am. Why not? If businesses in Bangkok are slow, the envelopes are lighter. There is no one more reliant on those envelopes for day-to-day living than the police. And you know it."

"The police hitting you... It's something they're totally capable of doing," Mint mused. "They don't care about anything but their bank accounts."

"That's right. And it has to be the ones from Bangkok."

"There are so many. How can we start to figure it out?"

Cake leaned forward and placed her mug down on the desk. "I want you to gather the other girls and start looking at business or even areas within Bangkok that have been affected the most by the slowdown. That could pinpoint a police station responsible for that area. They would be the most hungry and desperate."

After Mint left Cake's office, she'd begin to think about her conversation with Ped, wondering if he really could help. Cake wasn't even sure if she knew the best approach to utilizing someone like Ped. But at his level, his connections would be vast. The question in Cake's mind was whether he would play ball with a known drug dealer. He could have blown her off at the club, but he didn't. And she didn't get the impression it was out of politeness. He talked to Cake and Mint for a solid forty-five minutes before Phukdat's cousin intervened.

The Black Tigers didn't go around the neighborhood extorting business, nor could someone easily come to them and ask them to do something for payment. Cake assumed they would be very picky and careful of what they dipped their fingers into—very high-level stuff. Expensive stuff. She didn't get the impression they got involved with twenty or thirty thousand baht paydays. She actually wasn't sure how the money worked for members of the Black Tigers, but she was sure of one thing: they didn't survive on their monthly salaries.

Cake picked up her phone and sent a group text to her Fierce Five: *Find out the names of every member of the Black Tigers.*

Gun was having lunch at a local steak house known for their imported Wagyu beef from Hyogo, Japan. A young, beautiful woman sat opposite him, snapping selfies while she ate. Gun was enjoying his steak when Ped appeared near the entrance, grabbing his attention. Ped motioned for Gun to step outside.

"Excuse me," Gun said to his lunch guest.

Ped was waiting outside the restaurant, smoking a cigarette.

"This better be good. I was enjoying a steak," Gun asked.

"Cake, the Queen of the South, got hit at her home. The robbers took almost four million baht from her."

"So?" Gun shrugged.

"She's digging around."

Deep lines appeared across Gun's forehead. "What does this have to do with us?"

"Bunsong."

"You think Bunsong hit Cake to pay us off?"

"I'm just making sure we're covered, and there isn't anything that can come back to us."

"Even if Bunsong did hit Cake, she'll never trace the money to us."

"Maybe not, but it's a delicate situation at the moment. If

she keeps digging around, she'll make waves. It's not good. We need calm waters now, don't you agree?"

"How did you hear about this?"

"She told me."

Ped quickly updated his boss, Gun, about his run-in with Cake at Sing Sing.

"She's definitely looking for information," Ped said. "She also had dinner at Pacific City Club earlier. She won't stop. I could see it in her eyes."

"Sometimes these drug dealers can be smart, and sometimes they can be stupid. Why would she divulge this information to you? We could raid her place in a heartbeat." Gun snapped his finger. "And put an end to her reign in the south."

"I don't know what she's thinking. Maybe she's too cocky. A raid could put her back in her place. Whatever we do, we need to stay ahead of her."

Gun nodded. "Find out who she's been talking to, who is helping, and what she knows. But do it quietly; don't involve any one of the other men. Clear?"

Ped nodded as he took a long pull from his cigarette. "And what will you do?"

"Don't worry about me. Just focus on your orders."

26

Gray gripped the back seat of the motorbike tightly while Chet zipped around cars, and even once coming within inches of the giant tires of a cement truck. But Gray was too focused on the task at hand to nitpick Chet's driving. He was in the unique position of hunting for a criminal that he'd spent a great deal of time interviewing.

Approaching this investigation in the usual manner of drawing up a profile for local law enforcement wouldn't work. He was the local law enforcement. Well, he and Chet.

He had no access to FBI resources or manpower. It was just two men using their brains and their gut instincts. To make matters worse, Gray had to rely on a man he'd just met in a country where English wasn't the first language. Gray had to trust Chet's decisions and the process, one that had the potential to be unethical in many ways.

Chet pulled off the road and parked the bike next to a small noodle stand. "I'm hungry."

"Do you really think we should be eating?" Gray responded. "We should be running down as many leads as possible right now."

"I agree, but we also need to be smart about this. If we make too much noise around the wrong people, our investigation will die."

Gray took a seat at the table while Chet placed an order and returned with two cold water bottles.

"What are you thinking, Sterling?"

"Ever since yesterday, I've been trying to wrap my head around why Ritthirong would take Lillie."

Chet twisted the cap off his bottle. "What's the reason?"

"My gut tells me he took her just to toy with me. He has no interest in her, nor does he want to use her in exchange for something, like his freedom. I honestly believe he took her just to get to me. She's nothing but an instrument. He sees her the same way he sees all of the people he traffics: as objects for sale."

"If she's for sale, then he wants something. What else do you know about Ritthirong?"

It was then that Gray realized Chet hadn't been privy to his relationship with Ritthirong. He began telling Chet about the meetings they had while Ritthirong was being held in prison.

"I watched another inmate nearly kill himself by striking his head against a concrete wall because of Ritthirong whispering into his ear. He's very manipulative. It plays into his narcissism."

No sooner did those words leave Gray's mouth than a revelation popped into his head.

"Hmm," Gray said as his gaze fell to the road.

"What is?" Chet asked.

"Ritthirong smiled at the security camera while the other inmate banged his head into the wall. He wasn't focused on what was happening, even though he was responsible for it. He was focused on the camera. He just stared at it. I thought it was just his sick way of saying goodbye."

"I'm not sure I understand."

"In some weird way, I think it was a message for me. Like he already knew he would escape and I would find out. Maybe he thought I would bang my head against the wall trying to figure it out."

"You kind of are."

Gray's gaze focused back on Chet.

"You're right. I am. Maybe that's the reason why he took Lillie. He literally wanted me to bang my head against the wall."

Chet let out a big breath. "You think he actually planned it?"

"He's a master strategist. I think he did. He's playing a game. I'm not sure what it is right now, but he needs Lillie to do it."

"If he kills her, that will stop your search. So she's safe as long as you keep looking. If this is all about you and Ritthirong and nothing else, I believe what you saw and heard at the airport is true."

"I can't tell you how good it feels to hear you say that. Finally, someone who believes me, but that means you didn't believe me before, right?"

"You have to understand, even I saw Ritthirong on TV being taken to jail. We still need confirmation that there's an imposter in that jail cell. You need to understand, it is not easy to make something like this happen, even in Thailand, where money can buy anything."

"I agree, a lot of planning needed to be done in advance, but that's Ritthirong's strength. I wouldn't doubt for one second that he was anticipating his capture years ago and had already devised multiple plans. But if we can reveal there's an imposter in that jail cell, people will have to believe my story, at a minimum, follow up. That's good news for Lillie."

Chet nodded.

"I can't believe he's got this much control over the situation," Gray said as he stretched his legs out. "Ritthirong is nothing but a damn trafficker, a snakehead."

"They call them that in China, but this is Thailand; our snakes have many heads. And among them, Ritthirong is the king."

"I won't argue with that. Look, I know we have those guards working for us, but is there more we can do? The earliest they'll be able to confirm anything is tonight. I already feel like we've wasted too much time."

Chet shook his head. "I don't know if we have other options right now."

"I think we do. Whenever I asked Ritthirong about his upbringing or his family, he would shut down. Did you know they were the ones that tipped off the police in the UK?"

"So it's true. They do hate him."

"We might find more answers there. Do you know any members of his family?"

Chet smiled.

27

Arun Ritthirong was the patriarch of the Ritthirong family and the one who had held it together during their troubled times when his grandson Somsak Ritthirong, a.k.a. King Rong, claimed the title of largest human trafficker in Southeast Asia.

He despised Somsak for the permanent black eye he'd given the family name, the one that Arun had spent decades building up. He cast Somsak out of the family and forbade anyone from speaking his name. Any family member caught talking to Somsak, or helping him, would also be cast out.

The Ritthirong family wasn't the wealthiest, nor were they the most influential family in Bangkok, but they did have standing, and that was something Arun was immensely proud of.

The family also had Ploy Ritthirong, a twenty-eight-year-old influencer who was the cousin of Somsak. She was outspoken and opinionated, she rebelled against tradition, and she had been a constant thorn in Aurn's side, but he put up with her because she was famous. It added to the family's standing.

"This girl, Ploy; how well do you know her?" Gray asked as

the two walked on the sidewalk in the hi-so district known as Thonglor.

"Enough to meet up with her," Chet answered.

"Obviously."

"Let's just say I saved her butt a couple of years ago. She'd gotten herself into trouble, and I made the problem go away. Ever since then, we've been friendly."

"So she owes you."

"That too."

Chet stopped outside of a beauty clinic. Plastered across the windows were beautiful portraits of women with services being advertised.

"This is the place."

He pushed the door open and led the way inside. Sitting behind a white countertop were two young women dressed in matching skirt suit outfits.

"Sawadee ka," they said in union.

Chet had a short conversation in Thai with the women. They waited briefly while one of the ladies made a phone call.

Gray and Chet were escorted through a doorway that led into a hallway with multiple closed doors. The woman stopped at one and knocked twice before opening.

Inside the room, a woman lay on a medical table. She wore a paper gown, but it was clear that she had jeans on underneath. She had one arm raised above her head while a technician wearing a white overcoat and safety goggles performed a treatment on the woman's armpit. Even in that situation, her beauty did not get past Gray.

Ploy had silky black hair, fair skin, and hazel eyes with long lashes.

"Chet. So good to see you," she said in perfect English. No Thai accent like Chet.

"Ploy, do you have time? We can come back."

"Nonsense. I'm having laser hair removal. Talking to you will take my mind off the pain. Who's your cute friend?"

"This is Gray."

"Hello, Ploy. We appreciate you making time to see us."

"Of course. Chet is a good friend of mine. So what did you want to talk about?"

"Uhh..." Gray looked at the technician.

"Oh, don't worry. I know these women very well. Plus, they understand zero English."

"Oh, okay, well. Let me formally introduce myself. I'm FBI Special Agent Sterling Gray."

"Are you here to investigate me?" Ploy asked playfully.

Gray chuckled. "No, I'm not."

"Such is life," she sang playfully.

"I work in the Behavioral Analysis Unit."

"The what?"

"I'm a profiler."

"You mean like that character Jodi Foster played in that lamb movie?"

"Yes, like her."

"So impressive. I'm sorry. I'm sure you're busy. Please continue."

"Well, it's my understanding you're related to Somsak Ritthirong."

"Yes, he's my cousin. What do you want with him? He's already been captured."

"I'm aware of the news. I actually spent two months interviewing him while he waited for a decision on his extradition. I also accompanied him on the flight to Thailand."

"Seems like you already know a lot about him."

"Yes and no. During our conversations, he refused to talk about his childhood or anything with his family. I was hoping you could expand on that."

"His childhood or his family?"

"Both, if you could."

"Well, I didn't spend a lot of time with him when we were little, mostly at family gatherings. He seemed normal back then, but I was a little girl, so what would I know. But what I'm saying is that he didn't seem weird. I mean, I knew some weird kids at my school, and he wasn't like that. But once I caught him peeking up my skirt."

"Did he get along with the other children in the family? Was he quiet or outspoken?"

"Definitely more on the quiet side. He'd only talk if you spoke to him. He preferred to sit and watch. I never saw or heard of him fighting with anyone. I have other cousins who are so spoiled and they caused a lot of trouble."

"Did you see anyone bully him?"

"Um, sometimes those spoiled cousins would pick on him, but not too much. Khun Arun didn't tolerate any of that stuff."

"That's Somsak's grandfather, right?"

"He is."

"Did you attend school together?"

"There was one time we were in the same IBS for one year when we were teenagers."

"IBS?"

"It's what international schools in Bangkok are called. Anyway, he's older than me, so he went on to university after that one year. I didn't really hang out with him during that time. We had different friends."

"What were his friends like?"

"Hmm, I guess you could call them the weird crowd. You know, eccentric in a weird way, not a good way. You know what I mean."

"How well did you know his parents?"

"Well, they were always known as the strict parents. The

complete opposite of my parents, who were totally progressive."

"Which one of your parents is related to Somsak's parents?"

"My mother is the younger sister of Somsak's father. They got along okay, if you're wondering."

"So why are your mother and his father so different?"

"It's because Somsak's father was Khun Arun's favorite son. He had to be perfect, which meant his own family had to be perfect. You can imagine how finding out what Somsak was doing screwed that up."

"Did he get along with his parents?"

"The older we got, the more I heard him complain about them. He'd always said they were too traditional. Which is true. His father wanted him to go into the family business. It's a son's duty. Somsak wanted nothing to do with it."

"Why? It seems like it would be a path for a successful and comfortable life."

Ploy paused. "You know, there was something I heard from the other kids, but like only once or twice. I don't know if it's true, but I was told his father beat him a lot."

"Why?"

"I don't know. I just heard that's what happened. He would be locked in his bedroom for days before he was allowed to come out. Somsak never mentioned it, and I never asked. Do you think that's why he ended up becoming a human trafficker?"

"It might have contributed. What role did his mother play in all of this?"

"She listened to Somsak's father one hundred percent and always took his side. So yeah, they both mistreated him.

"Who else would know about these beatings and his confinements? What about his siblings?"

"Good luck getting any of them to speak to you. No one wants to risk being cut out of the family fortune. I'm probably the only one who would dare speak about Somsak, and to an FBI agent."

"Aren't you at risk by talking to me?"

"I don't care about Khun Arun's fortune. Neither do my parents. I was brought up to do what I wanted and to carve my own path. If I worried about that money, I would essentially be doing whatever he wanted. And that's just not me. He rules this family with an iron fist. There are times my parents have disagreements with him, but they are not afraid to walk away in the end. They refuse to be held hostage by his money."

"That's very noble of you."

"Thank you."

The technician turned off the laser and said something in Thai to Ploy.

"I hate to cut this conversation short, but I'm finished, and I have another appointment that I need to rush off to. Was I helpful, Agent Gray?"

"Yes, you were helpful."

"I'm sorry I don't have time to tell you more."

"Maybe we can schedule another time to meet."

"Sure. Chet knows how to get ahold of me."

Ploy got up off the table and stripped off the paper gown, revealing she only wore a lace bra and blue jeans. She was tall and in great shape. Both Gray and Chet looked away as she grabbed a crop top off a nearby chair. A second later, Ploy had cuddled up next to Gray, still only wearing her bra, and snapped a selfie of them together.

"Hey, what are you doing?" Gray protested.

"Aww, come on. You're the first FBI agent I've ever met. I promise I won't show this to anyone or talk about it." She batted her eyelashes at Gray.

"Uh, okay, so long as the photo is just for your eyes only."

"I promise. I hope we meet again, Agent Gray." Ploy put her top on slowly as she stared at Gray. She then blew him a kiss and left the room, her perfume the only sign that she'd been there.

Chet clapped his hands in front of Gray's face to grab his attention.

"Wow, she got you good," he said.

"What do you mean?"

"You know what I mean. Did you learn anything from talking to Ploy that can help?"

"I did. Ritthirong doesn't really want to play a game. I think he wants me to catch him. If the punishments Ploy spoke of are true, then he probably has issues of abandonment. I must have connected with Ritthirong in some absurd way during the time I spent with him back in the UK."

"He misses you?"

"Something like that. His tendency is to push me away when I get too close. But once I'm gone, or he even senses that I'm moving away, he will try to pull me back. Seeing Lillie must have given him the perfect idea on how to keep me coming back to him."

"Here you are."

"Yes, it worked brilliantly. I know Ploy said she thought no one else in the family would talk to me, but do you agree with that? Is there anyone you think we can get to speak with me? There must be someone in that family that might know where Ritthirong is hiding. And I know what you're thinking: no, I don't believe he's the man in that jail cell."

"Ploy is the only one I have a relationship with. She actually surprised me when she said yes. But even if we did approach another family member, it would be a bad thing."

"Why?"

"The more people we contact, the harder it will be to keep this quiet. We'll lose our advantage. You know, the one where no one suspects we're doing any digging."

Just then, Chet's phone chimed. He took it out and read the message and then said something in Thai that didn't sound great to Gray.

"Is there a problem?"

"Yes."

He turned the phone around so Gray could see it. "She tagged me in the post."

Gray was looking at Ploy's Instagram page, and she had posted the picture she'd taken of them earlier. The caption read *Helping the FBI catch a bad guy.*

"Why would she do that after... Wait, she has twenty-five million followers?" Gray shook his head.

"I thought I could trust her. I'll call her to delete them." Chet made a phone call. "She's not answering."

"How screwed are we? I mean, what kind of following is that? I'm not on Instagram. Is that considered small or big?"

"Sounds big to me."

"Okay, well, maybe it's just a bunch of hipsters following her, no one important."

"I hate to tell you this, but the population of Bangkok is ten million."

What the hell is wrong with you, Sterling? You should have ordered her to delete that photo. Of course she would post the picture. She's an influencer. Everything is content to people like her.

Gray couldn't stop beating himself up over what had happened. He put the blame entirely on himself, not Chet.

"Calm down," Chet said.

The afternoon sun began to fade as the two stood on the sidewalk outside of the clinic. Another day of making no progress on finding Pratt was passing by, and Gray had just tripped himself up.

"So are we or are we not screwed?"

Chet took a moment to think through Gray's question.

"Well?"

"I'm thinking. Those pictures won't help. I just don't know how much it will affect what we do?"

"What's the worst case?"

"I get reassigned. And you are forcibly put on a plane and forbidden from ever setting foot in the country again."

"Crap!"

"That's the worst case in a perfect world. But the worst case in Thailand is that this really is a big cover-up, and to keep it covered, we need to be dead. We have to prepare."

"What do you mean?"

"You need protection." Chet mimicked a gun with his hand.

"I can't for a number of reasons."

"I know, but you have no choice. I'm your only backup here, and I don't know if I can protect you. Don't worry, I know where we can get one that's not traceable. If you don't need it after a couple of days, you can toss it into the Chao Phraya River." Chet brushed his hands together for emphasis. "Come on, the sun will be setting soon. And I hate this place when it's dark."

"Where are we going? Gray asked as they walked back to Chet's motorcycle.

"The slums."

28

The Khlong Toei slums were roughly one square mile with nearly one hundred thousand people packed inside, living in makeshift shacks. The place was rife with a crime ranging from theft to prostitution to murder. Drug abuse was rampant, and to make matters worse, one of the city's sewage lines ran straight through the place, creating a putrid smell. Chet parked his bike in the parking lot of a Big C, a large, discount supermarket.

"It's safer to leave my bike here. The slums are about a ten-minute walk that way. But you should visit that ATM over there. It'll give you Thai baht."

"How much do I need?"

"Take out twenty thousand baht. That's about six hundred dollars."

After a quick trip to the ATM, the two made the walk to the slums, but instead of seeing squalor, Gray found himself moving through the largest wet market he'd ever seen. Stalls were selling every type of seafood imaginable, as well as a variety of poultry, pork, and beef. There were also vegetable and fruit vendors. Gray and Chet squeezed past crowds of people jockeying to make their purchases.

"Doesn't seem very slumlike to me," Gray said.

Chet continued to lead, and soon Gray took his words back as the wet market gave way to tin shacks that seemed to have the sturdiness of a standing domino.

The narrow walkway that cuts through the shacks had no rhyme or reason for their direction. Even Chet got confused, forcing them to backtrack. Some of the pathways were so narrow that Gray had to turn sideways to pass through, not to mention the number of dogs he had to step over. Curious onlookers sat in doorways or looked through open windows, many of them calling others to come and look. Gray could hear them all whispering one word over and over.

"What are they saying?" he asked Chet.

"They're calling you farang. It's what Thai people call white people. It's the Thai word for a fruit that is white on the inside. I think you call it guava. Foreigners don't come into the slums."

The sun had set by then and kerosene lamps, which seem to be a popular way to light the dwellings, shone a hot white light.

"What's that smell?" Gray asked.

"Sewage runoff cuts through the place."

"Well, that's hardly a way to live."

"It is in the slums."

"Who are we meeting here?"

"His name is Hia," Chet stopped and faced Gray. "If you feel like speaking, don't."

They continued until the path opened up into a small eight-by-eight-foot area. Lights from two nearby windows lit the area enough for Gray to see a bunch of shirtless men with tattoos covering most of their bodies. They were gathered around a small plastic table, talking and drinking. Lookie-loos quickly appeared in the windows.

The men at the table fell silent and stood as the attention focused on Chet and Gray. Only one remained sitting. He was the most muscular of them all and had long black hair that touched his shoulders.

Chet performed a wai.

The two had a brief discussion in Thai.

"Why did you bring a farang?" Hia said, switching to English. He walked up to Gray and looked him up and down. "What's your name, Farang?"

"You can call me Gray."

"Gray, like the color." Hia looked back at his men and laughed as he said something in Thai to them.

"Hia, can we talk?" Chet asked.

As Hia and Chet stepped off to the side, one of the men motioned for Gray to have a seat. Gray initially refused with a polite smile, but the man continued to point to the chair. Gray took a seat, and the men all sat down beside him.

The man who invited Gray to sit introduced himself with a thick Thai accent. "My name Moo."

Moo filled the empty glasses on the table with a familiar brown liquid. He pushed one over to Gray. The men held up their glasses for a toast. Not wanting to offend, Gray grabbed his glass and clinked the others'.

"Chon kaew," the men said in unison.

Gray slammed the drink. He immediately squinted his eyes and shook his head as he swallowed. Moo slapped Gray's back a few times as they all laughed. Within seconds, Moo had refilled Gray's glass for another round. Gray sucked it up and finished the drink.

Gray looked over his shoulder to where Hia and Chet had gone to talk, only they weren't there.

Moo tapped Gray's shoulder. "Don't worry. You stay with us."

"Where did they go?"

Moo shrugged and then laughed.

Gray stood up, and so did Moo and the other men. They surrounded Gray.

"Sit," Moo said.

"I should find Chet," Gray said.

"Sit. Everything okay."

Gray didn't like what he saw. Chet was gone, and he was outnumbered four to one. Chet's words from earlier haunted Gray. *Be careful who you trust in Thailand.*

Moo grabbed Gray by the arm aggressively. "Sit!"

Gray shook off Moo's hand before pushing through the circle of men. Thinking Chet and Hia needed more privacy, Gray walked over to the pathway that had brought him into the small area. He didn't see them. Gray then checked the other path leading out of the area. Chet and Hia weren't down that way either.

"Your friend is gone," Moo said as he smiled at Gray.

Two more men appeared from the other pathway. It was now six to one.

"Where did Chet go?" Gray asked as he took a few steps back toward a shack.

No one answered, and Gray didn't like how they were forming a half circle around him. Had Chet screwed him over? It was starting to feel that way.

Might as well get the jump.

Gray swung with a right hook, catching the jaw of the man nearest him and sending him to the ground. The other men moved in all at once, and Gray swung furiously to back them off. Multiple fists landed on Gray's head, but he continued to punch while trying to avoid being hit.

Out of nowhere, a kick caught Gray in the stomach, and he keeled over. Another snapping kick lay into his side. The pain was unbearable, but Gray fought to recover as more fists pummeled his body.

Gray exploded with an uppercut catching a man center of his jaw and knocking him out. A combination of more fist strikes dazed another man. Gray grabbed that guy by the back of his head and slammed his face into a knee strike. The man crumpled to the ground.

A fist caught Gray in the jaw, and then a spinning elbow struck Gray in the side of the head, causing his vision to go black momentarily before returning with a blur. Gray covered his face with his forearms, deflecting follow-up strikes. He stepped back, creating distance. He had immobilized three men, but there were still three left, and they all seemed to have Muay Thai training.

Moo moved in with a kick, and Gray caught his foot against his side and hung on. Gray then kicked Moo's other leg out from under him and followed with a stomp to the face.

Two more, Sterling. Hang in there.

No sooner had that thought crossed Gray's mind than five more men appeared. It was now seven to one. The only difference is these men were armed with bats and pointy machetes.

Gray raised his fists and stood in a defensive position. Chet had asked him earlier how comfortable he was with operating in the gray area. The way Gray saw it, people were dying that night. And he did not want to be one of them.

The men with the weapons took the first steps toward Gray.

This is it.

They raised their arms.

Do your best. Take down as many as you can.

Screams sounded as the men charged, followed by gunfire.

"Stop!" a voice yelled.

Everyone looked in the direction of the person who shouted. It was Chet and Hia, only Chet had an arm around Hia's neck and a gun pointed at his head.

Chet shouted at the men in Thai, and they slowly backed away from Gray. Chet moved around them toward Gray, still holding Hia hostage.

"You okay?" Chet asked.

"Yeah, I thought you had—"

"Leave? No way, my friend. Take this bag." Chet was holding a small duffel. "Inside is another handgun and ammo. Take the gun. Point it at them."

Gray opened the bag and took out a handgun. Chet let Hia go.

"You screwed up, Chet," Hia growled as he joined his men.

"We don't have much time," Chet whispered to Gray. "Others will come that have guns. How fast can you run?"

"Fast enough."

"Good. On the count of three, run through that opening. Don't stop for anything until you make it back to the market. Understand?"

"Yeah."

"One... Two..." Chet fired a single shot into Hia's forehead. "Run!"

29

Even though Gray saw Chet kill Hia right before his eyes, he wasn't about to stop and question the reasoning or the implications that could follow. He could hear Chet's footsteps slapping against the pavement behind him, and that was good enough for him. Gray pumped his arms and legs as fast as he could as he ran through the narrow pathway, leaping over a sleeping dog and running straight through a table and chairs like a rugby player.

Gray rounded a corner, and seconds later, a man with a bat jumped into the middle of the path. Gray tucked his shoulder down and barreled into the man, connecting with his chest. The man flew back through the air and crashed into the side of a shack.

Up ahead, the pathway forked.

"Left or right?" Gray called out.

"I don't know. Pick one!" Chet answered.

Gray tried to remember a fork on the way to meet Hia, but he couldn't. He had a fifty percent chance of choosing the right way. He went right and hoped for the best.

A gunshot rang out behind Gray. The men with guns were

giving chase. Another gunshot rang out, this one closer. Gray looked back over his shoulder and saw Chet taking aim and firing.

There was return fire, and a bullet whizzed past Gray's head. He crouched as he ran, trying to minimize the chances of his head becoming pulp. Up ahead, the pathway curved to the left, and Gray followed, only to hear Chet shout out to him that he'd gone the wrong way.

Gray put the brakes on and reversed course back to the start of the bend and saw Chet standing in an almost invisible path to the right.

"Hurry!" He waved at Gray.

Bullets punctured the shack next to Gray as he ducked and moved into the dark opening. He remembered it as the one place he had to turn sideways to pass through. Gray was right on Chet's heels when his shoulder slammed into something hard. The impact stopped him dead in his tracks, and pain exploded throughout his torso. A gunshot behind him pushed him to keep moving.

A few more lefts and rights and the two popped out into the market. Gray quickly tucked the handgun under his shirt and into his waistband. He looked back but didn't see any of the men chasing them.

"Are we safe now?" Gray asked as he walked hurriedly, perspiration raining down the sides of his face.

"Safer. We need to keep moving and get away from this area."

Gray walked alongside Chet. "Why did you shoot Hia?"

"Because he planned to kill me. Trust me. I could see it in his eyes. After he would take you hostage and see if an FBI agent was worth money."

"You told him I was an agent?"

"No, man. He saw the picture of you and Ploy on Instagram."

"Sheesh, that picture has the power to interfere at every step of the way."

"That's why I wanted to get you a weapon. You need it. You can't rely on your government to protect you while you're still inside the country. You have to leave if you want that."

"I can't leave Lillie here."

They exited the market and hurried back to Chet's motorcycle.

"Where are we heading to now?"

"We need to lie low in a safe place while we think. Word will spread about what happened in Khlong Toei and that I was connected."

"Don't you have any recourse, someone in the RTP you can go to? This can't be the way it works."

"If I do that, you can forget about Lillie. We have no choice but to keep moving as fast as possible. Let me worry about the fallout with the RTP."

When they reached Chet's motorcycle, Gray hopped on the back. "Hey, listen, Chet. Back there, I wasn't sure..."

"Don't worry about it. I would have thought the same thing. I hope you trust me one hundred percent now."

"I do."

"Good, because right now, all we have is us."

30

Chet pulled up to a tall luxury high-rise building. He flashed his police badge to the guard manning the security arm. The arm raised, and Chet drove inside and parked.

"Are we visiting someone here?"

"Nickle lives here. We need to see if he's heard anything."

Chet made a phone call. "I'm downstairs with Gray. Okay." He ended the call and shoved his mobile back into his jeans. "He's coming down."

A few minutes later, Nickle appeared at the entrance to the building. He waved them over.

"What the hell happened?" Nickle asked as they walked through the lobby to the bank of elevators. "I heard you shot up Khlong Toei."

"It's already out?" Gray asked in surprise.

"Yeah, well, for those who have their ear to the ground. Don't worry; something like this will never hit the media. No one cares what happens in the slums."

The three men stepped into the elevator. Once the door closed, Gray spoke.

"Agent to agent, what's my exposure?"

"Nickle, that all depends on how many more waves you make."

"I wouldn't have to make these waves if people would just do their jobs."

"People are doing their jobs. It's just not the jobs that are working in your favor."

The doors to the elevator opened on the twenty-second floor, and Nickle led the way to his apartment.

"Can I get you something to drink?" Nickle asked as he shut the door behind him. "How about a beer? Looks like you both could use one."

A few moments later, Nickle returned with three beer bottles, and they sat around the dining room table.

"Look, Gray, I've been digging around all day to try and find some evidence to corroborate your story."

"Sheesh, Nickle. Isn't the fact that I'm an FBI agent enough?"

"It is, but hear me out. For a cover-up like this to go into play, some powerful people in key positions need to be in on it. I'm sure Chet already explained this to you."

"I did."

"Gray, you just saw the value of your life back in those slums. If they had their way, you'd be handcuffed and blind-folded in the back of some shack while Hia and his men drummed up interest in you. If they can't, you're easily dumped into a river of sewage. Remember, you're not here on official business. You just tagged along."

"I get it, but my partner, Lillie... She is here on official business, and yet no one gives a rat's ass that she's missing."

"You need the right people to care."

"So what are you recommending we do?"

"Here's what I know: The Black Tigers were responsible for the security of Ritthirong. This is where we need to start looking. But these are dangerous people. Even someone like me needs to be careful of what rocks I look under."

"We paid off a few guards at the prison where Ritthirong is being held," Gray said. "They work the night shift, and they will try to confirm if that person being held there is really Ritthirong."

"Gray, have you thought about what you'll do if it is Ritthirong in that jail cell?"

Gray drew a breath and let it out slowly as he shook his head. "I'm not sure. I mean, it feels like I have minimal options now. I'll file the paperwork with my office back in the States and notify Interpol in the UK. Basically, try to get the UK involved as much as possible." Gray tapped his finger on the table. "You know what, let's get a board up on the wall."

Nickle fetched paper, some pens, and tape. Gray began writing down what they knew on pieces of paper and taped them to the wall.

Timeline

- *Masked gunman created chaos at the airport, and Lillie disappeared.*
- *Gray calls Lillie's phone, and she answers. Ritthirong comes on the line.*
- *Gray goes to Interpol's NCB office and notifies Lillie's contact, Suthisak.*
- *Suthisak informs Gray that Ritthirong is in custody and shows news media footage as proof.*
- *Shows no concern for Lillie's disappearance.*
- *Gray tracks down Nickle and informs him of the situation.*
- *Nickle brings Chet into the investigation.*
- *Gray and Chet hire prison guards to confirm the identity of the man believed to be Ritthirong.*

- *Gray and Chet interview Ploy, Ritthirong's cousin.*
- *Ploy reveals the troubled childhood of Ritthirong.*
- *Ploy posts pictures of her and Gray online, alerting all of Bangkok.*
- *Gray and Chet visit Hia. He's killed.*

"So this is our timeline," Gray said. "Now let's focus on theories."

Theories

- *Ritthirong is in jail, and someone else has taken Lillie.*
- *An imposter is in prison, and Ritthirong has Lillie.*
- *Ritthirong has taken Lillie to bait Gray into capturing him.*
- *Ritthirong has already killed Lillie and disappeared.*

"Last, what we know about Ritthirong's mindset," Gray said.

Who is Ritthirong?

- *Human trafficker*
- *High IQ. Able to plan and strategize down to the smallest of details.*
- *Dark triad: exhibits psychopathic, narcissistic, and Machiavellian traits.*
- *Fear of abandonment rooted in Ritthirong's traumatic childhood = reason for revealing himself on the phone. He wants Gray to find him.*

After taping up the last piece of paper, Gray stepped back and sat on the edge of the table. All three men quietly took in the information.

A few moments later, Nickle cleared his throat. "You really think Ritthirong wants you to come after him?"

"I do. Ploy mentioned Ritthirong was verbally and physically abused by his father. He was kept locked in a room for days at a time. This can create deep-rooted feelings of abandonment. During our time in the UK, I believe Ritthirong grew attached to me. Upon finding out that our time was over, he put together a plan to bring me back to him."

"So he was already planning to escape even while incarcerated back in the UK."

"Yes, I think once he knew I was flying to Thailand with him, it was a done deal. He knew he would take Lillie. Neither Lillie nor I would see it coming."

"How does he plan all this while locked up in another country?" Chet asked.

"You need to understand one thing with Ritthirong. He is capable of putting a plan in place years before it's needed. He'll plan on things going sideways and have contingency plans in place. His goal is to always control the outcome. The best way he can do that is to have a solution to every hiccup he can think of happening."

"And here I was thinking he was nothing more than a thug trafficking people." Nickle took a sip of his beer.

"He's much more than that. Ultimately, what he wants is ultimate control and to be in a position of authority over others."

"Like his grandfather Khun Arun," Chet said.

"Exactly, but on a much larger scale. In simple terms, this is his way of thumbing his nose at his family."

"What is he getting out of you catching him?" Nickle asked.

"That's a good question. I'm not quite sure, but the best

guess is he wants to keep our relationship going. It could be as simple as interaction."

"So keeping Lillie keeps you interacting with him. Does that mean he won't harm Lillie?"

"I'm inclined to believe that for the time being, Lillie is safe."

"Until he no longer wants to see you," Chet said.

Gray nodded. "Right."

Nickle rested his forearms on the table. "Okay, say we confirm that the Ritthirong being held at Bang Kwang is an imposter. How do we find the real Ritthirong? We clearly understand how this psycho thinks, but how does that translate to finding him? It's not like we can put out an APB and have every police officer in the city hunting for him. At best, we're working in the shadows."

Gray stood, walked up to the wall, and placed a finger on the line about Ritthirong wanting Gray to find him.

"He wants me to find him. So it can't be impossible. He had to have left a breadcrumb somewhere. We're just not seeing it yet."

Gray thought back to the conversations he'd had with Ritthirong while held at HMP Wakefield. Could he have been leaving clues back then? Gray thought about that last meeting he had with Ritthirong. Lillie had also been there.

During their chat, Ritthirong had made a big deal about Gray and Lillie dating. Even when told they were nothing more than colleagues, he continued to speak to them as if they were a couple. He even went so far as to suggest romantic places they could visit when in Thailand.

They'd also spoken about the travel arrangements to Thailand. Gray specifically remembered Ritthirong asking about the security detail and whether it was just the two men sent from the Thai government: Gun and Ped.

"Gun and Ped," Gray said. "They were the members of the security detail sent to escort Ritthirong back to Thailand."

"You remember something about them?" Nickle asked.

"You know, nothing unusual stood out. They were quiet, kept to themselves, but always maintained their professionalism."

"You think they had something to do with Ritthirong's escape?" Nickle continued his line of questioning.

"Everything is starting to point to them," Chet said.

"If there is an imposter, then they are responsible," Gray said. "It can't be anyone else."

"These are some lofty accusations," Nickle said. "I was always under the impression the Black Tigers weren't susceptible to corruption."

Chet laughed. "Everyone in Thailand can be bought for the right amount."

Just then, Chet received a message on his phone. "It's from the guard we hired. He was able to take a picture."

Gray and Nickle gather around Chet to look at the photo. Gray's knees nearly buckled as a sinking feeling filled his stomach.

"It can't be. It just can't be," Gray said.

The man in the photograph was Ritthirong.

31

Gray's mouth was agape, and his eyes were vacant as he sat motionless in a chair. Nickle and Chet were still looking at the photo of Ritthirong. They had only previously seen photographs of Ritthirong taken by the media or via arrest warrants. But the picture was clear, no blur. It had been taken straight on with decent lighting. Both Nickle and Chet had no doubts the man in the photograph was Ritthirong.

"Gray, you okay?" Nickle asked.

Nickle's question was enough to bring Gray out of the fog. He looked over at them and began to speak but stopped.

Nickle grabbed Gray's beer bottle from the table and handed it to him. "Take a sip. It'll do you good."

Gray finally managed to get a few words out of his mouth. "I know you guys think I'm crazy."

"I'm not thinking that at all," Nickle said.

"Don't bullshit me. I know how this all looks." Gray focused on Nickle. "But that is not Ritthirong in that picture. I heard him on the phone when I called Lillie."

"Maybe it was someone who sounded like him. Maybe someone—"

"I know what he sounds like! I spent two months interviewing the damn guy. Has either of you spent that much time with him? Have either of you even met him?"

Nickle and Chet remained quiet.

"This is a game. This is Ritthirong trying to get under my skin."

"Okay, let's forget about the photo. Explain to Chet and me why you're thinking what you're thinking."

"Don't you get it? He wants me to look crazy. More importantly, he wants me to question myself, to question my ability, my skills. I can't believe it."

"Believe what?"

"During our conversations back in prison, he constantly tried to trip me up, to undermine what I knew and how I classified him. He wanted to do it then, but of course, it didn't work. I was focused and in control."

"But now you're not in control," Chet said.

"Exactly. This is what he wanted all along. Having complete control over another person is classic narcissistic behavior." Gray popped up to his feet and walked over to the board. "I identified him as a psychopath with narcissistic tendencies. I'm not wrong here. I know Ritthirong's mindset better than anyone."

Nickle and Chet looked at Gray quietly.

"I completely understand if you doubt me. I get it. You're looking at the evidence, the photograph. And right now, it's trumping all this psychological babble that I'm spewing. But I know I'm right."

Chet cleared his throat. "How do you explain the photograph? You think it's fake, like made up with Photoshop or something?"

"I don't know. Maybe it's Ritthirong's face superimposed on another person's face. Look, I won't waste time trying to explain that picture. I know what I saw at the airport. I know I heard Ritthirong on the other end of that line. And the one thing that really continues to make my case is that Lillie is missing. Explain her disappearance. Can either of you do that?"

"You do have a point there," Nickle said. "I guess the million-dollar question is: What do we do now?"

"I need to see Ritthirong. I need to look him in the face with my own eyes. It's the only way I'll believe he's locked up. You two need to figure out a way to get me into that jail."

"Whoa there, partner," Nickle said. "That's a dangerous territory for you to be playing in. I might remind you that you have no jurisdiction here, hence no reason for you to visit a prisoner in that jail or even investigate anything."

"Yeah, I get that, but I need to look that man, whoever he is, in the face. There has to be a way. Chet, you keep telling me that everyone in Thailand can be bought. Can't we buy our way in there?"

Chet drew a deep breath and let it out. "It's true, but there are limitations. Keeping a visit to the jail by you quiet will be impossible, even if we pay people off. Just because someone takes payment from us doesn't mean they won't take money from another person right after."

"So what are you saying? Do we just give up? Say 'Good effort. We'll get 'em, next time, boys'?"

"I don't think Chet or I am suggesting that," Nickle said. "Look, I know you're heated right now—I totally get it. But attacking us isn't helping. We need to work together."

"I'm sorry, but it's just that I feel like I've been fighting an uphill battle from the very start."

"There might be one way," Chet said. "It's risky and dangerous... Things could go wrong."

"What is it, Chet?" Gray asked. "Right now, all ideas need to be considered."

"Okay. Let me lock you up in jail."

32

Gray and Nickle sat quietly as they absorbed Chet's plan: having Gray pose as a foreigner caught on the run. Chet reasoned that Gray needed to be held in jail while the proper paperwork was filed. No one at the prison would question it if Nickle, an FBI agent, and Chet, a detective inspector, brought him in. It was common for both agencies to work together to catch fugitives hiding in Thailand. Given the situation, Chet's plan was brilliant.

Gray looked at Nickle. "Do you think it can work?"

"Right now, I don't see any reason why it wouldn't. I've escorted numerous fugitives to jail. It's just that—"

"It's bullshit this time."

"That's right."

"Okay, set that aside. It's not out of the ordinary. If I were a real fugitive, you wouldn't be overthinking it right now."

"So you're totally okay with going through with this?"

"Yeah, I mean..." Gray caught Chet's eye. "What exactly did you have in mind? Are you literally locking me up?"

Chet nodded. "If we want it to look real. You need to be

processed and put in jail. But once inside, I'll contact the guards we have working for us and use them to gain access to Ritthirong's cell."

"Wait, so there will be a time when you won't have eyes on Gray?" Nickle asked.

"It's possible, but I'll do everything I can to make sure that doesn't happen. I'll try to get a private holding cell, something similar to what Ritthirong has. I'll tell them that Gray is a high-value fugitive and that we need to make sure he doesn't die or is hurt while being held."

"Gray, there is a risk. I want you to fully realize what you're signing up for here. Yes, there shouldn't be any problems, and everything should work out fine, but if things do go sideways, you could end up dead. I need you to understand that."

Gray took a moment to think about what Nickle said before nodding. "I'm okay with it. I trust you both."

"One other thing I recommend is that I part ways at the prison, that I'm just there to drop off. If things get crazy, you'll need me on the outside. I can't be compromised. You guys agree?"

"That's a good idea," Chet said. "One of us needs to be able to do something. It's risky for me too. But like you said earlier, this is normal. There shouldn't be any reason for someone to ask questions. Once you get a look at Ritthirong, we get out of there. The reason will be that we got word that you need to be transported to someplace more secure."

"So we can do this tonight, right?" Gray asked.

"Yeah, I don't see why not." Nickle looked over at Chet. "What do you think?"

Chet nodded. "Between midnight and early morning is the best time. The prison will be quiet. The inmates will be asleep, and the guards on duty will be relaxed."

Nickle looked at his watch and then at Gray. "Let's do it between twelve and one. It'll give you time to relax beforehand. I can't believe we're actually doing this."

"I can't either, but you both told me I can't approach this like a normal investigation. This is about as abnormal as we can get. Chet, is there anything we need to prepare before we go there?"

"We need a pair of handcuffs."

"I got that covered," Nickle said. "I'll need some time to work up a fake red notice document indicating that you're a wanted fugitive. It'll help sell the idea."

While Nickle went to work on the document, Gray mentally prepared for what he had to do. He was completely aware of the risks involved. Bang Kwang was by far the most dangerous prison in the entire country. The conditions inside were horrid, and it was not uncommon for guards to find inmates who had been killed during the night the following morning.

Chet placed a hand on Gray's shoulder. "Don't worry, my friend. I won't let anything happen to you."

"I trust you. But should something go wrong, do we have a contingency plan? Is it even possible to have one? Give me the honest truth. What will I really be up against?"

"It is possible you could die; I won't lie. But I don't think it'll go that way. I've transferred hundreds of foreigners and Thai people to the jails. I know how things work. We'll arrive. I'll check you in and explain your situation. You'll be processed and strip-searched. Your belongings will be taken from you. You'll have to change into a uniform. I'll be right outside the room when all this happens. And then I'll walk with you to the cell. I'll contact the guards working for us before we arrive at the jail so they'll know to expect us. We might have to separate for a few minutes, but I'll do my best to make sure that doesn't happen. How does all of that sound to you?"

Gray smiled. "Sounds like the perfect stupid plan."

33

The trio arrived at the Bang Kwang Central Prison a little after midnight. Gray had changed into some ragged clothing that Nickle had lying around. He also poured some beer over the shirt. In addition, Gray took a punch from Nickle to help sell the idea that he'd just been caught in a sting operation. Gray's crime: pedophilia. A serious crime was needed to give legitimacy to a joint operation between the RTP and the FBI. The story was that the US would want to petition to have Gray extradited, which the Thai government would have no issues with doing.

Since their arrival to the prison, every conversation was conducted in Thai, so Gray was out of the loop. It wouldn't be weird for a lawyer to translate, but Chet was the arresting officer, and everyone just thought Nickle didn't speak or understand Thai.

Once the situation was explained to the guards out front, Chet and Nickle escorted Gray inside through a series of locked steel doors. Nickle stayed with them until they reached the admission area to ensure the idea was sold and everything was proceeding as planned. Only then did Nickle part ways.

The admission area consisted of a desk with a man in a uniform sitting behind it. A few guards were milling around, caught up in their own conversations.

"Move, asshole," Chet said as he pushed Gray from behind, causing him to nearly trip. His hands were secured behind his back by handcuffs.

Chet's words gained the attention of the other guards, and their eyes settled on Gray. Gray was easily the tallest person in the room, not to mention the whitest.

Gray took a seat, and Chet proceeded to have a conversation with the admission officer. The officer filled out a bunch of paperwork. Chet signed a few pages before grabbing Gray's arm and standing him up.

Three guards joined them as they made their way to a doorway. The admission officer called out to Chet. They exchanged words. From what Gray could tell, it looked as if the officer wanted Chet to remain behind, but whatever Chet said, the officer gave in and allowed him to accompany Gray.

They were taken down a narrow hall. Gray noticed that what he'd seen so far of the prison didn't match the picture his imagination had painted. It appeared very well kept and clean. The air inside had a strong bleach scent to it. Gray expected a putrid smell, something closer to what he smelled in the slums. And most noticeable of all were the guards. They seemed pleasant, if not courteous.

In the hallway, they passed other guards, all eyeing Gray. He was the latest gossip, which worried him. The more attention he drew, the harder it might be for them to move around unnoticed later and eventually leave. Chet's plan for that was to simply have Nickle reappear to take them away. But Gray had to trust the process.

They entered another room that had a wooden bench.

Behind it was an open shower cell. A guard spoke to him in Thai.

"Take your clothes off," Chet said after uncuffing Gray.

Gray stripped down, and a guard proceeded to examine all of Gray's body cavities. He then pointed to the shower and handed Gray a small bar of soap. Gray showered off in cold water as quickly as he could. When he exited the shower stall, a small towel was given to him along with a change of clothes: a dark blue top with matching shorts that came down to just below his knees. No footwear was provided. Gray also noticed that his belongings, including his watch, were no longer sitting on the bench. One other thing he noticed: Chet had disappeared.

"Where is Chet?" he asked.

"Shut up!" a guard told him. "No talk."

"But I need to talk to him about my lawyer."

The guard slammed the end of his baton into Gray's abdomen, causing him to keel over in pain.

"No talk!"

Three guards then used their batons to direct Gray out of the shower room. Now that Chet wasn't around, their demeanor had changed.

"You like little boy and girl?" one of them said just before striking the baton against Gray's back hard. "Dirty farang. Go back to your country."

All three guards began to take shots at Gray with their batons as they shouted at him in Thai. Gray wondered if he'd made a big mistake coming to the prison. He took the beating like a man and continued to play his role in the charade, all while keeping an eye out for Chet. Surely, he would appear at any second. He did say there might be a time when they were separated momentarily. But Gray was only human. Doubt did creep into his head once again as he remembered Chet's words. *Be careful who you trust in Thailand.*

Gray was taken to an area of the prison that didn't have bright fluorescent lighting or the clean scent of bleach. The pungent smell of body order permeated the air. They stopped outside of a steel door. One of the guards fumbled with a key on a chain attached to his belt. He unlocked the door, and it squeaked as it opened.

The warm smell of BO mixed with urine slapped Gray's face as he looked into a dark room. Slowly his eyes adjusted, and a sea of men lying on the floor materialized.

"Move!" a guard said before striking him with a baton.

Gray walked into the room, almost tripping over a body in the process. The door slammed shut behind him and was locked. The room looked like a large warehouse with high ceilings a few windows near the top of the concrete walls. The space was rectangular and about half the size of a football field. There must have been hundreds of men lying across the floor. It dawned on Gray right then where he was. He had just been thrown into the prison's gen pop.

34

"Hey, you. Over here," a voice called out.

Gray turned and saw a white man with a beard waving him over.

"How you doing? The name's Mike." He stuck his hand out. "I'm American."

Gray hadn't anticipated making friends in jail, so he was a little taken aback at the introduction. While organizing the paperwork, Nickle had come up with an alias: Jerry Fletcher.

"Jerry," Gray said as he shook Mike's hand. "I'm also American."

"Man, I'm glad to have someone here from the States. I mean, I'm not glad you're in here... You know what I mean, right? There are some other foreigners in here, but you and I are the only Americans, as far as I know. So, what's your situation? Are you waiting for court?"

"I think so," Gray said. "And you?"

"If my lawyer does his job, I should be out of here in a couple of days."

"How long have you been in here?"

"Two weeks. Feels like months, though. Did you get a

lawyer yet? Don't wait on the embassy. They won't do shit. You need someone on the outside to contact a law firm here and pay them in advance. From what I hear, it's the best way to go. I can give you the name of my lawyer and the firm he works with. Don't go cheap, or else you get someone who'll just take your money and leave you in here. You have access to money, right?"

"Yeah."

"Whew, that's good, because if you didn't, you'd be screwed."

"How so?"

"Protection. There are serious people in here. You need to align yourself with the right people. I saw a dead Italian guy get taken out of here my first week. I mean, don't worry, they'll approach you and offer protection. You can say yes or no, but if you're not with someone, then you're free game for anyone in here."

"What do you pay?"

"Ten bucks a day. I have it transferred into their account that's attached to the commissary here. You don't want to give it to them all at once. The guards will get in on the action if you do that, and you'll still have to pay the gang their cut."

"How do you know all this?

"An Australian guy told me everything. He just got out yesterday. He was in here for a month and a half."

Just then, they noticed a group of men was making their way to them.

"Speak of the devil," Mike said quietly.

There were five of them, all of them were shirtless, and tattoos covered every inch of their bodies, including their faces. One of them walked right up to Gray. He had what looked like Thai writing tattooed on his face, plus a silly grin.

"Hey, farang. Welcome to Bangkok Hilton," he said with a

Thai accent. The men behind him snickered. "I can make your time here comfortable. You like?"

"What do you want?" Gray asked.

"You help me. I will help you. Okay?"

"Okay." Gray didn't think there was anything wrong with agreeing since, at any minute, Chet would appear and get him out of there.

"Fifteen dollar, every day."

"But he's only paying you ten dollars."

"You big man. More work to protect you. You pay tomorrow, okay?"

Gray nodded.

The men left.

"Tomorrow, you can make a phone call to my lawyer. The sooner they meet with you, the sooner you can get out of here."

"What about the charges?"

"Don't worry. He'll tell you how much you need to pay for that to go away. The bigger the crime, the more you pay."

"Hey!" a man shouted.

Gray turned, expecting to see the same man from before, but it was a different person with another gang of men behind him. He didn't have a friendly look on his face. In fact, he was snarling.

The man jabbed a finger at Gray's chest. "You pay twenty dollar tomorrow; we don't kill you."

Gray looked back at Mike, and all he offered was a shrug.

"I'm already paying someone else."

"So? Now you can pay me."

You little smarmy little shit. Gray was about to tell the guy to shove it when he realized Chet would be coming at any moment. The better response was to just agree to what anyone said to him. In fact, if every gang in the place came up to him, he should say yes to any demand because he'd be long gone before morning came around.

"Sure, I'll pay you tomorrow."

If Gray's answer came off as flippant, he wasn't aware of it.

"You think you better than me?" the man asked. Clear anger covered his face.

"I said I'll pay you tomorrow. Agree?"

"You dirty farang." The man got right up into Gray's personal space.

Gray understood alpha dynamics. If he let this guy step all over him, it wouldn't stop. It would only encourage him and possibly put Gray in a much more dangerous situation. There was no doubt in Gray's head he could squash the man with little effort. The only concern is how many of the men behind him would jump in. He had to assume all seven. That's a lot of ass-kickings, and it didn't look like Chet was walking through that door anytime soon.

Strike first. Strike fast.

Gray slammed a crushing right hook into the side of the man's face, buckling his legs in the process. The man dropped to the floor, unconscious. A second later, the seven men attacked all at once. Gray swung both of his fists as fast as he could. The men were striking him from all fronts with punches and kicks. A dogpile.

He needed to get a handle on the situation before it spiraled out of control. If the other inmates got in on the slugfest, it was over for Gray. Worst-case scenario, one of the men sticks a shank into him, and Gray ends up bleeding out in a Thai prison.

Gray ducked, avoiding a roundhouse kick to the head, and backed up, mowing down a man behind him and trampling him with heel strikes. A straight punch snapped the head back of an attacker. A quick left elbow crushed the face of yet another, but they were still coming at him.

A snapping kick to Gray's right rib cage stung and forced the air from his lungs. He did his best to fight through the pain, but it was too much. Gray dropped to a knee and covered his head with his arms to absorb the brunt of the strikes.

A moment later, Gray fought his way back to his feet and jabbed at his attackers to keep them at bay.

A second later, the men attacking him were now being attacked. Gray backed up against the wall. In front of him, he watched the Thai men battle it out.

"You okay?"

Mike had come up next to him.

"Look, your protection is already hard at work."

Gray then recognized the men who saved him. It was the first gang to approach him for protection money. A few seconds later, the fighting stopped. Gray had picked the superior gang as they had more men standing. The leader, the smiling guy who spoke to Gray, shouted out loud to everyone in the room and then pointed at Gray.

"What's he saying?" Gray asked.

"He's letting everyone know that you're his property. You'll be set from now on so long as you keep paying him every day."

Gray used his shirt to wipe the blood from his nose.

Mike looked him over. "A little bruising but no cuts. Can you move all your limbs?"

Gray nodded.

"No broken bones, then. I'd say you survived. I saw a man two days ago get the shit beat out of him by that second gang. They might have even killed him. But you're a tough bastard. No way they would take you down without getting a beating themselves. Where did you learn to fight like that?"

Gray looked over at Mike. "Air Force."

Just then, the door to gen pop opened. Gray squinted as he looked over at the door. At first, Gray couldn't tell who it was, as the person was backlit from the light in the hall. But as they moved closer, Gray recognized him. It was Chet.

35

It wasn't until Gray and Chet were standing in the hallway that he noticed the bruising on Gray's face and the blood on his shirt.

Chet looked Gray up and down. "What the hell happened to you?"

"What the hell does it look like? I got jumped. Where did you disappear to?"

Chet motioned for Gray to keep his voice down.

"Sorry, man. I had one more paper to sign. When I came back, you were already gone. I thought they took you to the private cells, which are far from here. I didn't think these idiots would throw you into gen pop. You're considered a high-value inmate. They should have known better."

"Apparently, those guards didn't get the memo. Now what?"

"Turn around. I need to handcuff you."

Gray did as Chet asked. After Chet finished, he walked over to the guard standing off to the side and had a quick conversation.

"I told him we need to go to the infirmary so the doctor

can look over your injuries because you have a meeting with a lawyer in the morning. The last thing they want is a high-value inmate telling his lawyer he's getting the shit beat out of him."

As he started to walk away, the guard caught up with him. Chet said something to him, and he backed off.

"Why do they listen to you?" Gray asked. "When I was taken to gen pop, they had no qualms with using their batons on me."

"I'm Thai. I'm the police. These men are just guards. They don't get paid enough to get into a fight with me or anything that happens here."

"Are we really going to the infirmary?"

"We're going there just in case someone asks, and it'll also look more believable. After, we'll meet up with one of the guards we hired." Chet looked back over his shoulder at Gray. "Do you need a doctor?"

"No."

"You sure?"

"I'm fine. I just want to get to Ritthirong's cell as soon as possible."

During their walk to the infirmary, only once did they pass a couple of guards. Chet barked an order at Gray to hurry up as they passed the guards. When they reached the infirmary, Chet poked his head inside, but the doctor wasn't at his desk.

"He might be on a break. This works for us. Let's keep moving."

Chet led Gray down a series of corridors, making a left and then a right.

"What's behind all these closed doors?" Gray asked.

"Storage. Meeting rooms. Private offices. Some are empty. Some are used for solitary confinement. Those double doors over their lead to the prison's morgue. It's always busy."

Chet made a left, away from the morgue. At the end of the hall, Gray saw two guards sitting on chairs. As they got closer, he recognized the men.

Chet said something to them as they approached and then removed handcuff keys from his pants.

"Turn around. We don't have much time, a couple of minutes at the most. Will that be enough for you?"

"It'll be fine."

One of the guards took off running to the end of the hall to keep watch. Gray looked up and spied a camera.

"What about that?"

"Don't worry about it. The guards will make sure the footage during this time disappears. Their ass is also on the line."

The remaining guard unlocked the door to the cell and pushed it open. Chet and Gray entered the concrete room. It wasn't very big, about ten feet deep and eight feet wide. There was a narrow bed against the right side wall, and a sink toilet combo tucked into the rear left corner. No windows, only fluorescent lighting above. Lying on the bed was a man wearing the same uniform as Gray. He had an arm draped over his face to block out the light above.

"Ritthirong, get up!" Chet said as he walked over to the man.

The man removed his arm and looked at them.

"Sit up!" Chet said. "Now!" He grabbed the man and pulled his shirt. The man sat up, swinging his feet over the side of the bed."

"He's all yours," Chet said.

From the moment the man removed his arm from his face, Gray recognized him. It was Ritthirong. His face looked a little gaunt, but that could just be from the treatment inside the jail.

Gray moved closer until he was standing right in front of the man whose gaze had settled on the floor.

"Look up," Chet ordered.

The man continued to stare at the floor. Chet lifted the man's jaw so that he looked up. Gray bent down so that he could look the man closer in the eye. Gray's initial thought was why wasn't Ritthirong acknowledging him. There was no reaction from him at all.

"Is he drugged?" Gray asked.

"I don't think so. What's your verdict? Is it Ritthirong?"

"I need to hear him speak. Somsak, it's me, Agent Gray. Do you remember?"

The man didn't say anything.

Chet slapped the back of the man's head. "Answer him."

"My name is Somsak Ritthirong. I'm thirty years old."

Gray looked up at Chet. "He may look like Ritthirong, but that's not him. It's an imposter."

36

Bunsong stood next to a standing marble bar and refilled his glass with a hundred-year-old whiskey. He bounced his head to the Thai music that blasted from the speakers hanging in the corners of the room. Rooster danced by himself while chugging beer from a bottle. Other armed men in the room were drinking and either talking or playing a game of cards. And finally, sitting in a leather recliner watching it all was Somsak Ritthirong.

He had a smile stretched clear across his face. He was dressed in a hip black suit. A large gold necklace hung from his neck, and impressive gold bracelets dangled from his wrists. He took a sip of champagne from a crystal flute. It was a festive time as the boss was back. And everyone was happy, but none more so than Bunsong.

He took a seat in the matching recliner next to Ritthirong. "I never thought this day would come."

"Why would you say something like that?" Ritthirong said, turning to his trusted lieutenant. "You know my word is guaranteed."

"You were gone for a long time. Longer than we had anticipated. But that is behind us now. What's important is that you are here and leading us in person."

"You did an excellent job of handling matters while I was away. I want you to know I appreciate your efforts."

"It was my honor to step up, but no one can fill your shoes."

"Now you're kissing my ass just to kiss it."

Bunsong laughed before taking a sip of his drink. "Have you given thought to what we'll do now? You're still not completely safe, at least not until the government kills your lookalike. After that, you'll be officially dead and free to do what you please."

"It was a brilliant plan, wasn't it, creating a lookalike."

"It was. I was skeptical at first, but as usual, you had the foresight to see things most people don't."

"Was his family well taken care of?"

"From the moment we recruited him, he and his family enjoyed a very comfortable life. But now, it is his time to do his part. And trust me, he is fully prepared to do it. We can trust him. And his family has enough money that he won't have to worry about them when he's gone."

"Good, good. I do have one request that I would like you to take care of right away."

"What is it?"

"Kill every member in his remaining family. Make sure the bodies are never found."

"Why? I just said you don't have to worry. He will do his part, and so will his family."

"The family can change their mind later. I don't want to take the chance. Do it!"

Bunsong nodded. "There are just his wife and two kids."

"I think you misunderstood me. I want you to kill every living relative that he has."

Bunsong looked at Ritthirong in disbelief.

"Am I clear?" Ritthirong said in a growl.

"Yes."

"Now I want to know about our operations. What are the problems?

"There really are no problems."

"There are always problems. Tell me everything."

Bunsong proceeded to give his boss a rundown of the traffic over the years. He talked about areas where they'd increased business and profits and spoke about other places where profits had slipped.

"The last problem was a few weeks ago. I lost an entire team and the cargo along the Thai–Laos border. The patrols have gotten really bad in that area. I think it's a good idea that we stop for now and let things cool down."

"No, we will continue.

"But..."

"You did a good job, but your problem is you're too soft."

"Soft?"

"If you let things slide slowly, it will reach a point where it can be impossible to fix. The answer isn't taking a break. The answer is better firepower, better training, and more men. We must crush our enemies. I don't care if they are Border Patrol agents working for the Thai or Laos governments. I will not let them dictate how I traffic my cargo, where I traffic my cargo, or when I traffic my cargo. Is that clear?"

Ritthirong grabbed a bottle of champagne from a standing ice bucket and poured himself another glass. "How is our guest doing? I've almost forgotten."

Ritthirong stood and walked to a bedroom on the first floor of the mansion. Bunsong followed, and when they reached the door, he unlocked it.

"Good evening, or shall I say early morning," Ritthirong

said. "I always get confused on how to greet someone if it's past midnight, but the sun hasn't risen."

Lying on the bed with swollen eyes, messed-up hair, and disheveled clothing was Lillie Pratt.

"Lillie, you look awful. Have you not been getting enough sleep?"

"Why are you doing this?"

"Why, she asks." Ritthirong looked at Bunsong briefly before focusing back on Pratt. "I'm surprised an analyst with Interpol can't figure it out."

"I've done nothing to you."

"You're absolutely right in that regard, but this isn't about you. It's never been about you. It's been about your boyfriend, Agent Gray."

"He's not my boyfriend," she shot back.

"Okay. I really don't care how you label your relationship."

"If this isn't about me, why am I here? Why aren't you spending your time with Gray?"

"You, my dear, are bait. Sometimes you British folk can be so thick. But as the saying goes, ignorance is bliss. And speaking of bait, your boyfriend is really not turning out to be the superb boyfriend I thought he would be. A couple of days have already passed, and I don't think he's done much of anything. To be honest, I'm very disappointed in his efforts. The big bad FBI agent is failing miserably. Did you know your embassy isn't even aware that you're missing?"

Pratt remained quiet.

"Cat got your tongue? I bet you weren't expecting to hear that. I suspect you were thinking that at any minute, the cavalry would come crashing through the front door to rescue you. I hate to burst your bubble, but no one has saddled up. I'm afraid you're stuck here with me, which worries me because I'm not really interested in keeping you around."

"Then release me, and we can both go our separate ways," Pratt said with a smile.

"If only life were so easy." Ritthirong took a sip of his champagne as his gaze moved slowly across Pratt's body. "You know, you're not a bad-looking woman. I could sell you for a lot of money. Perhaps I'll do that. I have clients in East Africa who are extremely fond of having white women as their sex slaves. Most of their slaves are Eastern European, so a British woman would be a prize. What do you think, Bunsong?"

"I think we can easily start a bidding war and drive up the price."

Ritthirong drained the last of his champagne. "I think sex slave isn't quite right. There's always the chance that she can talk later."

"You can cut her tongue out and promote her as a 'no-nagging model,'" Bunsong said.

Just then, they heard an elephant trumpet in the distance. Ritthirong snapped his fingers.

"I got it!" Ritthirong looked at Bunsong with excitement. "We can let an elephant have its way with her. What do you think, Lillie? Have you ever been trampled by an elephant? Don't answer. It's rhetorical."

"That's a great idea," Bunsong said as he clapped.

"When an elephant tramples a human, all that's left is a red pulp mushed into the ground. Imagine pouring red Slurpee onto the dirt. Did that paint the picture well enough?"

"How long do you want to keep her around while waiting for Gray?" Bunsong asked.

Ritthirong let out a breath. "Sadly, I'm already bored with her."

37

One of the things that stood out to Gray when he had gotten to know Ritthirong was his command of English. It was perfect, and he could go back and forth between American and British English, complete with accents. The man sitting on the bed might have looked exactly like Ritthirong, but he spoke with a heavy Thai accent. And after more questioning, it was apparent he wasn't fluent in English. Ritthirong was highly educated. The man in front of Gray wasn't.

Chet did his best to pry information out of the man: What deal had he made with Ritthirong? Would Ritthirong rescue him later? Anything they thought could provide them with a lead on Ritthirong's whereabouts. But shortly after discovering the decoy, the guard came into the room and told them they had to leave. A new shift of guards would be arriving at any minute.

Gray put his hands behind his back and Chet quickly handcuffed him as they made their way down the hallway.

"Ritthirong must be planning to come to the jail," Chet said. "We can sit on the place and grab him or his men when they show up."

"He's not coming, nor is he sending any men. He doesn't care about that man taking his place. He's here to take the fall. That man had to have had extensive plastic surgery. That's not something that's thought of and done in a couple of months. This has been in the works for years. It's textbook Ritthirong, planning years ahead for all possibilities."

Chet ran a hand through his hair. "Thinking about this years ago and having it work." Chet shook his head in defeat. "How do you catch someone like that?"

"You play their game. That's how. Remember, Ritthirong wants me. He's expecting me to find him. That's the challenge that's been issued."

"So we have to find him."

"That's right. We can't give up. Not now. Not ever. He's counting on it."

Just as Chet and Gray rounded a corner, they bumped into a group of guards. With them was the admissions officer.

"Detective Inspector Chaemchamrat. Can I ask what you are doing in this area of the prison with this prisoner?" This time he spoke in English.

"I was escorting my prisoner to the infirmary to have the doctor look him over. As you can see, his face was injured by the incompetence of the guards here. He is a high-value inmate and was placed in gen pop."

"I apologize for that mistake, but the infirmary is nowhere near here."

"We took a wrong turn. Maybe you should escort us there. My prisoner is meeting with his lawyer first thing in the morning. If he looks like this, it will make us all look bad. I spent a long time hunting for this bastard. If he is released because of your men's mistake, I will not hesitate to launch a full investigation on you and your men. I'm sure you don't want that with your busy schedule."

The admissions officer was almost as tall as Gray. He moved in closer so that they were eye to eye.

"You understand me, yes?"

"I do."

"I looked over your paperwork and found something interesting."

"What's that?"

"For the FBI and the Royal Thai Police to work together, there must be a red notice issued by Interpol for your arrest. But I can't seem to find any evidence of its existence online, just the copy submitted to me. I'm wondering why that is so?"

Gray shrugged. "How would I know?"

"Hey, it's probably a technicality. We gave you the correct paperwork when we arrived."

"Yes, you did, but all that exists are the copies you provided."

Chet moved in closer to the admissions officer. "Are you trying to say something?"

"I am only doing my job," the officer answered. He looked back at Gray. "Mr. Fletcher, it's probably a misunderstanding, like the inspector said. I'm sure we'll be able to clear this up in the morning. You should have your face looked over."

Gray nodded.

"Can we go now?" Chet said.

"Of course." The officer moved to the side.

Chet grabbed hold of Gray's arm, and as they took a step forward, but the officer quickly stepped back in front of them, blocking their path.

"I just remembered I have one more question for Mr. Fletcher. After that, you can be on your way." The officer tapped at his mobile phone and pulled up a photo of Ploy and Gray. "Mr. Fletcher, why do you look exactly like this FBI agent?"

38

Chet let out a laugh. "You think my prisoner is an FBI agent? Have you been drinking? Why would Ploy Ritthirong, a hi-so, be messing around with a pedophile?"

"I'm just looking for an explanation."

The officer's men spread out as they lifted their batons.

"Are you threatening me?" Chet asked in a low voice. "I would answer very carefully."

"Detective Inspector Chaemchamrat, you know I have the authority to hold you and your prisoner if you have broken any laws or protocols associated with this prison. Mr. Fletcher, would you care to explain this photo?"

"I can, but it's a little embarrassing. Can you lean in, and I'll whisper the answer?"

The officer leaned in, and Gray slammed his forehead into the man's face. He let out a howl as he covered his face with his hands. Gray then kicked him in the stomach, sending him back into the man behind him.

Chet attacked the man nearest him with a double fist strike and a jumping kick that put him to sleep. He immediately deflected a baton strike and countered with rapid punches backing his man up. Body blows sent the man to the floor, and Chet finished him off with an elbow to the back of his head. Gray watched in amazement as Chet single-handedly took out all five guards in rapid succession.

"Why did you head butt him?" Chet said, a little out of breath.

"We were toast, and I don't have time to play games with men who think they have power."

"Actually, he does have a lot of power," Chet said as he looked at the officer lying unconscious on the ground. "He controls the jail."

"Oops, my mistake. Uncuff me."

"No, we still need to get out of here."

"Are you kidding me? The ruse is up. It's over."

"Come on." Chet led the way.

"You like keeping me handcuffed, don't you?" Gray asked as he followed.

"I like preventing problems. Knocking that officer out makes more problems."

The two rounded a corner and bumped into three guards.

Chet shouted angrily at them in Thai while pointing at Gray. All three guards gave Chet a wai and stepped out of the way.

"You see? The story is still good."

"Do you have a plan on how you're going to walk me out of here with no questions asked?"

"It should be easy now that the admissions officer is lying on the floor and not at his post."

"So I didn't create a problem. I actually eliminated one."

The two entered the admissions area calmly. A guard came up to inquire, and Chet had a conversation with him while smiling. Chet then showed him his phone, but Gray couldn't tell what he was showing him. Eventually, the guard cracked a smile and allowed them to pass. Once clear of the doorway leading out of the building, Gray asked Chet what he said.

"I showed him the photo on Instagram and said I had made a big mistake and I needed to free you right away or else I could lose my job."

"He bought that story?"

"Ploy is a very popular influencer. Of course, he did. We just need to get through the gates up ahead and we're good."

Armed guards stopped Chet and Gray at the security gates that surrounded the prison grounds. Chet talked to them and showed them the photo of Gray with Ploy, only these guards weren't as easily persuaded. They looked at the picture and had a discussion between themselves before talking more with Chet.

Come on, fellas. What's the holdup?

The final exit was only feet away. Gray could smell the freedom.

Then one of the guards walked off to the side and made a phone call.

Sheesh, this is it. Surely that officer and his men have recovered or were discovered by other guards.

"Chet, what's he doing?" Gray whispered.

"He's calling the admission officer for clarification."

"But?"

"I know."

"Can't you just pay them and be done with it."

"I offered, but they still wanted to make the call."

Chet laughed and said something to the guards.

Finally, the guard shrugged and ended his call. They talked between themselves, and then one of the guards signaled for the gate to be opened. Slowly, the large security fence rolled along its track. Chet and Gray stepped forward, waiting for enough space for them to slip out. And just when they did, a wailing siren sounded.

"Run!" Chet shouted.

39

Gray hustled as fast as he could with his hands behind his back. He jumped onto Chet's bike and clamped his legs around it just as Chet twisted the throttle and rocketed their asses out of there.

It took every ounce of strength for Gray to stay on the bike. He could feel the burn in his thighs intensifying, but he wasn't about to tell Chet to stop and uncuff him, at least not until he could no longer hear those sirens.

Chet drove like a superbike racer competing in the Isle of Man TT. He leaned into turns and exploded out of them all in poorly lit areas while avoiding soi dogs sleeping in the middle of the road. Eventually, Chet brought the bike to a stop under a large mango tree.

"You okay?" he asked as he got off the bike so he could remove the handcuffs.

"Yeah, man, I'm fine." Gray stretched his arms over his head. "How screwed are we? Did we just fake break out of jail?"

"Don't worry, the paperwork is fake too, so they'll look like idiots if they try to pursue it."

"Well, now that we got our answer on Ritthirong, can we finally make a move on the Black Tigers?"

Chet drew a deep breath as he thought about Gray's question.

"What is it about these guys that gives you such pause? So far, we've broken out of prison, taken out an arms dealer in the slums—heck, we even watched an influencer get the hair removed from her armpits. Nothing phases you except the Black Tigers."

"I have no sway over them. They have more powerful connections than I do. If I'm not careful, they can make me disappear."

"Fair enough. I don't want that to happen, but..."

"I know. They're a part of this. I just don't know what the best way to get information from them is. Interviewing them will only result in denials, and then they'll be watching us twenty-four seven if they aren't already doing so. I still believe taking them head-on is the quickest way to kill your friend. We can't give them a reason to start a cover-up, because when they do, it involves getting rid of people."

"Okay, then, we focus on finding Ritthirong. He's got to still be inside the country. Can't you use your contacts? Aren't there known locations where he might be that we can run down? What about the men that work for him? Someone has to know something."

"Ritthirong is one of those guys that has managed to keep his business from many. We know of him and what he does, but when it comes to the inner workings of his organization, there is very little to say. You said he's an excellent planner. That's why he's hard to track down. And I hear the men that work with him are very loyal."

"Still, every organization has a disgruntled employee. I refuse to believe he's untouchable. I get that you're worried about blasting it out there that we're hunting down a man who supposedly is locked up."

"I'm glad you can understand my predicament. You have no idea how dangerous the power players in my country can be. I want to go after them, but it's simply not worth it to start a war."

"I agree. The focus should be on finding Lillie and not investigating the Black Tigers."

Chet yawned, and Gray followed suit.

"I will drop you off at your hotel," Chet said. "We both could use some sleep. We can come at it fresh tomorrow."

———————

Back at Bang Kwang Central Prison, the admissions officer sat at his desk with a bruised face and a battered ego. He had been taken for a ride. Not only that, when he discovered it, he tried too hard to posture his cleverness in front of his men, and it got the best of him. Detective Inspector Chaemchamrat and Agent Gray had gotten away.

It wasn't lost on him as to why they were there. They'd come to confirm whether that was Ritthirong being held in the cell. Because he was well aware that it wasn't.

The door to the admissions area opened. The guards who had helped Chet and Gray gain access to the Ritthirong's cell were brought in and made to kneel before the admission officer. He walked around his desk to the men and spat on them. They had caused the admissions officer to lose the respect of his men. He needed to rectify that. He nodded at one of the guards, and he handed the officer a pistol. He then shot both of his men in the head.

"Get rid of them," he said to the guards.

He took a seat at his desk and made a phone call.

"It's been done," he said when the other person answered.

"Good. Now, you know what to do?" said the man on the other end. "Mess this up, and you'll be the next one shot."

The admissions officer hung up and gathered some more men. They made their way to Ritthirong's cell, where they found him lying on his bed.

The admission officer gave his men the go-ahead, and they quickly subdued the man and wrapped a piece of cloth tightly around his neck. After a brief struggle, the imposter lay motionless on the floor. The officer watched as his men tied the bedsheet around the imposter's neck and then secured it to the bed frame.

The officer told one of his men to fetch the doctor. "Tell him there's been a suicide."

40

Cake had been holed up in her office all day and night. She'd been studying the robbery footage again, determined to find out who had wronged her. A knock on her door grabbed her attention. It was Mint.

"You're still looking at that?"

Cake leaned back in her chair and rubbed her temples. "I won't stop until I find out who did it."

"I fixed you a mango smoothie." She placed a glass down on the desk. "Take a break. It's late." She cleared away dirty plates and utensils.

Cake took a sip of the smoothie. "It's good. Thank you."

Mint sat down. "Why does it matter so much to you that you find this person? The money stolen isn't much to you."

"It's not the money. It's the disrespect. I can't let it go."

"Will it kill you if you never find out? Wait, I have a better question—is it really worth killing yourself over?"

"I know you're right, but I feel violated. Someone came into our home and trashed the place and stole my money. Look at them in the video. They don't seem worried at all about getting caught." Cake rearranged the messy bun on top of her head.

A smile formed on Mint's face. "Now I get why you can't let this go. You don't like their cocky attitude."

"You're right. I don't."

"What have you learned from looking at those videos all day?"

"Nothing."

"And what about the names of businesses doing poorly and the names of police officers who rely on them for brown envelopes?"

"Nothing."

"And what about the names of all the Black Tigers? Learn anything there?"

Cake shook her head.

"You might have to accept that it happened, and there is nothing you can do about it except move on."

Just then, there was another knock on Cake's office door. This time it was Chompoo poking her head inside.

"Cake, you have a visitor."

A crinkle formed on Cake's forehead. "Who's coming by so late at night?"

Chompoo took a step back as she opened the door wider. Ped stood next to her.

"Ped? I wasn't expecting you. Come inside."

Ped took a seat, and Mint and Chompoo left, closing the door behind them.

"Did the girls offer you something to drink?

"I'm fine."

"Why are you here? I don't recall us having a meeting scheduled."

"If I remember, I told you if I heard anything about your problem, I would let you know."

Cake leaned forward, rested her forearms on her desk, and smiled.

"We were paid to do a job. I believe the person who paid us took the money from you."

"And why do you think this? Where is your proof?"

"I have no proof. It's just my gut."

"I'll need a little more than your intuition."

"The man people saw escorted to the jail by my boss and me was an imposter. The real Somsak Ritthirong is free."

Cake leaned back as she took in what Ped had just told her.

"He's free? Are you sure?"

"Positive. I don't know where he is, but I know the Ritthirong at Bang Kwang is not the real Ritthirong."

"So Ritthirong paid the Black Tigers to help him escape? It doesn't make sense. People would know it's not him in jail."

"Ritthirong's men provided us with a man who looked exactly like him. His job was to take the rap for Ritthirong. Blaming people for crimes they didn't commit is common. Either the guilty find a scapegoat to blame it on, or they find someone they can pay. With enough money, it's easy to orchestrate this."

"Yes, I know. It's just that I find it hard to believe since Ritthirong and I have a long-standing business agreement. We don't interfere. In fact, I have never had any problems with him, ever."

"I heard about your arrangement with him. Unfortunately, it was Charong Bunsong who hired us. That is the truth. We gave him less than a day to come up with six million baht. I guess he was short and thought of you. According to your timeline, both things happened around the same time."

"Why are you telling me this? What's in it for you?"

"I'm just helping. Maybe in the future, you can find a way to repay the favor."

"And the money?"

Ped smiled. "The money will not be returned. Forget about it. Focus on getting answers to all your questions. You know where to go for them."

"Are you still working with Ritthirong?"

"No. Our job is over. We are not involved with him or anyone from his organization. But I can't guarantee Ritthirong won't flee Thailand real soon. If I were you, I would visit him as soon as possible...if you want answers."

Cake escorted Ped back to his vehicle and thanked him once more before rounding up her Fierce Five back in her office. She relayed the information that Ped had given her.

"That little rat," Chompoo said. "I can't believe after all these years he would pull a stunt like that."

"His business must have been hurting with him being away for so long," Tukta said. "You would think he'd have six million baht to pay off the Black Tigers."

Mint crossed her arms over her chest. "It's so strange that after all these years, Ritthirong would do that."

"I agree," Cake said as she leaned back in her chair. "It's out of character for him. Trust me, I know he's a psycho, and I would never turn my back on him in a room, but stealing four million baht... that should be pocket change for him."

"How do you want to handle this?" Chompoo asked.

"If what Ped said is true. I need to settle this right now."

Cake stood and took a custom-made machete off a stand she kept behind her desk. It belonged to her father and was one of the few things she had to remember him by. The handle was inlaid with mother of pearl and gold, and a Thai inscription ran the length of the blade. It was one of her father's favorite Buddhist sayings. It read, *Don't run from your problems. There is always a way to solve them.*

Cake's father always believed every problem could be solved, no matter how difficult. He had passed that thinking on to Cake, and that's why she never gave up on solving the problem at hand.

Cake looked at her Fierce Five. "Gear up and prepare for war. We're going to Saraburi tonight."

41

Gray didn't put up much of a fight at Chet's suggestion that they call it a night. They'd been grinding steadily since early that morning. A few hours of rest would help. On the ride back to Gray's hotel, the adrenaline flowing through his body had slowly subsided, and he'd begun to feel the need for sleep.

But Gray being Gray, his mind refused to shut off. The ride was filled with a ton of *what if*s. Gray couldn't help but replay the meetings with Ritthirong over in his head, searching for anything that might have suggested that he was planning to escape. He didn't put it past Ritthirong to throw out a clue. Ritthirong always seemed to be testing Gray. But if he had done so, Gray wasn't able to pin it down. Nor was there any indication Ritthirong intended to kidnap Lillie.

Lillie's abduction could have been a last-minute addition, but the escape? No way. That was planned well in advance.

The more Gray gave it thought, the more he accepted that there were no hints given. Everything had gone to plan the way Ritthirong had intended.

Chet brought the bike to a stop in front of Gray's hotel.

"I'll pick you up first thing in the morning," Chet said.

"All right, buddy. See you then." Gray placed a hand on Chet's shoulder and squeezed. "Thanks for everything. I would have gotten nowhere without you."

"Thank me after we've rescued Lillie." Chet then handed Gray his wallet, key card, and watch that he'd been able to get from the guards. "This is everything except your clothes."

No one paid any attention to the prison clothes Gray wore when he entered the lobby or the fact that he was barefoot; they probably weren't even aware. He walked quickly to the elevators and headed up to his floor. Gray entered the room and fumbled with placing the key card into the power switch. The lights turned on, revealing Gun sitting in a chair near the window.

"Whoa!" Gray jumped back. "What the hell are you doing here?"

Gray then noticed a few of Gun's men standing off to the side. Outnumbered in a small room, Gray spun around to exit but found more men waiting outside, blocking him.

"Agent Gray, it's okay," Gun said. "Come back inside. I just want to talk."

Gray walked back into the room.

"Please sit." Gun motioned to the bed. He looked at the clothing Gray wore but gave no indication of whether he recognized it.

"What do you want from me?" Gray asked.

"Nothing, but there is something you want from me?"

"Where's Ritthirong?"

"If I give you that information, what will you do?"

"He kidnapped my colleague Lillie Pratt."

"So you want to rescue her? I think that's a good idea. After you do that, my advice is that you leave the country as soon as possible."

"Why are you telling me all this?"

"Agent Gray, you and I both know what happened after you landed in Bangkok. Look at the clothes you're wearing. There is only one place I know where you can get an outfit like that. Were you able to confirm the identity of the person purported to be Ritthirong?"

"It's not him. It's an imposter."

"You're right. Ritthirong is free, and he has your friend."

"Are you going to help me rescue her?"

"No. That is your responsibility. But I will help by giving you information. Ritthirong is in Saraburi. It's a province north of Bangkok."

Gun motioned to one of his men, who then handed Gray a paper with Thai writing on it.

"Those are directions to Ritthirong's home. He lives in the jungle. Call your friend Detective Inspector Chaemchamrat. He'll be able to find it. Don't wait. I can't guarantee Ritthirong will be there long."

"You think you're a righteous guy, but I see through your facade. You're as corrupt as they come, and you abuse your power to your advantage."

Gun smiled.

"You really think you're getting away with this, don't you?"

"Agent Gray, I already have. Take my tip and go rescue your friend."

"You could be sending me into the jungle to disappear. How do I know this isn't a trap?"

"You don't. But you have no other options. What little progress you've made until now will not help you find Ms. Pratt. Don't lie to yourself that you're getting somewhere. I just handed you the location of Ritthirong. And still, you are sitting there having a conversation about what I've done. Your priorities are mixed. I am allowing you to save your friend and yourself."

Gun looked at Gray's balled fists.

"What, you want to fight me?" Gun laughed, and so did his men. "I admire your tenacity, Agent Gray, and your ability to stand firm on your moral beliefs. You are probably an excellent agent back in your country, and there is no doubt you have put a lot of people in jail, but you are in Thailand. Here, you are nothing but a fool."

Gun stood. "You have twenty-four hours to find your friend and leave Bangkok. Do the smart thing, Agent Gray."

42

Gray didn't have to wait long in the lobby after calling Chet and informing him of his visit from Gun. Chet walked through the entrance, holding up his arms.

"I still can't believe it. That bastard had the nerve to come to you."

"It's a power play," Gray said as he stood. "He's trying to control the outcome. He's worried you and I will reveal his part in Ritthirong's plan."

"Of course, it's the only reason for him to come to you. I'm actually surprised he didn't kill you, but he probably thought that would bring additional worries. Thank your badge for that."

"Here are the directions." Gray gave Chet the paper. "Are you familiar with Saraburi?"

Chet nodded. "I think I can find it."

"We should leave right away. I'm not interested in testing the deadline Gun gave me. I left my handgun at Nickle's place. I tried calling, but he's not answering."

"Don't worry, I have an extra handgun. I want to warn you.

This is dangerous. Ritthirong has men, and they're probably well armed. And we have no real plan except to show up."

"Any suggestions?"

"Aside from turning this into a real operation with a team of men from the RTPs special ops unit, no."

"Are you okay with doing this?" Gray asked. "You've already put your life in danger, and now I'm asking you to do it again with the odds stacked against us."

"I've come this far. I need to see it through."

Across the street from the hotel, Gun and his men stood in the shadows watching Gray's hotel.

"You think Gray will bite?" one of Gun's men asked him.

"If he has a chance to save Lillie Pratt, he'll do it. He can't help but do the right thing."

Ten minutes after Detective Inspector Chaemchamrat arrived, he and Gray exited the hotel and rode away on his motorcycle.

"There they go, off to save the day." Gun chuckled.

His phone buzzed. It was Ped calling.

"How did your meeting go with Cake?" Gun asked.

"I gave her the information about Ritthirong stealing her money. She believed me. I'm sure she is on her way to Saraburi right now."

"Good, good. I had an equally positive conversation with Agent Gray. He and the inspector have just left his hotel and are off to rescue the woman. I also have news about the decoy. It seems he committed suicide as planned."

"That's great news. Now we don't have to wait until his trial. I was worried he would crack beforehand or someone would discover he was a fake. Having him killed sooner was the right decision."

"You never know with this government, they might have decided not to give him the death penalty but keep him alive so they can continue to show him off as a success."

"You're right. I still can't believe the plan has happened just as you said it would. It's really working."

"You doubted me?"

"No. I'm in awe. You are the true mastermind here. Not Ritthirong. We are tying up all of these loose ends. Soon any involvement we had in Ritthirong's escape will disappear. The fake Ritthirong is dead. Cake's digging around has stopped now that she knows Ritthirong stole from her."

"And with luck, she will kill Bunsong, silencing that man's loose mouth," Gun said. "She might even do us a favor and get rid of Ritthirong."

"That would be a coup. We'd be in the clear. It'll make it easier for Agent Gray to rescue that woman and leave the country. I wish I could be there to see it all play out."

"You will."

"What do you mean?"

"Agent Gray knows too much. He's a loose end that needs to be dealt with. Gather a team of men and gear up now. We're going to Saraburi."

43

It wasn't often Cake ordered her crew to mobilize, but they trained daily. If the call came, they were ready. Cake and her Fierce Five were prepared to move in thirty minutes. They hit the road and sped toward Saraburi, making excellent time due to light traffic on the highways.

Cake and the girls were dressed in black from head to toe with body armor and combat belts carrying extra ammo, a flashlight, zip ties, pepper spray, and a sheathed knife. Cake had her father's machete. They wore drop-leg holsters with Beretta M9s tucked inside outfitted with a suppressor. The girls also carried HK G36 assault rifles.

There was zero conversation inside the black Land Rover. Everyone was focused on the task at hand. They weren't driving to Saraburi to chat with Ritthirong. Blood would be spilled.

The crew arrived at the dirt road that led into the jungle in the early morning, the perfect time for an assault. They all climbed out of the Rover and made their way in by foot. Cake peered through night-vision binoculars.

"There's a guard station up ahead," she said. "Four men.

But they aren't paying attention. Chompoo, Nok, I want you guys to approach from the right flank. Joke and Tukta, stay here and cover Mint and me. Everyone clear?" she asked as she screwed a suppressor onto her handgun. She and Mint left their assault rifles with Joke and Tukta and concealed their handguns.

With their orders given, the girls moved out. Cake's plan was to approach the men head-on and tell them she had an appointment to see Ritthirong. She was sure the men knew who she was, or at the very least had heard of her.

"Sawadee ka," Cake called out.

The men stood quickly, guns aimed at Cake and Mint.

"Please, we come in peace. My name is Cake. Somsak Ritthirong is expecting me."

"No one told us Khun Ritthirong was expecting guests," one of the men said as he approached Cake and Mint.

"Well, I'm sure there's been a mix-up. Have you heard of me?"

The man nodded. "I've heard of you. I will need to make a call. Wait here."

As he walked away, fumbling to get his phone out of his jeans, Cake shot him in the back of the head with her handgun. Mint followed by planting two rounds into the chest of the man nearest her. Chompoo and Nok dropped the other two.

Once Tukta and Joke caught up with Cake and the rest of the girls, they continued on the road farther into the jungle. It took another twenty minutes on foot for the wall surrounding Ritthirong's mansion to come into view. Cake had visited Ritthirong twice before, so she was familiar with the layout of his home. She also knew there were armed guards on top of the wall.

The easiest way into the mansion was through the front of

the house. It was a combination of floor-to-ceiling glass windows and French doors. They could easily see inside and eliminate targets as they approached.

"Are we killing everyone?" Chompoo asked as she knelt down next to Cake.

"I haven't decided yet. I want to talk to Ritthirong. I want answers."

"So kill what is necessary to make that happen?"

"Yes."

Chompoo relayed the message and coordinated with the other girls while Cake observed the men guarding the wall. Much like the four guards from earlier, the ones on the wall were distracted by their phones or liquor. Cake could hear the faint sound of music coming from the other side of the wall, indicating that Ritthirong was still awake. Maybe they were celebrating his return. Whatever was taking place worked in Cake's favor.

Chompoo returned to Cake's side and recommended eliminating all the guards on top of the wall.

"I count five. We can do it quickly. That front gate looks like it's open a bit. We should be able to walk right in."

Cake nodded in agreement and gave Chompoo the go-ahead.

The girls spread out and took aim at their targets using their handguns. Chompoo gave the signal, and they fired.. Just like the men guarding the road, the men on the wall were taken down at once. Cake and the girls moved quickly to the gate and pushed through. As they approached the home, a guard on a second-floor balcony spotted them and opened fire.

Cake and the girls split up as they returned fire with their assault rifles. Covert operations were over. Cake pushed forward, firing at the large French doors lining the front of the home before entering. She dropped down behind a sofa. The rest of her girls entered the mansion and took cover.

Armed men appeared on the double sweeping staircase and fired. Cake popped up and returned fire, taking one of the men out. More armed men burst through a closed door toward the rear of the large living room area.

Both sides continued to trade shots. Cake knew she needed to push through that door that the men had come from. Through that doorway was the entertainment room and where the music came from. That's where Ritthirong would be if he wasn't sleeping.

Cake motioned to Chompoo that they needed to head through that door. Chompoo immediately took the lead, gunning down two men as she advanced. Cake and the rest of the girls provided fire cover. They all made it to the door one by one, taking out all their attackers on the stairs.

Chompoo shot the handle off on the door before kicking it open. Rapid gunfire erupted, forcing Cake and the rest of her gang to fall either side of the door. They'd get cut down if they tried to funnel in through the narrow doorway. As Cake thought about another way in, Ritthirong called out.

"Cake, my friend. Hello to you, too."

"I appreciate you stopping by. A welcome fruitcake would have sufficed. You didn't need to shoot up my home."

"You think I would bring you a gift after what you did to me?"

There was a moment of silence before Ritthirong responded. "What are you talking about?"

"The money. Don't play dumb. It's the reason why you're walking around free right now."

More silence followed.

"Cake, I'm calling a truce. Don't shoot. Come inside."

Cake peeked quickly through the doorway and saw Ritthi-rong standing in the middle of the room unarmed.

"Come, Cake. We're old friends. Let's discuss this, because I'll be candid: I know nothing about this stolen money you're talking about."

"It could be a trap," Chompoo whispered.

Cake peeked once more through the doorway. Ritthirong was still there with his arms up in the air.

"I'm not going to shoot you, Cake. Do I have your word that your girls won't shoot me?"

"Deal."

Cake motioned for her girls to lower their guns, and she stepped through the doorway. Ritthirong smiled at her.

"Come, Cake. Have a drink with me. I just opened a bottle of champagne."

Bunsong stood off to the side next to a leather recliner. He did not look happy to see Cake. Ritthirong handed Cake a glass of champagne.

"To our successful ceasefire."

Cake took a sip of the champagne, but her eyes never left Ritthirong. Nor did his leave Cake.

"Tell me what happened," he said.

Cake told Ritthirong about the hit at her home and four million baht that was stolen and how it happened right around the time the Black Tigers received payment for their help.

"You seem to know an awful lot. How did you come to know this information? I ask because four million isn't a lot of money, and I'm still not sure why you think it was me. Yes, I hired the Black Tigers, but I did not steal your money."

"You're right. You didn't steal it. But Charong Bunsong did."

"You're crazy. Don't listen to the crap coming out of this ladyboy's mouth," Bunsong said.

"But is it true, Charong?"

"Do you really believe her?"

"Ped visited me earlier tonight," Cake interrupted. "He was the one who informed me about the deal. He told me he and Gun had given Charong less than a day to pay them or the deal to help you escape was off. That same night my place got hit. Why would Ped come to my villa with no warning to tell me that?"

"I don't know. That's a good question," Ritthirong said.

He turned to Bunsong. "Is what Ped said true?"

"What do you want me to say? My job was to execute the plan the way you had intended. I did just that. And that is why you are here right now and not in a filthy jail cell."

"Who else was involved?" Ritthirong asked, but Bunsong kept his mouth shut. "Rooster, I know you were involved. Get over there now!"

Rooster put down his beer bottle and moved over next to Bunsong. One by one, the men who went along with Bunsong's plan were weeded out.

"Now I know you were all simply following orders. Charong was in charge while I was away, but I did give explicit instructions to everyone after making this arrangement of convenience with Cake. Now my business in the south is jeopardized." Ritthirong turned to Cake. "These men are yours. You're free to do with them as you wish."

44

After bringing his bike to a stop, Chet checked the map on the phone.

"The road we're looking for is around here... There it is."

"Should we walk in?" Gray said.

"Good idea. I can hide the bike in the bushes over there."

With the bike stashed, they did quick weapons check. They each had a handgun, a Sig Sauer P320, with seventeen rounds in the magazine.

"It's not a lot, but it'll have to do," Chet said. "Shoot wisely."

The two started their walk along the dirt road until they spotted the stilted house. They crouched near the side of the road.

"Do you see anyone?" Chet whispered.

"I don't see any movement, but someone could be sitting inside the house, away from the window. There's a good chance they can see us if we're not careful."

"Then we better be careful."

They remained crouched as they made their way forward, stopping and listening every five feet or so until Chet stopped.

"What is it?" Gray asked quietly.

"Look over there. Is that someone on the ground?"

"Looks like it now that you mention it."

They moved a little closer.

"Yeah, that's a body," Gray said. "There's another one a little over to the right."

They relaxed a little as they moved forward. A total of four dead men lay on the road with AK-47s beside them.

"The body is still warm," Gray said as he touched one of the men. "Someone blasted through here not too long ago. Does Ritthirong have any known enemies?"

"Everyone has enemies. Grab a rifle and any ammo you find on them."

Chet and Gray continued farther into the jungle. The jungle canopy wasn't very thick and allowed the full moon to cast a silvery light everywhere. Walking on foot wasn't a problem. Their eyes had adjusted, and they could easily see. All around them, they heard scurrying in the trees and the brush. Insects were singing, chirping, and, as Gray had referred to it, barking.

"That long burping sound is a tokay gecko. They can easily grow to double the size of your hand."

"Are there elephants in the area?"

"Yes, but they're usually farther in. Thailand's largest national park is Khao Yai, and it's not far from here. If you drive through the park, you usually see the elephants. You'll have to come back for a real holiday."

"Will I be allowed back in?"

"Maybe, maybe not."

After thirty minutes, Gray and Chet spotted the perimeter wall.

"Looks like we found his home," Gray said. "It's secured, but I'm guessing whoever gunned down the men back here did the same here." Gray pointed to a dead man draped over the top of the wall. As they moved in closer, they found more dead men. The entrance gate was open, and they proceeded inside cautiously.

The lights inside the two-story mansion were on, and most of the windows on the French doors were shot out.

"Someone with serious firepower hit the place," Gray said. "Some of those doors are barely hanging on."

They moved up closer and took cover behind a couple of large potted plants. From there, they could easily see more dead men inside on the floor and the stairwell. Chet suggested they move around to the left and see if they could look through the windows rather than enter the house just yet.

They heard voices as they made their way forward. It had sounded like a man crying or whining. Take a pick. When they reached the windows, they saw five men on their knees. Standing behind them were five women in tactical outfits and body armor. Each one had the barrel of an assault rifle pointed at the back of a kneeling man's head. Standing off to the side was another woman, dressed similarly. She was talking to someone Gray recognized immediately.

"Ritthirong," Gray said. "It's surreal to see him standing there like a free man. Do you know who the woman is?"

"I recognize her. She's a drug dealer—the Yaba Queen of South Thailand. Her name is Cake."

"I guess we know who killed Ritthirong's men. She must have had a big beef with Ritthirong, maybe an old score to be settled now that he's back. Strangely, she's holding his men hostage but not him."

"And there are other armed men who aren't being held hostage," Chet said. "This makes no sense at all."

"I wonder how she discovered the Ritthirong in jail was an imposter."

"She might have had a connection in the jail."

"If they were speaking just a little bit louder, we'd probably be able to make out what they're saying."

Just then, Cake gave a signal to her women, and they fired their rifles, blowing holes in the backs of the kneeling men's heads.

"Looks like they've come to an agreement and settled their differences," Chet said.

"I don't see Lillie anywhere in the room," Gray said. "He might be holding her in a bedroom, possibly on the second floor."

"The place is big; a lot of spots to lock up a woman."

"We may be outgunned and outnumbered, but they aren't expecting us. We have the advantage."

"The women with Cake look trained. If we target them first, we might have a shot. Maybe Ritthirong's men will give up and run. They just watched five men get executed."

"Yeah, that's Ritthirong. People mean nothing to him."

Chet held up his rifle. "Are we doing this?"

"I think so. Count of three?"

Chet nodded.

Gray began the count. "One. Two..."

"Don't move," a voice behind them said.

45

Four black SUVs were parked on the side of the highway in Saraburi, not far from the access road that leads into the jungle and Ritthirong's home. Gun and Ped sat quietly in the first vehicle with a few men in the back seats. The remaining SUVs were filled with other members of the team, twenty in total.

"There he is," Ped said.

The man climbed into the back seat with the other men. Ped shifted around so he could look at him. "What did you find out?"

"There's a guard station farther down the road. They've all been shot. Also, I found a motorcycle hidden in the brush at the entrance to the road. It looks like the Detective Inspector's motorcycle."

"And his home?"

"More dead men around the perimeter wall. The gate is unsecured, and the lights are on inside the home."

"Did you see anyone?"

"Not from my position."

Ped looked over at Gun, who was sitting in the front

passenger seat. "That Rover we passed is Cake's. She and her girls are here."

"Excellent," Gun said.

Ped radioed for the rest of the team to meet them at their SUV. Once gathered, Gun addressed his men.

"We have a critical mission tonight. Inside there"—he pointed to the jungle—"are our enemies. We must silence them all. Leave no man standing and no man breathing. Do you understand?"

The men answered yes in unison.

"What about Ritthirong?" Ped asked.

"Kill him. I never liked that guy."

"You have your orders," Ped said to the men. "Check your weapons, check your ammo, and prepare yourselves."

Ped turned back to his boss. "This is it, the final push to tie up any loose ends that can connect us." He gave Gun a hearty slap on the back. "We'll breathe easier tomorrow."

Ritthirong stared at Bunsong, who was lying at his feet. The blood that had pooled around his head popped against the white marble floors.

"He was your second-in-command," Cake said.

Ritthirong shrugged. "Was." He looked up at Cake. "You happy? Are we all squared away?"

"We are."

"Good, because I have a lot of work to do. Bunsong failed to grow my business as much as I had expected. As Napoleon once said, 'If you want something done, do it yourself.'"

"Boss!" one of the men shouted, and pointed at the doorway to the entertainment room.

Standing with their hands above their heads were Gray and Chet.

"Agent Gray!" Ritthirong called with surprise. "I can't believe it. You made it. Welcome to my home." Ritthirong turned to one of his men. "Don't just stand there. We have important guests. Pour them a glass of champagne."

Ritthirong walked over to Gray.

"I honestly did not think you'd ever come. I was feeling a little hurt."

"Where's Lillie? Where is she?"

"Your girlfriend? I think you might have arrived a tad bit too late."

"You bastard!" Gray shouted.

The man standing behind him struck him in the back of his head with the butt of his rifle. Gray fell to the ground, dazed.

"Bastard? You of all people should know I'm not a bastard. My mother was married when she had me. Speaking of family, I saw the photo of you and Ploy. You look cute together. Is there something brewing between you too? I don't blame you. She was always the pretty one, even when we were kids. Did you know Khun Arun, the fearless leader of our clan, raped her repeatedly when we were young? Did she mention that to you? Probably not. I think she was only ten when he started—at least, that's when he began having intercourse with her. Who knows what those lovebirds did beforehand."

Ritthirong's man approached with two flutes filled with champagne. He handed one to Chet and placed the other on the floor next to Gray.

"Come on, Agent Gray...to your feet. I have other guests, if you aren't aware." Ritthirong looked back at Cake and smiled.

"Is he really an FBI agent?" Mint whispered to Cake.

"I have no idea."

"Hold on." Mint pulled out her phone navigated to Ploy's Instagram account. She showed Cake the photo. "The caption says 'Helping the FBI catch a bad guy.'"

"Why is the FBI here? And why does it look like they already know each other? Who's the other man with him?"

"I'm not sure."

"Chompoo, do you know that other man?"

"I don't. Maybe he's with the FBI too."

"Cake, I don't like what's happening," Mint said.

"I agree," Chompoo said. "Whatever is going on with Ritthirong and the FBI, that's one thing you don't want any part of."

"We got what we came here for," Mint said. "It's time we leave."

"What could Ritthirong and the agent have in common," Cake mused. "It's bizarre. I wonder if he was involved with the extradition?"

"It makes sense," Chompoo said. "If that's true, then he came here to catch Ritthirong, but showing up with one other person doesn't make sense either. I don't like this one bit. Cake, we need to get out of here."

Ritthirong waved at Cake, grabbing her attention. "Come over here. I want to introduce you to someone. Don't be shy."

Cake joined the group of men.

"Special Agent Sterling Gray, please meet my dear friend Cake."

Gray got to his feet and brushed off his hands on his pants.

Cake smiled. "It's nice to meet you, Agent Gray."

"Agent Gray works in the FBI's prestigious Behavioral Analysis Unit. He's a profiler. It's his job to catch people, well, like me." Ritthirong laughed.

"So was Agent Gray the one who caught you in the UK?"

"No, it was those pesky, oh, what's the nickname for them... Bobbies! That's it. On the other hand, I got to know Agent Gray while I was being held in prison. We met once a week for two months, isn't that right, Agent Gray? We learned an awful lot about each other, but I suspect he didn't realize I'd use what I learned against him."

Ritthirong picked the flute up off the floor and handed it to Gray. "I would like to propose a toast." Ritthirong raised his glass; so did Cake. "Come on, you two, don't be party poopers."

Chet and Gray relented and raised their glasses.

"I want to thank everyone for coming to my home for my welcome-back party. I am deeply grateful for it. I also would like to thank Agent Gray and his friend, whose name I don't know and don't care to, for finding my home. That's some excellent detective work. Would you mind telling me how you managed to put two and two together?" Ritthirong smiled.

"Where's Lillie?"

"Must we discuss that? It's so boring. Tell me, how did you find my home? It's in the middle of the jungle."

"Answer the question," the man behind Gray said just before a bullet tore through his head.

46

The windows along the side of the room exploded as a hail of bullets flew through. Gray and Chet dove to the ground and scurried behind the bar for cover. One of Ritthirong's men was also behind the bar. Chet grabbed the rifle from the dead man who had been standing behind them. He then shot Ritthirong's man.

"Gray, take his rifle," he said.

"Who's firing on us? More enemies of Ritthirong?" Gray asked.

"I have no idea, but shoot anyone who comes to us."

Chet peeked around the side of the bar and returned fire. Gray did the same from the other side.

Cake also dove to the ground. She fired at the windows as she slithered across the floor back to where her girls were. Mint had ducked behind a sofa.

"Cake, over here," she said. "Who is shooting?" she asked as Cake joined her behind the sofa.

"I have no idea, but they're shooting at everyone, not just us." She motioned to Ritthirong and his men. They were crouched behind a large marble table they had pushed over for cover and were firing back. "Where are Chompoo and the others?"

"I saw Chompoo and Nok take cover over there, behind the pool table. I don't know where Joke and Tukta are."

Cake and Mint fired back at the windows.

"Whoever it is, they came prepared," Mint said.

"This sofa won't protect us much longer." Behind them was a short hallway. "Come on. Follow me."

Cake and Mint scooted back into the hallway toward a closed door. Cake reached up to the doorknob. It was locked. She fired at the knob, destroying it. She and Mint then slammed their shoulders into the door at the same time, forcing it open. Inside the room, they spotted a woman peeking at them from behind a bed.

"Who are you?" Mint shouted while pointing her rifle at the woman.

The woman didn't answer, and Mint walked over to her and aimed the rifle right at her head. "Answer my question."

The woman shielded her face with her arms as she shouted. "My name is Lillie Pratt. I work for Interpol. Please don't shoot me."

Mint looked back at Cake. "This is getting even weirder."

Cake approached the woman. "Why are you here?"

"I was kidnapped by Somsak Ritthirong while handing him over to Thai authorities at the airport. Please, it's the honest truth."

It all immediately made sense to both Cake and Mint. Agent Gray wasn't there to arrest Ritthirong. He was there to rescue Pratt.

"Does the name Sterling Gray mean anything to you?" she asked

"Yes! Yes! He's the FBI agent that accompanied me. Do you know him?"

"I don't, but he's outside in the middle of that firefight."

"What is happening?"

"We're not sure."

"Cake, this is out of our control. We need to get out of here." Mint pointed at the window.

"You're right. Stay here with her. I'll get the others and return."

Cake left. Mint and Pratt were alone.

"Your friend Agent Gray came here to rescue you," Mint said.

Relief appeared on Pratt's face.

"But don't get comfortable. He only brought one other person with him, that's it."

"May I?" Pratt gestured to the bed.

Mint nodded, and Pratt took a seat on the edge. "Where is all the shooting coming from?"

"From outside. We were having a conversation with Agent Gray and Ritthirong when we were all attacked."

Pratt gave Mint a full once-over. "Do you work for Ritthirong?"

Mint shook her head. "I work for the woman who was here with me earlier. We're not associated with Ritthirong. We were here to clear up some business."

"I see. You...uh, I couldn't help but notice... You're transgender."

"Yeah, and what's it to you? You have something against the LGBTQ community?"

A small smile appeared on Pratt's face. "If I did, it would be awkward, because I'm gay."

"It's the damn Black Tigers," Chet said as he pulled his head back around behind the bar. "Son of a bitch. I should have known it. They set us up. They set everyone up."

"Eliminate Ritthirong and us at the same time. It ties up loose ends. No one will be able to tie them to Ritthirong's escape."

"That's right. The imposter in jail will be convicted and killed by the government. No one left to say a single word."

"Those corrupt bastards," Gray said. "You think that Cake woman had anything to do with it?"

"I don't think so. They were shooting at her, too."

Just then, Cake came sliding behind the bar right into Gray. They both pointed their rifles at each other.

"Don't shoot," she said. "I'm a neutral party here." Cake lowered her gun and then pushed Gray's rifle out of her face. "I found your friend Lillie Pratt."

"Where is she? Is she okay?"

"She's fine."

"Why are you helping us?" Chet asked. "Why should we believe you're not a part of all of this?"

"I had nothing to do with his escape. I'm here because his men stole money from me to pay off the Black Tigers, who I'm guessing are the people shooting at us."

"Did the Black Tigers tell you to come here tonight?" Gray asked.

"Yes, that's how I found out Ritthirong's men stole from me. They said they weren't sure how long he would be here and I should hurry. They told you to come here too?"

Gray nodded. "We already knew the real Ritthirong wasn't in jail, but I had no idea where Lillie was. Gun surprised me in my hotel room and told me to come here tonight."

"They want to kill us all to cover their asses," Chet said.

"That won't happen. Not if I can help it," Cake said. "Agent Gray, your friend is in a bedroom down that hallway over there. I already told her you were here for her. One of my girls is watching her. My advice to you is to go get her and get out of here. There's a window in the bedroom you can use to slip out of unnoticed."

"What are you going to do?"

"I'm grabbing the rest of my girls, and we're doing the same thing. This is Ritthirong's fight, not ours."

Gray and Chet looked at each other and nodded.

"Good luck," Gray said to Cake before heading to the hallway.

He and Chet crawled across the floor and into the hallway. "There," Gray pointed at the door with the doorknob blown off. Into the room they went, but it was empty.

"Wait," Gray said.

He quickly stuck his head out the door and looked into the hallway.

"This is the only door. It has to be the room Cake talked about."

Gray began searching the room, looking for anything that could identify Pratt or signal that she'd been in the room, but there was nothing.

"Gray," Chet pulled the drapes back from an open window.

"Why would she leave?" Gray asked as he walked over to the window. "She knew I was here. And where's the person Cake said was with Lillie?"

"I don't know, but they left, so I think we should do the same."

"What about Ritthirong?"

"What about him? Let Gun and his men deal with him.

There will be no justice with Ritthirong or the Black Tigers. Our goal is to get Lillie. This was always a search and rescue mission."

"You're right. But it burns me up that they're getting away with it."

Just then, a large explosion went off and shook the home.

"They haven't gotten away with it yet. But if we don't move, neither will we."

47

From the hallway, Cake took a moment to observe the situation. It was out of control. Complete chaos. The damage to Ritthirong's home was immense. There must have been over a thousand rounds fired so far. The windows and French doors along the wall were utterly destroyed, and the Black Tigers were making their way inside the house. Ritthirong had no shortage of men putting up a good fight, but the Black Tigers were relentless in their advance. Both groups appeared to be fighting to the death. That was something Cake wanted no part of.

While the Fierce Five were highly trained and Cake had complete confidence that they could handle themselves, she had put them in the middle of Ritthirong's battle, and that wasn't the plan. Cake sent a text message to her girls, instructing them to pull back and meet at the Rover right away.

Behind the sofa she had taken cover from before, she spotted Tukta, the youngest of the Fierce Five. Cake made her way over to her.

"Are you okay?" Cake asked.

"I'm fine, but you've been shot." Tukta pointed to Cake's shoulder. A bullet had grazed her and she hadn't even noticed.

"I'll be fine."

"It's the Black Tigers. They're attacking us."

"I know. We need to get out of here. Where are the rest?" Cake asked.

"I was with Joke, but she moved away to flank the Tigers. I don't know where Chompoo and Nok are."

"I want you to go to that hallway over there. There's a bedroom in there. Stay there until I come. I'm going to find the others."

Tukta nodded and left Cake.

Cake crawled over to the pool table. There she found Chompoo and Nok lying in a pool of blood. Cake checked for a pulse, but both women were dead. A sinking feeling overcame her, and she felt like she'd just been slugged in the gut with a bat.

Surely they were killed by gunfire from the Black Tigers, but she blamed Ritthirong. It was his man Bunsong that got her involved in this mess. She never would have come to Ritthirong's place if it weren't for him. And even though she was able to give Bunsong the punishment he deserved, it wasn't worth losing Chompoo and Nok.

Cake could feel the boil in her bubble intensify as she clamped her jaw tighter. She made her way back to the sofa. From there, she could see Ritthirong behind the table. His men were not with him. Cake headed straight toward him and knelt down beside him.

"Cake," Ritthirong said. "Glad to see you're still here. We have uninvited guests. I wish you had waited to kill Bunsong and the others. We could have used them right now. Where are your Fierce Five? Are they enjoying the fight?"

Cake may have held her tongue, but her eyes burned a hole right through Ritthirong.

"This is like old times, isn't it, Cake? You and I, partners to the end, right?"

"Right," Cake said.

She grabbed the handle of her machete and pulled it from its sheath. In one sweeping movement she swung the blade and took Ritthirong's head clean off his shoulders. His body stood kneeling for a moment before collapsing.

"The end came," she said.

Cake scooted back across the floor and into the hallway. She made her way into the bedroom, where Tukta was waiting for her.

"Where are the others? Mint, the FBI agent, the woman with Interpol, they should have been in here."

Tukta shrugged. "There was no one here. The room was empty."

"They must have left already."

"Where are Chompoo, Nok, and Joke?"

"Chompoo and Nok... They didn't make it. I didn't see Joke. I hope she got my message. Out the window, let's go."

"I don't think we should have left," Pratt said to Mint as they made their way through the dark jungle.

"We're safer on the move. And anyway, my boss sent out a message for everyone to meet back at the vehicle."

"But what about Agent Gray? He came all this way to rescue me. I can't leave him back there."

Mint stopped walking and turned around to face Pratt. "I know he's your friend, but if we stayed, there would be a chance we'd die. If he doesn't make it out, then he's already dead."

"But you don't know that?"

"We were outnumbered and outgunned by the Black Tigers. They are the RTPs special operations team—highly effective at eliminating their targets. What will you do? Show them your Interpol badge and tell them to stop?" Mint laughed. "They are there to kill everyone, including you."

"Why me? I don't understand."

"The Black Tigers were behind Ritthirong's escape."

"That much I know."

"They're getting rid of anyone they see as a threat, anyone who could expose what they've done. That includes Ritthirong and his men, Agent Gray, and you."

"But were you also involved in Ritthirong's escape?"

"Not exactly."

Mint explained how Bunsong stole from Cake to pay the Black Tiger's fee. After hearing that, Pratt understood the reason why they were there.

"But what happens now? I mean with us here," Pratt asked.

"I don't know. Cake will decide that, but we should keep moving."

A branch cracked nearby. Mint put her finger to her lips and pulled Pratt down.

"Someone's coming," she said as she aimed her rifle in the direction of the noise.

Footsteps could clearly be heard.

Then voices...speaking English.

"Sterling?" Pratt whisper-shouted. "Is that you?"

"Lillie?"

A beat later, Gray emerged from behind a tree.

Pratt shot to her feet. "I'm here. Don't shoot."

"Lillie, my God, it's you." Gray picked Pratt up in a bear hug. "I can't believe I finally found you."

"That makes two of us."

Gray lowered Pratt. "Are you hurt?" He gently patted her down.

"I'm fine. A little hungry and a little thirsty, but other than that, I'm fine. Where's Ritthirong?"

"Back at the house. We came looking for you. This is Inspector Detective Chaemchamrat."

"Call me Chet. I've heard so much about you, Ms. Lillie Pratt. I'm happy to see you're okay."

"Please, Lillie is fine."

"Yes." Chet smiled.

"This fierce woman is Mint," Pratt said as she patted Mint on her back. "She helped me escape."

"Thank you for getting Lillie out of the house," Gray said.

Mint nodded. "Where is Cake?"

"She told us to get out," Gray said. "Then she went to get the rest of your team."

Just then, an explosion went off in the distance.

"That's the second one," Gray said. "They must be using grenades."

"We need transport," Chet said. "How big is your vehicle?"

"It's a Land Rover, but Cake must make that decision."

"It's fine. Where is it?"

"It's off the highway just before the road heading into the jungle."

"Can you get there from here?" Chet asked.

"I think we need to go that way." Mint pointed.

"We have to get away from here," Gray said. "We can work out the details later."

Just then, bullets ripped through the trees, forcing them to the ground. In the distance, they heard men shouting.

"It's the Black Tigers," Mint said. "We need to move quickly."

Mint and the others moved while crouching. More bullets ripped through the trees around them. One struck Mint in the leg, causing her to drop to the ground in pain. Chet and Gray opened fire.

"Where were you hit?" Pratt looked Mint over.

"My leg."

"Can you walk?"

"Barely."

Pratt grabbed Mint's arm and slung it around her neck. "I'll help you. Come on, get to your feet."

Mint tried to stand, but the pain was unbearable.

"I can't. You guys go."

"I'm not leaving you," Pratt said. "You're coming with us."

"I'll slow you down."

"The jungle's dark. We can lose them," Pratt argued.

More bullets hit their location.

"They're getting closer," Chet said.

"You need to go. I'll be able to hold them off. Don't worry about me. Cake will be here soon."

"But..." Pratt pleaded.

"Go!" Mint shouted.

Chet grabbed Pratt by the arm. "We have to leave."

Pratt stood up and backed away from Mint as Gray and Chet continued to fire at the Black Tigers until they spent the last of their bullets.

Mint smiled at Pratt. "I'll be fine. I'm fierce, remember?"

"Yes, you are."

48

Gray, Pratt, and Chet moved as fast as they could in the jungle, which wasn't very fast at all. Chet led the way, thinking he had an eye on where Mint had pointed. Moments later, a barrage of gunfire erupted behind them, followed but a few single shots, and then quiet. They all knew what had happened and what it meant. Gray gave Pratt's hand a squeeze as they moved in step with each other.

Eventually, the jungle opened up, and more of the moon-light above made its way through the canopy. That gave them hope that they might pop out of the jungle at any second and see the highway in the distance. But as the minutes wore on and the jungle moved back and forth between dense and open coverage, their hopes for a quick getaway diminished.

Chet stopped and leaned over, resting his hands on his knees as he drew deep breaths. Gray and Pratt followed suit.

"I think we're lost," Pratt said, through quick breaths.

"Sorry, guys. I thought I knew exactly where Mint pointed at." Chet straightened up so that his chest could open.

"There's good news," Gray said as he looked around. "I don't think we're being chased anymore."

As the trio continued, Gray and Pratt took the opportunity to catch each other up.

"One minute I was on the phone on hold, the next thing I know, there's gunfire," Pratt said. "A few seconds later, Gun came up to me and told me there was an attack and that he needed to get me out of there. He moved me quickly to the van with tinted windows. The side door opened, and I was guided right in. There were other members of the Black Tiger inside, so I didn't think to question it. I expected to see you there, or that you would be right behind me," Pratt said.

"At what point did you realize that wasn't the deal?" Gray asked.

"When the door slammed shut, and the van took off, I hollered at the driver to stop, that you weren't with us. He kept driving, and right about then, I heard someone laughing behind me. I turned around and saw Ritthirong sitting in the last row. A second later, I had guns pointed at me."

"It was that easy and quick," Gray said. "It's no wonder I couldn't find you. As soon as the gunfire died down, I searched, but you were already gone."

Gray walked Pratt through everything he'd gone through in the beginning to try to get people to believe him.

"Everyone had seen the news footage. I looked like a mad man. Thankfully, Agent Nickle believed me, sort of. He gave me the benefit of the doubt and put me in touch with Chet. If not for Chet, I wouldn't be here right now."

"Like I said earlier, don't thank me yet," Chet said. "We're lost in a jungle."

Gray told Pratt about his encounter with Ritthirong's influencer cousin, as well as their run-in with the arms dealer in the Khlong Toei slums, but left out that Chet shot Hia.

"Did you have to use the gun?" Pratt asked.

"I didn't. Not until we were in Ritthirong's home did I

discharge a firearm. I know what you're thinking, Lillie. I broke more laws during the past few days than I care to count. But I saw no way around it."

Pratt put her hand up to stop Gray. "I would have done the same. How did you finally get confirmation that the person arrested wasn't Ritthirong?"

Gray smiled. "Our friend here arrested me and threw me in jail."

Gray told Pratt how he pretended to be a pedophile on the run named Jerry Fletcher and that Chet and Agent Nickle captured him.

"What was it like in Bang Kwang?"

"Most of the prison isn't like what you'd expect. It was fairly clean and sterile. I couldn't say the same for the area where gen pop is housed."

"Were you careful about not dropping the soap," Pratt said, which caused Chet to laugh out loud. "Seriously though, I can't believe you two did all of that just for me. I can't even begin to express my gratitude."

"If we gave up, you would have disappeared for good," Gray said. "I couldn't let that happen. Did Ritthirong bring you back to his place right away?"

"Yes. Shortly after that brief call after I was taken, I had a black bag placed over my head. I had no idea where we were heading until it was removed, and I was standing outside his place. He kept me in the bedroom from that moment on. For the longest time, he didn't check on me or even try to speak to me. The only contact I had was with his other men. They'd brought me something to eat and drink."

"Oh my God!" Pratt slapped a hand against her forehead.

"What?"

"Evie! Does she know? She must be worried sick from not

hearing from me. I'd sent her a brief text message right when we landed and that was it."

"Who's Evie?" Chet asked.

"My wife."

"Lillie, I held off on telling her right away as I wanted more information. There would be a ton of questions, and I wanted to at least have some information. But things moved so fast and never let up, and now we're standing here."

"I understand. Ritthirong took my phone. Do either of you have one? I want to send a quick text to Evie just to let her know I'm okay."

Gray and Chet checked their phones. Both devices were dead.

"Evie will have to wait a little longer," Gray said. "As soon as we're able to, we'll find a phone so you can contact her."

"The most important thing is for you two to get to the embassy," Chet said. "It doesn't matter if it's US or UK. It's the only place I think you'll be safe. The Black Tigers are very well connected, but they don't have influence there."

"What about my contact at Interpol, Khemkhaeng Suthisak? He might be able to help."

"The embassy is the only place. Interpol can't keep you safe."

"I had a conversation with Suthisak," Gray said. "As far as he's concerned, Ritthirong is in jail—end of the story. I don't think he cared one way or another about my claims that you were abducted. I hate to say that, but that's the reaction I got from him."

"I've had a couple video calls with him," Pratt said. "He always seemed pleasant, but you never really know a person, do you?"

"He answers to people more important," Chet said. "It's as

simple as that. If he is told to move on, he'll do that. End of story."

"But, Chet, what about you? The Black Tigers had you in their sights back there," Pratt said. "You're also not safe."

"Don't worry about me. I'm Thai. I know how things work, and I know my country. I'll be able to keep myself safe."

"But for how long?" Gray asked. "So long as the Black Tigers feel there are people who can expose them, I don't think they'll stop."

"I might have to convince them my memory is terrible." Chet smiled.

"I'm serious, Chet."

"I know, my friend. But like I said. This is my country, and I know how things work."

As they continued to talk and walk alongside invisible critters scurrying in the dark, they heard an elephant trumpet in the distance. Chet assured them they were in no danger of an apex predator. The biggest threats were the elephants, but they were usually sleeping at night.

"Any large snakes in the area, like pythons?" Pratt asked.

"There are pythons, but short of stepping on one, rarely do they attack humans, unless they're big. Then..."

"Define 'big,'" Pratt said.

"Big would be six meters or more."

"That's like twenty feet," Gray said. "Do they really get that big?"

"Sure. At that size, they hang from trees and prey on animals passing under them. Gray, not to alarm you, but don't move."

"Hilarious, Chet."

"I'm serious. Don't move. Because I almost forgot that they hang from tree limbs until I spotted the one above you."

Gray looked up and jumped back immediately as a python lashed out at him like a spear. Its mouth clamped down on Gray's forearm, and its body followed, coiling itself around Gray.

Chet leaped into action, grabbing hold of the python right below the neck. Gray struggled to try to unwrap the snake's thick body, but it continued to tighten its grip.

"We can't let it get itself fully wrapped around you. Keep fighting it until it tires."

"What should I do?" Pratt shouted.

"Find a rock or something and slam it into its head. Gauge its eyes. Anything to cause pain so that it releases its grip."

The weight of the python caused Gray to drop to his knees. Chet continued squeezing the snake's neck with all his might until it unlatched from Gray's forearm. Chet fell back and began to pull the python away, slowly unwrapping it.

Pratt returned with a hand-size rock. Chet pinned the python's head against the jungle floor, and Pratt laid into it with the stone, striking it over and over again. The snake uncoiled from Gray in seconds, but it began to secure itself around Pratt's legs just as quickly.

Gray grabbed the rock from Pratt and started slamming it into the python's skull with deadly accuracy. After the third strike, the snake's body relaxed its grip around Pratt, and she was able to move away. Gray, however, didn't stop his attack until he had crushed the snake's head, killing it.

"It's done. Stop," Chet said while breathing hard.

Gray tossed the rock and fell back on his hands, his chest heaving up and down.

"Damn, Chet. I really thought you were bullshitting me in the beginning," Gray said in between breaths.

Gray crawled over to the python. "This thing must be close to twenty-five feet." He moved the body. "And it feels like it weighs a ton."

"How's your arm?" Chet asked.

Gray checked. "The teeth punctured my skin. Other than a stinging pain, I think I'm okay."

The three took a moment to stretch the snake out fully and lift it up.

"This thing is heavy," Pratt said. "I wish we had a phone to take a picture. Evie will never believe I almost got eaten by a snake in the jungle."

"Better than a souvenir," Chet said.

"No doubt about that. Gray and I have a story we can tell at every dinner party we attend from now on."

With the snake ordeal behind them, they continued, this time keeping watch for any moving vines hanging from a tree. It wasn't until the sun had started to rise that Chet could navigate the jungle more accurately. An hour after sunrise, they broke out of the jungle and saw a highway in the distance.

"Is that the highway we drove on to get to Ritthirong's place?" Gray asked.

Chet looked around to try and get his bearings. "It looks like it, but I don't think we're near where I left my bike. We'll have to hitch a ride."

Gray and Pratt remained crouched in the brush while Chet flagged down a passing vehicle. He managed to get a truck hauling sugar cane to stop. After a brief conversation, he called Gray and Pratt over.

"He's willing to take us to the next town. Climb up. We're riding in the back."

49

Gray, Pratt, and Chet tucked themselves down into the cane stalk so that they were out of view of passing vehicles.

"How far is the next town?" Gray asked. "Is it on the way to Bangkok?"

Chet nodded. "It's more like a rest stop outside of a village. There will be a couple of restaurants and cafés, maybe a convenience shop and a place to buy gasoline. We'll have to try and hitch another ride from there. We're about two hours from the city limits of Bangkok."

"Do either of you have any cash on hand?" Pratt asked. "I'm starved."

"I have a little money," Gray said.

"There will be some food stalls there. It won't cost much to get something to eat."

"You think the guy driving the truck will let us use his phone?" Gray asked. "I want to give Nickle a heads-up and see if he can lend any support. We still have a long way to go without a sure way of crossing that distance. I wouldn't discount that the Black Tigers are still in the vicinity."

"If they found my bike, they'll know we have no transport," Chet said.

"They might think we're lost in the jungle," Pratt said.

"That would be the best-case scenario," Gray said. "It'll either keep them occupied back at Ritthirong's place, or they've already given up and have headed back to Bangkok. If they're smart, which I think Gun and Ped are, they'll assume our destination is one of the embassies. They'll have men stationed nearby to intercept us."

No sooner did those words come out of Gray's mouth than Chet motioned for them all to duck. He pointed behind them. In the distance, identical black SUVs were approaching the truck.

"Is that them?" Pratt asked.

"They drive around in black SUVs," Chet said

The SUVs came upon the truck fast, but they pulled into the oncoming lane to pass instead of coasting behind. Gray could clearly see the driver and the front passenger inside the first SUV as they drove by. It was Gun and Ped.

The four SUVs passed. No one inside the vehicles paid any attention to the truck or its cargo.

"That was close," Gray said.

"They were probably searching for us all night," Pratt said. "I wonder what happened to Ritthirong and his men."

"I don't think the Black Tigers would have left with them still alive," Chet said. "From the number of men in those SUVs, they won."

"What about Cake and her team?" Gray asked.

"Hard to tell if they survived."

"It may be wishful thinking, but I do hope they got out safely," Pratt said. "Especially Mint."

The rest of the ride was relatively quiet as they all kept to their own thoughts on what had taken place in the recent twelve hours. But with no cover above them, even the morning sun had the intensity usually associated with the afternoon. If it weren't for the wind blowing on them, they might have crisped up like bacon.

Chet glanced at his watch. "We'll be at the rest stop soon. It's up ahead."

"Great. I need a toilet," Pratt said.

The truck began a series of downshifts to reduce speed. It then turned off the highway into a lively rest stop filled with multiple restaurants and cafés occupying a U-shaped building. The gas pumps were out front, near the highway. The driver stopped near the right side of the building, and they climbed out.

Chet went to have a conversation with the driver before meeting up with Gray, who had gone inside a nearby bakery.

"I thought I'd pick up some snacks for us," Gray said as he held up a bag. "Any luck with the phone?"

"He was low on his minutes."

"Lillie's in the restroom. When she comes out, we should hit up one of these restaurants," Gray said as he walked toward the exit of the bakery.

A second later, Chet grabbed Gray's arm and pulled away from the door.

"What?" Gray asked.

"Over there," Chet pointed. "The black SUVs."

"Damn. Talk about rotten luck. They stopped at the same place we did."

"They're probably eating."

Pratt walked in front of the bakery, looking around, and Gray popped his head out the door.

"Lillie, in here."

"Are we buying pastries?" she asked.

"The Black Tigers." Gray pointed.

"Are you sure it's them?"

"Black SUVs. Probably a good guess. Maybe we should move closer for a better look."

They left the bakery and followed the walkway out front before moving in between two cars and crouching. Straight ahead, they had a clear view of the SUVs.

"Those are definitely the SUVs that passed us earlier," Gray said as he chomped on a curry puff.

Pratt kept quiet as she worked on a banana muffin.

"They must be eating in that Thai restaurant over there." Chet bit into a curry puff. "I have an idea, but you won't like it."

"I'm used to your ideas, so try me," Gray said.

"I think we should steal an SUV."

50

"Are you nuts?" Gray whispered-shouted at Chet.

"Hey, we need transport. Those guys are busy stuffing their faces. They won't even see us pull out of here."

"I suppose next you'll tell me you can hot-wire a car."

"Of course."

"Those look like newer models. Is it even possible?" Gray asked as he popped the last bite of his curry puff into his mouth. "Besides that, how do we get in? Break the window?"

"That's not a bad idea."

"I dunno. I know we need wheels, but what you're suggesting seems problematic. I say we wait here and let them finish their meals. When they're done, they'll climb back into their cars and drive off. After, we'll have time to sort out transport and have one less thing to worry about on our way back to Bangkok."

"Sorry, Chet. I'm with Sterling on this one," Pratt said. "We just need to be patient and wait it out for a bit."

"All right. We'll wait."

Just as they were making their way out from between the cars, behind them, a Black Tiger exited a coffee shop carrying a cup of coffee. He stopped directly in front of them.

It was like time had frozen. The Black Tiger and the trio locked eyes. Neither said anything, but Gray could see it on the man's face. He recognized them but couldn't quite place how yet. A beat later, realization exploded across his face, and Gray jumped up at him, leading with a solid right hook that slammed into the side of his face. His knees buckled instantly, and he was out before he hit the ground. Gray quickly pulled the man in between the cars.

"What are we going to do now?" Pratt asked as she stared at the man.

Chet patted the guy down. He stuck his hand into the man's front pocket and removed a set of car keys.

"Guys..." He dangled the keys.

Gray couldn't believe it. Not only was an idea to steal an SUV from the Black Tigers back on the table, but it was also the only option. He had just knocked out a Black Tiger. It was only a matter of time before the rest of his team realized he was missing, especially since he was one of the drivers.

"Any second, this guy will wake up," Chet said. "Are you going to keep punching him every time he does that?"

"Sterling, I don't think we have a choice this time around," Pratt said. "We need to move now. Those men will be finishing up soon."

"You're right. What about him?" Gray said, looking down at the unconscious man.

"Forget about him," Chet said. "Let's go."

"Wait," Gray said.

He took the man's phone and used his finger to unlock it, and then navigated to the phone's settings and dismantled the security function. "Now we have a phone."

The three stood up and walked as quickly as they could

toward the SUVs without drawing attention. As they reached them, Chet pressed the unlock button on the key fob. The lights of the SUV closest to them blinked twice, and they heard the doors unlock.

"Hurry, get inside," Chet said as he climbed into the driver's seat.

Gray and Pratt climbed into the back seat and kept watch on the restaurant where they thought the Black Tigers were eating while Chet started the engine. He gave the engine a quick rev and released the parking brake.

"Go! Go! Go!" Gray said.

Chet stepped on the gas and drove the SUV straight to the rear of the rest stop.

"You see anyone?" he asked as he waited for a break in traffic so he could pull onto the highway.

"So far, so good," Gray said. "Drive along the shoulder if you have to. Don't just sit here."

Chet drove along the shoulder and merged into traffic. A few seconds and they were speeding on the highway toward Bangkok.

"Holy crap. I can't believe we just pulled that off," Gray said.

"My idea worked," Chet said proudly.

"I thought this one was crazier than throwing me in jail, but it worked."

"It sure did," Pratt added as she looked through the rear window. "It's still clear. The longer it stays that way, the better it is for us."

"How are we on gas?" Gray asked. "Enough to get us to Bangkok?"

"It's possible. Depends on how fast the car eats gas. We might need to ditch the car before we reach the city."

Pratt and Gray checked the rear seats for supplies. They

found rifles and ammo. Pratt climbed back to the storage area and found half a case of bottled water, a first aid kit, and a box of paperwork. She brought back the water and gave Gray and Chet each a bottle.

"Even warm, this is so refreshing," she said after a long gulp.

Gray finished his water in one long swig.

"The weapons will come in handy if we need them," Chet said.

"How much farther to Bangkok?" Gray asked.

"If we keep moving at this speed with no interference from the Black Tigers, about an hour and fifteen minutes. But we could run into traffic, and that's just as bad."

Gray grabbed another bottle of water and twisted the top off. Just as he was about to gulp, the phone he'd taken off the Black Tiger rang. Both Chet and Pratt shifted their eyes to Gray.

"Answer it," Chet said.

Gray answered and switched to speakerphone. No one said a single word as they stared at the phone.

"Agent Gray," a voice said. "I know you're there."

51

Everyone recognized Gun's voice. Pratt batted Gray's arm, urging him to say something. He cleared his throat.

"This is Agent Gray."

"It seems our relationship has taken a turn for the worse," Gun said. "I don't understand why you're running from me. I thought we were friends, colleagues at a minimum."

"You think we're colleagues? Sorry, pal. There is no relationship between us."

"You surprise me, Gray. I did you a favor. I told you where your friend Lillie was when no one else wanted to help you."

"Please, don't placate me. You didn't do that for her or for me. You did that to save your own skin."

"Do the exact reasons really matter?"

"They do to me. You're not getting away with this."

"You are aware that SUV you stole belongs to the Thai government, right? I can help with that problem, but you need to stop running. Let me help you, Gray."

Gray laughed. "Are you serious? That question was rhetorical, by the way. Since we're pointing out the obvious, I'll go next. You are aware that shooting at a federal agent with the intent to kill is not only considered first-degree murder but also a crime against the United States—terrorism, namely. Let's not forget you helped Ritthirong escape."

"Ritthirong?" Gun laughed. "Nobody cares about him. And he's dead. Anyone who can back up your story is dead. The truth is you have no jurisdiction in my country, Agent Gray. You can talk about the laws that I may or may not have broken, but there is nothing you can do about it."

"You see, that's where you're wrong. Not only did you commit crimes against my government and myself, but you also committed crimes against an Interpol investigator. At its worst, this can be considered a crime of war. You also committed crimes against one of your own, a detective inspector with the Royal Thai Police. That's bottom of the barrel... One who would turn on his own to pad his bank account. I would list the number of crimes committed by you and your men, but I don't think we have the time."

"Agent Gray, you forget one important detail. No one but you and I know any of this has happened. No one knows where you and your friends are. No one cares. This information is useless in your hands."

"You think you can stop us from exposing you for what you are? A corrupt, spineless official who hides behind a gun and a badge that he doesn't respect. You are the epitome of scum...a bottom feeder."

"Enough! Do you think you can speak to me that way? I am the chief commander of the Black Tiger Special Operations Unit. You have no idea the power I wield."

"You have no power. All you have is a following of men who are as spineless as you. I bet given a chance, they would turn on you in an instant, as it would be impossible to honestly and voluntarily respect a man of your character.

Don't fool yourself. You are no better than the man you escorted back from the UK."

"I promise you, Gray," Gun said in a low, gravelly voice. "You and Pratt and Chaemchamrat will all die slow, painful deaths. They can thank you and your big mouth for that."

"Can't wait," Chet shouted out mockingly. "Sounds like a great time."

"I agree," Pratt added. "Shall we bring a bottle of champagne?"

Gun exploded into a Thai tirade with English expletives occasionally mixed in.

"We're breaking up," Gray said as he replicated the sound of static. "Send us an email if you need to follow up." Gray hung up. "You think we got his attention?"

"I'm not sure who's more of a psycho, Gun or Ritthirong," Pratt said.

"Gun is a casebook psychopath," Gray said. "Morally depraved, radiates superficial charm, shows disregard for others, is manipulative, has a blurred division between what's right and wrong. Being in that power position only amplified those characteristics. He's just as dangerous and as evil as Ritthirong. But he's not stupid. We cannot underestimate him."

"It doesn't sound like Cake and Mint made it out," Pratt said.

"There were others, six total in her gang," Gray said. "They helped us when they didn't need to. Gun could have left Ritthirong's place a long time ago. Only one reason to stick around for so long."

"He made sure no one was left alive," Pratt said. "What do you think, Chet?"

He shrugged. "I'm not sure. We have more important things to worry about than a drug dealer. We're making good time. It won't be long before we reach Bangkok. It'll just be tricky getting to the embassy. Do you care which one we go to?"

"I'm thinking the US Embassy because of Nickle. I'll call him."

Gray dialed, keeping the phone on speaker, so everyone in the car was privy to the conversation.

"Come on, Nickle, pick up," Gray said quietly as the phone continued to ring.

"Nickle speaking."

"Nickle, it's Gray."

"Sheesh, Gray, where the hell have you been? I've been calling you all morning."

"We got Lillie."

"That's great. I thought for sure you and Chet were... Well, it doesn't matter at this point. Everything is fine. Where are you guys now? Where's Ritthirong?"

"We're driving back to Bangkok. We were in Saraburi at Ritthirong's place. We're pretty sure he's dead. Listen, Nickle. We're not out of the woods yet. Gun and his men are chasing us. They ambushed us at Ritthirong's. There was a huge fire-fight, but we managed to escape. We stole one of their SUVs."

"Let me guess, Chet's idea."

"Yes," Chet shouted out. "And it worked."

"I don't have time to get into the details right now. We're on our way to you. Is there anything you can do to help our situation? Maybe rally reinforcements from the RTP that can, at a minimum, run interference between the Black Tigers and us? Gun is out for blood. He won't stop unless we're dead."

"I'll be honest. I don't think involving the RTP would be helpful, even if I did have that sort of pull. I can try, but I want to manage expectations here. You can double-check with Chet on the likelihood that they will help."

"I think Nickle is right," Chet said. "I'm worried that Gun has too much power, and somehow the men sent to help us will be working for him. I wouldn't trust them."

"Any other ideas?" Gray asked.

"Besides hauling ass to the embassy?" Nickle asked. "No. That is your best plan right now. Gun's reach is long, but he can't touch you if you're at the embassy behind the gate. That goes for all three of you. You need to do your best to get here as quickly as possible. I'll make sure the men stationed at the front know you're coming, and they'll be ready."

"Good, because we'll be coming in hot."

52

Gun's eyes bulged, and spit hung from his pressed lips as he pounded his fist against the dashboard repeatedly. He was furious and in complete disbelief at how Gray had spoken to him. Being the unit commander, he wasn't used to insubordination. In fact, he wasn't used to anybody questioning anything he said or did, let alone blatantly insulting him.

"Drive faster!" he shouted at Ped.

The SUV moved in and out of traffic, using both the shoulder and the oncoming lane to pass slower moving vehicles.

"They can't be that far ahead of us."

"They only had a fifteen-minute head start," Ped said. "We'll catch up soon."

Ped's mobile phone rang, and he answered it.

"Where are you now? How many men did you bring?" Ped looked at Gun. "It's the men. They are on their way from Bangkok, ready to intercept Gray. They have two vehicles and ten men. How do you want to handle it?"

"I don't care about the others," Gun said. "Tell the men to do whatever is needed to capture Gray alive. I want to make him suffer. I want him to see that Americans are not above me. No one is."

Ped returned to the call and gave his men the orders.

"We still need to deal with Cake. She and a few of her girls got away," Ped said.

"I'm not worried about Cake," Gun said. "We can deal with her later. But Gray and Pratt, they can hurt us. We need to stop them from reaching the embassy."

"If they leave the country, we might not have a way out of this." Ped glanced at Gun.

"They won't. Not if I can help it. We should have never agreed to let Ritthirong take Pratt. That was our mistake. Even the extra money Ritthirong gave us isn't enough for the trouble it caused."

"You're right. We wouldn't be in this mess if he left Gray and Pratt alone."

"I wish it was me who took Ritthirong's head off." Gun stretched his legs out. "That guy should have been executed a long time ago by us."

"It's done. We need to focus on Gray and Pratt. You think they'll go to the Interpol office?" Ped asked.

"If they do, it'll be easier for us to get to them with our connections there. We need to have men stationed at all three locations. But we'll go to the US Embassy. I believe Gray will want to go there. That's where he'll feel safe."

"Hey, look!" One of the men in the back seat pointed. "The SUV."

Up ahead was the SUV.

"I can't believe we already caught up," Ped said.

"Get ready," Gun said as he checked his weapon.

"What's the plan?" Ped asked. "You want me to run them off the road?"

Gun thought for a moment. "No, we can't take any chances. Let's kill them all."

Ped stepped on the gas, and the SUV rocketed forward toward the other SUV. Gun's men in the back seat were locked and loaded with their windows down as they approached the vehicle. Ped pulled up alongside it, and everyone in the car, including Gun, aimed their weapons at the car.

"Gray!" Gun shouted. "You lose!"

The rear passenger window lowered, and a little Thai boy appeared with a smile on his face. Sitting next to him was a girl who looked not much older. The boy made a gun with his hand and pretended to fire back at the men. Then the driver's window rolled down, revealing a middle-aged Thai man driving the SUV. A woman, who was probably his wife, sat in the passenger seat screaming at them.

"That son of a bitch!" Gun said as he pulled his rifle back into his vehicle. "He switched cars!"

Gun yelled at the man to pull over to the side of the highway. Ped stopped behind them and went to talk to the family. He returned a few minutes later.

"They had a silver Toyota two-door. Just like every car driving around Bangkok. They'll be harder to find."

"Call the men, tell them to set up a roadblock right now. I want them to stop every car driving on this highway."

53

"This will buy us some much needed time. Great idea, Sterling," Pratt said from the back seat of the small Toyota.

"Hey, I couldn't let Chet keep coming up with all the good ideas. Plus, now we don't have to worry about Gun calling us." Gray held up a new mobile phone. He'd also traded phones with the family.

"And no chance at all of tracking us," Chet said.

"That's right."

They'd also taken the rifles and the remaining ammo with them, as well as all the bottled water. The pastries they had earlier kept them content for the time being.

Gray went ahead and called Nickle to update him on their new phone number and the make and model of the vehicle they were now driving. Nickle assured them he had everything ready on his end. They just needed to make it there."

"Where are you guys now?" Nickle's voice emanated from the speakerphone.

"We're almost at the city limits of Bangkok," Chet answered.

"Good. Stay safe. I'll see you guys real soon."

Just as Gray ended the call, Chet began to pump the brakes and slow the car.

"What's up ahead," Pratt asked.

"Crap! I was hoping this wouldn't happen," Chet said.

"Is it an accident?" Gray asked as vehicles ahead slowed to a crawl.

"Just traffic. Up ahead, another highway merges with the one we're on. It causes a bottleneck."

Pratt looked out the rear window. "I don't see any black SUVs. So far, so good."

"Well, if we're stuck in this traffic, then that means Gun and his men are stuck in it as well," Gray said.

"Not really." Chet motioned to the cars starting to use the shoulder as a lane.. "I think we need to keep moving."

Chet waited for a break and then pulled into the line of cars driving on the shoulder.

"This beats the stop-and-go alternative," Gray said. "Chet, keep doing whatever it takes to get us to the embassy."

After few seconds of zooming past the parking lot of vehicles, their makeshift lane began to slow.

"Is that an accident up ahead?" Gray asked.

Chet braked and brought the car to a stop.

"It can't just be traffic," Pratt said. "I see emergency vehicle lights. Plus, traffic in the oncoming lane seems to have slowed."

Chet shifted the gear into the park and engaged the parking brake. "I'll be back."

Chet made his way to the shoulder on the other side of the highway.

"I hope this isn't a multivehicle pileup with casualties," Gray said. "We could be stuck for a while."

"It's certainly starting to look that way. No one is moving."

Gray kept an eye on Chet as he stood on the other shoulder while shielding his eyes from the sun. A beat later, he came running back to the car.

"What is it?" Gray asked.

"Black Tigers. They have a roadblock ahead and are checking every vehicle. Gun will be using the oncoming lane to get here. We can't stay still."

Chet started the car and threw it into gear. He stepped on the gas and pulled off the shoulder.

In that particular area, the highway was sandwiched between sunflowers fields that extended for miles.

Chet slammed his foot down on the accelerator and drove right into the field, creating a path of squashed destruction. The undercarriage of the car scraped the ground as it bounced up and down across the field.

"Hang on," Chet yelled as he drove straight ahead toward the roadblock.

As they neared, they spotted members of the Black Tigers searching vehicles. They definitely noticed them as they started pointing and shouting. A few climbed into an SUV and drove into the field, straight toward the Toyota.

"Chet, what are you doing? Now isn't the time to play chicken with an SUV," Gray said as he gripped the grab handle above the door.

Chet slammed on the brakes, and the car skidded to a stop. Chet threw the gear into reverse and hit the gas. The Toyota drove backward down the same path it had cleared out.

"They're catching up, Chet. We need to do something else."

The sun glinted off the SUV's chrome grill as it barreled down on them. A beat later, the man leaned out of his window with a rifle.

Don't tell me this guy is actually going to start shooting with all these civilians around.

He opened fire. All three of them ducked as bullets hit their vehicle. Pratt was the first to lower her window and return fire.

Gray picked up his rifle, leaned out of his window, and fired at the engine, trying to disable the vehicle. The SUV driver doubled down and revved the engine as the dust cloud behind the car ballooned in size.

Chet slammed on the brakes and turned the wheel, so the car's front swung around and came to a stop, pointing directly at the highway. Chet shifted out of reverse and into first gear. The wheels of the tire spun around as it tried to grip the loose soil.

"Chet, we're about to get T-boned here."

Slowly the car began to move forward as the tires gained traction. Chet turned the wheel from side to side to help, and a moment later, the car shot forward toward a line of vehicles. The SUV missed them by feet and skidded to a stop.

Chet drove straight toward a small opening between two cars. He slammed his hand down on the horn, warning the driver not to close the narrow gap.

"Will we fit?" Gray shouted.

"No choice."

The Toyota squeezed through the two cars, ripping off the vehicle's front bumper as they passed. Chet pulled the parking brake, and the car skidded to the side and aligned perfectly with the oncoming lane.

Gray looked out his window. The SUV sped toward the same narrow opening. No way they'd make it through clean.

Chet punched the gas, and the wheels chirped before sending the Toyota down the highway.

Behind them, the SUV slammed into both vehicles as it

tried to thread the needle. The SUV skidded as it turned, but the momentum was too much, and it rolled over onto its side, sending vehicle parts flying into the air.

"Whoo-whee!" Chet cheered as he looked in the rearview mirror. "One down. We just need to get past the other one up ahead."

The remaining Black Tigers had already mobilized into their SUV. They were backing up to drive around a couple of cars and cut over to the oncoming lane.

"This will be close," Chet said as they approached the roadblock.

"Chet!" Gray pointed.

Driving straight toward them was a large truck hauling a tractor-trailer.

"Chet, he doesn't look like he's stopping."

"I'm not either. I got a plan."

Chet floored the accelerator, and the six-cylinder engine whined.

"Are you crazy?"

"Trust me, Gray."

The Toyota drove straight toward the big rig. At the last moment, the driver of the truck swerved to avoid an accident. The trailer began swinging left and right, eventually jack-knifing and flipping over onto its side, sending hundreds of beer bottles crashing onto the highway. With no room to maneuver, the SUV slammed into the side of the trailer.

Chet cranked the steering wheel to the left, and the Toyota skidded sideways onto the shoulder before straightening out. Chet punched the gas once more, and they cleared the wreckage and drove toward the open highway in front.

"How the hell did you know that would happen?" Gray shouted as he looked back at the wreck.

"I didn't. I just hope I'm lucky."

Gray laughed as he reached over and rubbed Chet's belly. "Whatever kind of luck you got, I want it."

54

The Toyota crossed into Bangkok's city limits without any further interference from the Black Tigers. Even though Gun probably knew the exact make and model and most likely the plates, they could now easily blend into the busyness of Bangkok.

"How far are we from the embassy now?" Gray asked, feeling a bit like a kid on a long road trip with the family.

"It's not that far, but Bangkok traffic is hell. Forty-five minutes."

"It's not that bad, considering not too long ago we were lost in a jungle."

"We traded one jungle for another," Pratt said.

They were still on a highway, and it was stop-and-go traffic at that point. All around them, tall office buildings rose straight up, reflecting the sun back at the vehicles. Pratt moved to the other side of the seat, away from where the sun penetrated the window.

"Does the car have air-con?" she asked.

"Yeah, it's already on," Chet said.

Pratt lowered her window, but the exhaust fumes were too

much, forcing her to raise it right back up. Slowly they trudged along, making it past the merger of two highways. Traffic loosened up, and they moved a bit faster.

Gray made another call to Nickle. "We're in Bangkok, about forty minutes out from your location."

"Good to hear. You're almost home free. Keep me posted if plans change."

Gray disconnected the call. Pratt wasn't sitting behind him, so he pushed his seat back and stretched out his legs.

———

Gun and his men had watched the semi-trailer jackknife on the highway from a distance. They didn't bother to stop and see if their men were okay. Gun was too focused on trying to catch up with Gray.

"The only men we have available are the teams we have at both embassies and the Interpol office," Ped said.

"Tell all the teams to move toward the Don Muang Toll-way. It's the most direct route to the embassy. Tell them to cover the Din Daeng, the Phetchaburi, and the Sukhumvit exits."

Ped made the call and gave the orders. Gun and his men had just hit the same bottleneck that Gray and the gang had maneuvered through a bit earlier.

Ped looked over at Gun and noticed the tension in his jaw. "We'll get them, boss. This is our town. We run it."

———

Chet merged over to the far left side highway and took the Din Daeng exit.

"I think it'll be faster if we take surface streets," he said as he followed a couple of taxis off the exit ramp. They ran straight into a traffic light. Right above the signal, the time to when the light would turn green was counting down. They had a hundred and sixty seconds left. Every second felt like a minute. Gray had started tapping his finger on the inside of the door, loud enough that it prompted Pratt.

"That won't make the light turn faster," she said.

"I know, but I can't help it." He cracked a small smile. "It just feels like every foot forward is a battle."

"We're almost there, friend," Chet said.

One hundred seconds.

Ninety seconds.

Eighty seconds.

Are all the lights this long?" Gray asked.

Chet nodded. "Some of them are manually controlled by a police officer in a little station. "You see that tiny structure across the intersection at the corner?"

"Yeah."

"That's where the traffic officers are."

"Wait, you're telling me they manually switch the light from red to yellow and then to green?"

"Yes, but this one is automated. But sometimes, you get an officer who is either older and loses track of time or is too involved with his phone to care. You can sit for two and half minutes before they look up and realize they need to switch the light."

"Why on earth would the government think in this day and age that would be useful?"

"No rhyme or reason to decisions that are made. Sometimes it's best to accept and not get upset over things. In these situations, we say 'mai pen rai.' It's used when you want to convey that everything's okay, or 'never mind.' Make sense?"

"Yeah, it's the equivalent of 'fuggedaboutit'?"

"Yeah, like the Mafia," Chet said.

"There's something we can't forget about," Pratt said. "To the right, black SUV."

"You think they see us?" Gray asked.

A beat later, the front passenger window lowered, and a Black Tiger pointed right at them.

"Shit!" Chet hit the gas and rammed the taxi in front of him so that he could get around it and enter the intersection. He punched right through and made a right onto the boulevard.

"They're on us," Pratt said.

Within seconds the SUV had caught up and was right on the Toyota's rear. Seconds later, the SUV rammed the car, sending it swerving left to the right. Chet hooked the steering wheel to the left and turned down a side road. The SUV overshot the turn and slammed on its brakes, quickly reversing and continuing its chase.

"He's going to ram us," Pratt shouted.

Chet slammed on the brakes, hooked the steering wheel, and drifted into another turn. He downshifted as he came out of the turn and slammed his foot on the gas pedal.

"One-way street," Gray shouted. "Not in our favor."

Chet narrowly avoided a head-on collision with a taxi by driving up onto the sidewalk.

"Noodle cart ahead," Gray noted.

Straight ahead was a noodle stall where diners were sitting at small plastic tables and eating noodles. Chet laid into the horn, and the people jumped from the seats just as the Toyota took out the tables sending bowls of noodles flying everywhere.

Chet switched on the windshield wipers to clear a glob of noodles that had splattered across the windshield.

"They're still right on us," Pratt said.

Chet moved back onto a road, almost taking out a rank of motorbike taxis as he shot across to the opposite sidewalk that wasn't loaded with food vendors. The sidewalk was narrow, forcing Chet to drive half on the road, half on the sidewalk. He continued sounding the horn to warn oncoming traffic, primarily motorbikes. He was coming.

"These guys don't give up," Pratt said as she kept watch.

Chet made a hard left and into an alleyway that connected with the next street over. The Toyota sped down the narrow lane and sideswiped plastic garbage cans as they passed by. As they approached the alley's exit, an old woman pushing a fruit cart on three wheels stopped and blocked the path. The front wheel was stuck in a pothole.

Chet laid into the horn, and the woman raised her arms in protest. Chet shouted outside his window at the lady to move, but she refused to try her best to get her fruit cart out of the way. At the urging of people around her, she relented at the last second.

The Toyota slammed into the glass pushcart sending a rainbow-colored explosion of cut fruit flying into the air. Pineapple, watermelon, guava, dragon fruit, mangos, and more rained down on the windshield, forcing Chet to use the wipers again.

"All this food and not a single bite," Pratt said.

The tires of the car squealed as it turned onto the street. An oncoming bus clipped the backside of the car, spinning it around in circles until it came to a stop. Chet put the car into gear and floored the gas pedal. The tires screeched, and the vehicle took off just as the SUV exited the alleyway.

The SUV rammed the back of the Toyota, causing the entire rear bumper to fall off. Again the SUV rammed the car, crushing the rear of the vehicle.

"We can't keep taking this damage," Chet said.

Just then, the SUV pulled up along the driver's side of the Toyota. The front passenger window lowered, revealing a smiling Black Tiger. A beat later, he produced a handgun and took aim.

Chet slammed on the brakes just as the man fired. Gray grabbed his rifle, popped out of his window, and fired. The SUV swerved away and then slammed into the Toyota. The impact caused Gray to lose his grip on the car roof, and he fell back. Gray hung from the vehicle, his head inches from the road and only the strength of his legs hooked around the doorframe to hold him there.

"Hang on, Gray," Chet shouted as the SUV slammed into the side of the Toyota once more, causing it to move into the oncoming lane.

Gray looked ahead and stared down, a lorry coming directly at him. The swerving of the vehicle made it difficult to pull himself up and back into the car.

Chet tried to move back into his lane, but the SUV forced the small Toyota to remain halfway in the oncoming lane. Pratt latched on to Gray's pants and pulled with all her might.

"Chet, do something!" Pratt screamed.

Chet slammed on the brakes and moved behind and around the SUV, just as the honking lorry passed by. The momentum was enough to help lift Gray up and back into his seat.

"You okay, buddy?" Chet said.

"Considering I was a few seconds away from becoming a pancake, yeah."

Chet made a left at the next turn, breaking away from the SUV. The car raced down the road and made another left and then a right.

"We might have lost them for now," Pratt said as they looked out the back window.

"How far are we from the embassy, Chet?" Gray asked.

Gray took a moment to get his bearings. "We're farther away now."

"Damn!"

"That's not all; we're almost out of gas. Plus, this car won't last long."

"There." Gray pointed ahead to a parking structure.

Chet drove inside the building and up a couple floors and found a spot in the corner. He shut the engine off, and everyone took a collective breath of relief.

"Everyone okay?" Gray said after a few moments.

Chet and Pratt nodded.

"This car is done. Maybe we use one of the cars in here."

"Chet, exactly how far are we from the embassy on foot?" Pratt asked.

"I think maybe an hour. Maybe faster if we run a little."

"You thinking moving on foot is better?" Gray asked as he turned around in his seat to face Pratt.

"Assuming Gun has his men on high alert and combing the city for us, it might be easier to stay out of sight. We just left a trail of destruction and had a gunfight in public."

"That's a good idea. What do you think, Chet?" Gray asked. "Is it doable to get to the embassy while staying hidden? You know, taking back roads, cutting through buildings or parks, anything that's off the main roads."

"I think so."

"So we all in agreement?" Gray asked.

Chet and Pratt nodded.

"Okay, let's move out."

55

Gray and the others used the stairway to exit the parking structure. From that point on, Chet led the way. They crossed over to the other side of the street hurried a couple of blocks before being led into an office building, where they took the escalator up one floor. From there, they were able to leave the building and access an elevated walkway that moved above the busy road below.

"What is this?" Gray asked.

"This connects the stops of the elevated trains system."

"Can we use the train to get to the embassy?"

"It's risky. Gun is too connected and could have the guards working the platform looking for us. This walkway follows the path of this train line. We just have to cover the distance by walking."

They moved inconspicuously along the walkway until it ended. They entered another office building and made their way down to the ground floor. They were just about to pop out of the office building when Chet stopped abruptly. Parked directly out front was an SUV with body damage. The man in the front passenger seat was on the phone.

Chet, Gray, and Pratt stepped back and moved into a small convenience store near the entrance. From inside, they could look out a window and observe.

"What are they waiting for?" Gray asked.

"I'm not sure."

A moment later, a Black Tiger walked right past them and stopped just before reaching the exit door. Gray, Chet, and Pratt froze. The man had his phone pressed against his ear as he stepped off to the side, out of the way of people coming and going.

Don't turn around. Don't turn around was the only thought running through Gray's mind.

A moment later, the man hung up and left the building. The three watched as he climbed into the back seat of the SUV, and it drove off.

"That was a close one," Pratt said.

"I wonder if they know we bailed on the car," Gray said.

"It's possible, but it's eerie that he happened to be in the same building as us."

"It could have been a bathroom break," Chet said. "Let's keep moving."

They slipped out of the building and moved with their heads down. Most of the foot traffic on the sidewalk was office workers going about their day. Gray stood out the most as a tall white man among the short Thai men.

Farther down, Chet led them back into another building. They made their way through the ground level, filled with various shops and eateries until they left the building on the opposite end.

They mixed in with a group of office workers, crossed the street, and walked right into another office building.

"If we can keep using these buildings as cover, we'll be good," Gray said as he walked alongside Chet.

"We're about two kilometers from the embassy. There aren't any large office buildings like this in that area, so we'll be exposed as we get closer."

"Of course there aren't," Gray said.

"Actually, the boulevard the embassy is located on is called Wireless Road. There are many embassies located there."

"So it's all contained properties," Gray said. "No place to maneuver except out in the open."

"Yup."

"We could hop into a taxi when we get closer," Pratt suggested.

"That's an idea. We can crouch down inside and have it deliver us to the embassy's doorstep," Gray said. "Chet, can you think of a reason why that idea won't work?"

Chet shrugged. "No available taxi?"

"The restrooms are over there. I need to go," Pratt said.

"We'll wait for you here," Gray said.

———

Pratt headed down the short hallway and entered the women's restroom. She looked at herself in the mirror. *You look terrible, Lillie.* She had dirt smudges all over her face, and her hair was a mess. *Why didn't Sterling mention this to me?* Pratt turned on the faucet and splashed cool water on her face. When she finished, she leaned in to the mirror for a closer look at her face.

A toilet flushed, and the door to one of the stalls opened. A woman appeared, wearing black pants, a uniform top, and a black beret. Around her waist was a standard officer rig complete with a holstered handgun.

Pratt bit her bottom lip. The woman didn't react to her standing at the sink. Instead, she walked casually to the sink next to Pratt and proceeded to wash her hands. That's when Pratt noticed the golden emblem sewn on the woman's sleeve: the face of a tiger.

Pratt shut off her faucet and walked calmly over to the paper towel dispenser, pulled two sheets out, and dried her hands. When Pratt turned around, a punch landed on her face.

Pratt fell back into the wall, dazed but able to avoid a second strike that connected with the towel dispenser. Pratt deflected the following two punches and then countered with one of her own, knocking the woman back. Pratt remained on the offensive, drilling the woman's face with multiple strikes.

The woman ducked and connected with a straight punch into Pratt's belly and then swept Pratt off her feet. She fell flat onto her back hard and groaned. The woman pounced on her and gripped both hands around Pratt's neck and began to choke her. Pratt batted at the woman's forearms with her fists, but they wouldn't move. She then struck both sides of the woman's ears, causing her to loosen her grip. Pratt slammed her palm into the woman's face, snapping her head back. Another quick right, and she knocked the woman off her.

Pratt gasped for air as she rolled over once. She looked back at the woman and saw her reaching for her weapon. Pratt kicked at the woman's hand as she removed the handgun from the holster and sent the gun skidding across the tile floor and under the stalls.

The Black Tiger grunted as she kicked Pratt in her face. Pratt rolled away, avoiding a second kick, and got to her feet just in time for the woman to plant another kick directly into her chest. Pratt flew backward into the stall and landed on the toilet. She let out a yell as her back hit the metal flush valve.

The woman rushed into the stall. Pratt kicked her, stopping her in midcharge. Another swift kick and the woman flew back out of the booth and landed on the floor. Pratt fought the intense pain in her back and made her way to the woman. She had already gotten to her hands and knees.

Pratt grabbed the woman by the hair, dragged her into the stall, and slammed her face down onto the toilet seat twice, knocking her out before shutting the door. She made her way back to the mirror; she looked worse now than when she first came into the restroom. She grabbed a couple towels, wet them, and cleaned the blood off her nose and lip.

Gray and Chet were sitting on a bench when Pratt appeared in front of them.

"Sheesh, Lillie," Gray said, giving Pratt a once-over. "You look terrible. What happened?"

The commotion behind Pratt caught Gray's and Chet's attention. A Black Tiger stumbled out of the women's restroom, dazed and clearly beaten.

"That's what happened."

56

Gun and Ped continued to cover the surface streets, slowly making their way toward the US Embassy.

"Where the hell did they go?" Gun asked out loud.

"We got every man looking for them," Ped said. "Plus, we have cooperation from our friends at the sky train. They have to be moving around by foot."

Ped's phone rang. "Yes? When? And? Where are you now?"

"What is it?" Gun asked.

"It's Sitwat," Ped answered. "She just encountered the woman, Pratt."

"And Gray?"

"He got away."

"But she has the woman, right?"

"No, she got away too."

Gun slammed his fist repeatedly against the dashboard. "How can they keep escaping us?"

"She said they're on foot. They were last seen near the Krungthai Bank Building."

"They're close to the embassy. Notify the others and get us over to Wireless Road now!"

Chet felt they were close enough to the embassy that it made sense to flag a taxi. But it was also the start of rush hour traffic. The streets were quickly becoming bogged down, and every taxi that had passed by was already occupied. Gray and Pratt remained inside of a convenience store, watching Chet struggle to find a cab.

"It was a good idea in theory," Pratt said.

"Timing is rotten," Gray said.

Chet came back to them in the store. "I got another idea. We'll take motorbike taxis."

"Won't we be exposed on the back of the bikes?"

"Look at the streets. They're slowing to crawl. Motorbikes can drive in and out of the cars. That's something Gun and his SUVs can't do."

"You're right. Where do we get them?"

"I know a place nearby. They're a special group of motorbike taxis."

Chet led them to the next block over, where a bunch of motorbike taxis was located. The men were either standing next to or sitting on their bikes. They each wore bright orange vests with their identification number on them. Gray had seen the taxis all over Bangkok since his arrival, especially while riding around on the back of Chet's motorcycle. But the bikes these men had were different. They looked like super-charged mopeds.

"These aren't normal bikes, are they?" Gray asked.

"Nope. When they're not taxiing people around, they're street racing. My advice is to hang on tight. I told them we needed to get to the US Embassy as fast as possible."

They all put on a helmet and then hopped on the back of the bikes. The men fired up their bikes and revved them, creating a high-pitched trumping from the exhaust pipe. Gray gripped the seat of the motorcycle tight as it shot forward.

Riding in single file, the motorbikes zoomed down the side of the road, moving on and off the sidewalk when needed to avoid other bikes. The pickup on the bike was insane. Gray felt his stomach shoot back with every gear change. He kept his legs pinned against the bike, fearing he might catch the corner of a car and have them ripped off. He looked back over his shoulder at Pratt, and she was still hanging on to the back of the bike. But that's not all he saw. In the distance, he spotted black sport bikes approaching quickly. Each one carried two men, all dressed in black: Black Tigers.

The taxis slowed as they zigzagged around the cars.

"Chet!" Gray called out. "Behind us."

Chet peered back and spotted the Black Tigers. He said something to his driver, who then shouted to the other drivers.

"Hang on tight!" Chet shouted to Gray and Pratt.

The motorbike taxis drove up onto the sidewalk and rocketed forward, moving in and out of pedestrians with deft control. Some didn't even realize a motorbike was approaching until it zoomed by. Up ahead, a packed crowd had gathered around a street vendor. A crash of epic proportions was the only thought running through Gray's head.

"Watch out!" he shouted to his driver, but he didn't let off the throttle, nor did Chet's driver, whom he was following.

Gray watched Chet's bike head straight toward a two-wheeled cart that was tilted down. The bike hit the makeshift ramp and launched itself into the air. A second later, Gray's bike hit the exact same ramp and shot up into the air. Gray looked down as the bike wheels passed over the small grill with various skewered meat grilling. His driver cheered as he cleared the grill. The bike hit the sidewalk on the other side.

Gray looked back over his shoulder to see Pratt's bike clear the grill while she screamed.

Gray slapped his driver on the shoulder. "Good driving!"

He looked back again, and Pratt had survived the landing. A beat later, a motorcycle with two Black Tigers hit the same ramp and sailed easily over the grill.

"Chet!" Gray called out.

"I know, I know." Chet tapped his driver on the shoulder and pointed to the motorcycles racing toward them.

The motorbike taxi made a sharp left and cut across the three lanes, with Gray and Pratt following. The lead taxi drove over the grassy island separating the boulevard and into the oncoming lanes. All three bikes were now moving in the wrong direction, having to avoid collisions with other motorbikes. It slowed them down, but they were quickly running out of options.

A few seconds later, Chet's motorbike came to a stop, and he jumped off.

"We're on foot from here."

Gray and Pratt got off their bikes.

"Lillie, you okay?" Gray asked.

"I'm fine. Where are we?"

"Wireless Road is half a block up away," Chet answered. "These guys are gonna do us a favor and give us a head start."

The motorbike taxis cut off the routes between the cars, forcing all the motorbikes to move onto the sidewalk and making it impossible for the Black Tigers to gain ground that way.

Gray, Chet, and Lillie ran through a narrow lane between cars like their lives depended on it. They did. Chet cut left between two vehicles, narrowly avoided being run down by a motorbike.

"That's Wireless Road," Chet shouted as he pointed at the corner up ahead. "We're almost there."

57

Ped leaned in on the horn as he shouted at the taxi in front of him to move. The driver stuck his head out of his window and looked back at Ped with an angry face. Ped waved a handgun at him, and the driver started maneuvering his car out of the way.

"Boss, they're on motorcycle taxis." A Black Tiger sitting in the back was receiving an update on his phone. "Kongthong and the others are chasing them now."

"Get around this guy, Ped. We can't let them get to the embassy."

Ped crashed into the rear corner of the taxi as he drove around it. He then slammed into another small car and bull-dozed it out of the way before driving up onto the sidewalk. The large SUV barreled down the sidewalk, destroying the vendor carts that lined the road. People scattered to avoid being run down, and a lazy soi dog popped to its feet and ran away in the nick of time.

Ped continued their path of destruction until they approached Wireless Road. Near the corner was a team of road construction workers. A large hole in the sidewalk had been dug.

"Shit! We need to get back onto the road to get around this," Ped said.

No sooner had he uttered those words than he and Gun spotted Gray, Chet, and Pratt running toward the corner on the opposite side of Wireless Road.

Gray locked eyes with Gun as he approached the corner. Call it their moment. Each man knew what the other thought: that he had won and the other had lost. Gray smiled at Gun as he rounded the corner. The final sprint lay ahead of him, and Gun was stuck in traffic with no way to get around the construction blocking his path.

The sidewalks along Wireless Road were narrow and often blocked with trees or vendors. It was easier and faster to run on along the side of the road. Gray's steps felt light as a new burst of energy flowed through his body, propelling him forward.

He looked to his right at Pratt. She had a look of easiness on her face, one he hadn't seen since their reunion. She had also accepted that they had won and that this madness would be over at any moment. Gray shifted his sights to Chet on his left. The man whose introduction was made with a right hook while drunk had deftly guided Gray through the perplexing intricacies of Bangkok. And finally, in the distance was Nickle, a colleague who had introduced him to the hallucinogenic effects of ya dong. He stood in the middle of the road, waving his arm with the gusto of a third base coach giving the runner the go-ahead to home base. Was this a nirvana moment?

The rev of an engine punched through Gray's happily-ever-after and yanked him back into reality. He looked back over his shoulder. Speeding straight toward them was a black SUV.

Gray checked on Pratt. Her face had tightened as she breathed heavily in and out of her mouth.

"You got it, Lillie. We're almost there."

They were forty yards out.

Nickle shouted at them to hurry as he waved his arm and pointed at the gate. At that moment, Pratt lost her footing and fell forward, tumbling end over end. Gray grabbed her arm and yanked her back to her feet, dragging her as he yelled to keep moving.

"My leg!" she shouted in pain.

Chet moved around, grabbed Pratt's other arm, and slung it over his shoulder. Together, he and Gray ran while carrying Pratt.

Thirty yards.

The engine of the vehicle grew louder with every step. Unable to turn his head around, Gray had no idea the distance between them and the SUV. He just knew it was getting closer.

Twenty yards.

The burning in his thighs and calves was unimaginable, and his lungs felt deflated as every breath he drew seemed to do less and less for his body.

"Gray!" Gun used a PA system in the SUV. "I got you."

The combination of the engine and Gun's voice made it seem like the SUV was literally right behind them. At any minute, Gray expected to be mowed down. It didn't help that Nickle's eyes had grown more expansive as he shouted at them to hurry.

Ten yards.

They ran at an angle toward the gate. *Come on, Gray. You're almost there.*

"Take her, Chet," Gray said as he let go.

He then continued running straight as Chet and Pratt made their way toward the gate. Gun wanted him. He would continue after Gray and give Chet and Pratt the time they needed to make it inside.

Gray finally looked over his shoulder. The SUV was nearly upon him.

Wait...

Wait...

Wait...

Now!

Gray juked to the left just as the SUV was about to hit him. A rush of air passed across his back as the SUV drove by. The screeching of tires pierced his ears as the SUV slid to a stop. Gray ran past the bollards and US soldiers with their rifles raised and aimed at the SUV. Once past the gate, Gray turned around. The SUV had stopped in the middle of the street with the passenger side facing the embassy and Gun staring straight at Gray.

Both men kept their eyes locked on each other as the steel doors closed. Right before Gun went out of view, Gray gave him a playful salute.

58

Nickle spirited Gray and the others to a small conference room inside the embassy where they could eat and drink and have a doctor look them over without curious onlookers. In return, Gray unofficially debriefed Nickle on their car, motorcycle, and foot chase on the streets of Bangkok. Nickle seemed to take it all in stride.

"That's it? I think we'll be okay," Nickle said.

"You're kidding, right?" Gray asked. "Let me be clear. I fired a weapon from our car, at another car, in broad daylight. How on earth can something like that be swept under the rug?"

"You were in an unmarked car. The other vehicle was unmarked. Plus, the higher-ups will find out very quickly about Gun and Ped's chase through Bangkok. I wouldn't be surprised if things were already put into motion to get ahead of any reports hitting the news or social media. Vendors that had their carts or stalls destroyed will receive a visit from the local police telling them that the culprits have already been apprehended. The government wants to help them rebuild their business by paying for the damage. Word will spread quickly that cash is being doled out, and those affected will keep their mouths shut while they wait their turn to have a conversation with the police."

"This is unbelievable."

"This is reality. You think cover-ups don't exist in the United States?"

"Of course they do, but not of this magnitude."

"People tend to move on fairly quickly when a wad of cash is shoved into their hand by a smiling person who apologizes." Nickle looked over at Chet, who was halfway through a sandwich. "You want to back me up on this?"

"Everything he said is true," Chet said through a full mouth. "What happened out there is the least of my worries. I'm more interested in how Gun and Ped are handled. Are they considered a liability by people more powerful? If they are, they're done. If not..."

"And if they are, what does that mean for you or even Nickle? Surely, they'll be able to connect Nickle to us."

"Like I said before, don't worry. I'm Thai. I'll get through this."

"Same here," Nickle said. "I know enough people who matter that Gun and his men wouldn't dare come after me. Plus, I'm an FBI agent. Coming after me in any way would only muddy their situation."

"Do you think they'll get away with it?" Gray asked Nickle.

"Honestly, this will be hard for them to bounce back from. It won't surprise me if they're already planning their own disappearance."

"You're saying they'll give up their positions with the Black Tigers and go on the run?"

"It's like self-exile. Better to handle your own punishment than let the powers that be decide. I'm sure they have more than enough money tucked away in a secret bank account outside of Thailand. I know what you're thinking. Losing their powerful careers doesn't begin to satisfy the crimes they've committed. And you're right. But take solace that your efforts got rid of two nasty individuals. In due time someone else will step into that role. But, hey, that's life, right? There's always someone willing to sit in the driver's seat and see how far they can run with things before they crash the damn car. Listen, Gray, I won't tell you how to do your job, but if you want to file a report, update your supervisor, that's up to you. But nothing will happen on my end. There'll be no official investigation into what happened, and I won't meet with my RTP counterparts. Chet, will you be doing anything different?"

"No. I already forget this happened."

"I don't know if you heard," Nickle said, "but the Ritthirong that was being held at Bang Kwang is dead, apparently by suicide. There's no need for that charade to continue. It's already starting to go away."

"It doesn't surprise me," Gray said. "Why go through the trouble of a trial and risk people figuring out that's a fake Ritthirong? Both Ritthirongs are dead."

Gray looked over at Pratt, who was munching on potato salad. She'd been quiet during the entire discussion, except for answering a few questions from Nickle.

"Lillie, what do you make of all this?"

"Sterling, the more you work with Interpol on investigations outside of the countries like the US or the UK—essentially, countries that are not part of the G8—you'll find that they operate in ways that are very different. I would say the one G8 exception is Russia. But like you said earlier, corruption and cover-ups happen everywhere. Transparency is really the divider. You just got a taste of what true transparency really is."

"You've seen this before?"

"Not to this degree."

"Your counterpart at Interpol here. You'll just move on like how he was ready to move on when I reported you were abducted."

"I will because that's how things work. You can't watch out for everyone. You watch out for the select few that mean something."

When Gray heard Pratt say that, it triggered a memory from when he served as a Pararescue in the Air Force. His job was to save people. It didn't matter who they were, what they were doing, how they ended up in their predicament. His objective was to recover and medically treat. And that's what he did. When he failed, and it happened, Gray always took it personally. Because he believed that was his job...to save everyone, to make things right.

The reality was more along the lines of what Pratt said. It's impossible to worry about everyone. So one had to pick their battles. Clarity hit Gray at that moment. He was continuing to push into a battle that no longer needed to be fought. He'd already won. It may not have been the knockout he wanted, but it was definitely over.

"Gray, I hope you realize you came out on top here," Nickle said. "If it were not for you and Chet, Lillie wouldn't be here with us. She was the mission. So let's take our wins however we can, okay?"

"You're right. What's the plan from here on?"

"It's best you and Lillie take the first flight back to the UK tonight. I'll make sure it happens. We can arrange for an armed escort to the Suvarnabhumi and make sure you two get on your flight safely. In the meantime, forget about your luggage and belongings at the hotel. You'll both stay put here until flight time."

"I need to make a call that's long overdue," Pratt said.

"Sure, I'll set you up in my office."

Nickle and Pratt left, and Gray and Chet were alone.

"I know I'm starting to sound like a worried mother, but are you sure you'll be okay?" Gray asked. "I can't help but think I'm the worst. I used you for everything you had, and as soon as I got what I needed, I'm leaving you high and dry."

"Gray, I'll be fine. And for the record, I had a hell of a time with you. These are stories I'll tell years later over shots of ya dong."

"Watch yourself. I heard you can end up fighting a stiff suit in the middle of an alley if you drink too much of that stuff."

"We make a good team," Chet said.

"You're my brother from another mother. I won't forget you or what you did. If you ever need my help with anything, you call me. Deal?" Gray stuck his hand out.

"Deal."

59

Two SUVs came to a stop at the curb outside of international departures at Suvarnabhumi. Four men in suits exited the first SUV and looked around before nodding at the second vehicle. Nickle, Gray, Pratt, and Chet exited, and they were escorted into the departure hall. They checked into the flight quickly and then made their way to the first security checkpoint. That's where Nickle and Chet had to say their goodbyes.

Gray gave Chet a pat on the back as they shook hands. "It's been a wild ride, my friend. It was an honor."

"Same for me," Chet said.

"If you ever make it to the UK, look me up. I'll take you to my favorite pubs."

"Sounds like a good plan."

"Nickle, you're one agent I won't forget. I have to admit, you've adapted well here in Thailand while still keeping the Bureau's integrity intact. Job well done. Thank you for all your help."

Gray gave Nickle a hug.

"Take it easy, pal, and shake loose all the bad habits I taught you here. They won't work where you're heading."

Pratt held her arms open and gave Chet a big hug. "I can't thank you enough. You went above and beyond the call of duty to rescue me. You will always have a special place in my heart. And please take care of yourself."

"You're welcome, Lillie. I hope I never have to rescue you again."

"Lillie." Nickle opened his arms and hugged Pratt. "May we meet under better circumstances next time."

"I won't argue with that."

As Gray and Pratt walked toward security, Nickle called out with a Southern twang, "Y'all come back now, you hear?"

An hour and a half later, Gray and Lillie were settled in their business class seats next to each other. They buckled up and prepared for takeoff. When the Boeing 777 took off, it banked to the right, giving Gray and Pratt a beautiful view of the Bangkok skyline.

"I think we can both finally breathe easily," Pratt said.

"I was just thinking the same thing," Gray said. "I meant to ask, how did the call with Evie go?"

"I held back and told her I'd lost my phone and got so caught up with work and bunch of other excuses. Let's just say she wasn't happy with my silence."

"Why didn't you tell her the truth?"

"I'll tell her what happened, but that's a conversation that is better had in person, not over the phone. But you and I never did discuss what our official story would be. We both need to be on the same page when we fill out our reports on the extradition. I know you will also need to update your supervisor back in the States."

"You're right. Well, Nickle said nothing will happen officially on his end here in Thailand. Essentially, everyone will move on. Both Ritthirongs are dead. If what Nickle said about

Gun and Ped is true. They probably already disappeared. You think we should stay quiet?"

Pratt shrugged. "I'm opening the discussion for debate."

"Well, in a week, it'll be like it never happened, as far as Thailand is concerned. It's really up to us if we want to keep it alive. And if all parties involved are really out of the picture...it begs the question, what do we hope to gain from filing reports about what actually happened?"

Pratt made a zipping motion across her lips. Gray smiled and did the same thing before stretching his legs out. A few moments later, both were fast asleep.

Later that same night, Gun and Ped were making last-minute preparations to flee the country. They knew they had lost big time. Their only hope to save their skins was to leave under cover of darkness that night. They had already arranged for a border crossing into Cambodia to take a flight from Phnom Penh to Bahrain. Flying out of Suvarnabhumi was too risky.

Their remaining assets in the local Thai banks had already been transferred to their Swiss accounts. They had direct conversations with the bank branch manager who handled their money. He assured them that their accounts would be wiped off the bank's ledgers, as if they never existed. Their homes, cars, and other local material possessions were taken out of their names and divided up among their men. It was the least they could do since they were bailing on them.

Gun kept a luxury apartment in the city he wanted to visit before he and Ped left for the border. There, he kept a safe that held half a million dollars in gold jewelry.

Ped brought the car to a stop outside. "You want me to come up with you?"

"It'll only take me a couple of minutes."

Gun opened his door, and as he slid out of the vehicle, he came face-to-face with the barrel of a gun.

"Hello, Gun."

It took a moment for Gun to recognize the woman pointing the gun at him. It was Cake.

There was a tap against Ped's window. Standing outside were three other women, Mint, Joke, and Tukta, pointing guns at him. One of them motioned for Ped to lower his window.

"What do you want?" Gun asked as he sat back down. "Money? How much will it take? I have a safe upstairs that is filled with gold jewelry. I'll hand all of it over to you right now. No questions. You leave quietly, we'll leave quietly, and we'll both forget any of this took place."

"That's not how this works," Cake said. "Your men killed two of my girls. It was almost three, but I was able to rescue Mint. She's the pretty one with green eyes on the other side of the car. Ped, you remember her, don't you?"

"How much do you want for each girl?" Gun demanded.

"I don't think you understand. I'm not here for the money."

"Then why are you here? You want to kill us? Do you think you can kill a Black Tiger and get away with it? Be smart, Cake. I'm giving you a way out. How about a million baht for each girl? Will that settle things?"

"You really are a stupid man, more than I had originally thought."

"Watch your mouth, Cake. I can have your entire operation shut down with a snap of a finger."

"No, you can't. I know exactly what you're doing right now. You and your friend here are getting ready to disappear. You screwed yourself so bad that you no longer have other options or friends to turn to. You're an outcast. Not even your loyal men will lift a finger to help you."

Cake looked over at her girls and nodded. They each fired a shot into Ped's head. An explosion of blood, brain, and skull matter landed on Gun.

He put both of his hands up in defense. "Cake, wait. Let's work something out. There is always a price. Name it, and it's yours."

"There is one thing that might satisfy me."

"What is it? Tell me, and you'll have it."

Cake pulled the trigger and shot Gun directly in his face, blowing the back of his head out.

"Killing you," Cake said, as Gun lay slumped over the dashboard.

"Do you feel better?" Mint asked as she and the others came around to Cake's side of the car.

"I do. Let's go before the stink in this car settles on us."

THE BUTCHER OF BELARUS
A STERLING GRAY FBI PROFILER NOVEL

As a brutal serial killer terrorizes a migrant camp on the Polish border, an FBI profiler must get inside his twisted mind before another little girl is killed...

On the border between Poland and Belarus, thousands of migrants are struggling for survival. But illness and unsanitary conditions aren't the worst of it.

The first girl's death is too brutal to be an accident. The second sends a wave of panic through the camp.

When the third body is discovered, there's no escaping the horrifying truth: a serial killer is on the loose inside the camp, and the local authorities are powerless to stop him.

FBI profiler Sterling Gray is an expert at reading troubled minds. On loan to Interpol, he is called in on behalf of the Polish government to assist in identifying the killer. Gray goes undercover as a member of the Doctors Without Borders program, using his time inside the camp to profile the killer, but quickly finds other dangers lurking around every corner...

Gray's profile of the killer leads to a swift arrest, but something doesn't feel right. And when a new shocking truth emerges, Gray must risk everything to return to the camps...or another little girl will die.

Get your copy today at SevernRiverBooks.com

JOIN THE READER LIST

Never miss a new release! Sign up to receive exclusive updates from author Brian Shea.

Join today at
SevernRiverBooks.com

Sign up and receive a free copy of
Unkillable: A Nick Lawrence Short Story.

YOU MIGHT ALSO ENJOY...

The Sterling Gray FBI Profiler Series

Hunting the Mirror Man

The King Snake

The Butcher of Belarus

BY BRIAN SHEA

The Boston Crime Thriller Series

Murder Board

Bleeding Blue

The Penitent One

Sign of the Maker

Cold Hard Truth

The Nick Lawrence Series

Kill List

Pursuit of Justice

Burning Truth

Targeted Violence

Murder 8

Never miss a new release!

SevernRiverBooks.com

Sign up and receive a free copy of

Unkillable: A Nick Lawrence Short Story

ABOUT THE AUTHORS

Brian Shea has spent most of his adult life in service to his country and local community. He honorably served as an officer in the U.S. Navy. In his civilian life, he reached the rank of Detective and accrued over eleven years of law enforcement experience between Texas and Connecticut. Somewhere in the mix he spent five years as a fifth-grade school teacher. Brian's myriad of life experience is woven into the tapestry of each character's design. He resides in New England and is blessed with an amazing wife and three beautiful daughters.

Ty Hutchinson is a USA Today best seller. Since 2013, Ty has been traveling nonstop worldwide, all while banging away on his laptop and cranking out international crime and action thrillers. Immersing himself in different cultures, especially the food, is a passion that often finds its way into his stories.

4:22